D1045384

# The Night Rainbow

# The Night Rainbow

CLAIRE KING

BLOOMSBURY
LONDON • NEW DELHI • NEW YORK • SYDNEY

First published in Great Britain 2013



Bloomsbury Publishing, London, New Delhi, New York and Sydney

50 Bedford Square, London WC1B 3DP

A CIP catalogue record for this book is available from the British Library

ISBN 978 1 4088 2467 2
10 9 8 7 6 5 4 3 2 1

Typeset by Hewer Text UK Ltd, Edinburgh
Printed in Great Britain by CPI Group (UK) Ltd, Croydon CR0 4YY

www.bloomsbury.com/claireking

A story for when you're older, in case time makes you forget.
To remind you that you have always had the wisdom to know what's important, and the hope that brings dreams to life.

For Amélie and Beatrix, with all my love.

## *Chapter 1*

Maman's belly is at the stove, her bottom squeezed up against the table where we are colouring. Her arm is stretched forwards, stirring tomato smells out of the pan and into our socks. She isn't singing.

It is mostly cool in the kitchen, but half of me is sunny and hot because I'm sitting in a ribbon of outside. The rest of me is in the stripy shade of the socks and knickers that dangle from the wooden airer above our heads. They have been there for five sleeps already, since that rainy afternoon when we couldn't stop getting under Maman's feet even when we were in a different room altogether.

A fly lands on the edge of the butter dish, and another on my empty plate. Then one jumps on to my arm, making the hairs stand up. Margot watches them. Her eyes roll around so they are mostly white and her eyebrows waggle. Two more flies skid to a stop on the oilcloth.

The flies think our house is an airport, Pea, she says.

Margot is like me and she is not like me. I am five and a half, Margot is only four, but she's tall for her age. We both like cuddles and insects and cuddling insects and we both have freckles and green eyes, like Maman, with sparkles of blue and brown. In the sunlight Maman's eyes are kaleidoscopes.

Margot and I are not the same, you can tell by our dreams. I am always dreaming about witches chasing me, or picnic-days at the beach before all the dying happened – those are the best ones. Margot dreams about tiny people that live in the cupboards and have parties on Thursdays, and about jigsaws that make themselves.

Ladies are like cars and men are like motorbikes, Margot says.

You have to listen to Margot because she explains things.

Motorbikes don't have doors, but cars do, to put the people in, she tells me. You can put people inside ladies too. And they have doors for the going in and out.

I stare at Maman's big fat belly, imagining the door. I have never seen it, which is strange. I have seen the doorknob, though, sticking out through her clothes where her belly button used to be.

Go and knock on it, Pea, the baby might answer, says Margot.

In my head I can see the baby opening up Maman's tummy to say hello, or to sign for a parcel. Before I can stop it my laugh bubbles out of my lips like a raspberry. Maman's head turns to look at me.

Peony, she says (because that is one of my names), and her face is grey clouds. Then she turns away again and stirs faster.

Maman, I say.

She turns back. But I have forgotten to think of something important to say, so I quickly say the first thing I can think of.

There is a fly stuck to your foot.

Well, there is. Maman has bare feet and under one of her heels I can see a little fly leg sticking out. And a little fly bum.

Maman stares at me for a moment with eyes that say 'this is all your fault', and then leans on the table so she can inspect her feet. She lifts one off the tiles and cricks backwards to look at it over her shoulder, her hair falling down her back like a red curtain. The bottom of her foot is black. Maman's feet get dirtier than mine even though we both walk barefoot on the same floors.

The other one, I whisper.

She swaps feet. There it is: the squashed fly. She peels it off with the tips of her fingers and puts her foot back down slowly. Her mouth wobbles as though it can't decide what shape to make. She looks at the floor, her eyes moving over the crumbs, the small bits of onion and garlic skins, the cat hair and the outside dirt. The table is not very clean either. We do try not to make too much mess, but if we do I can't reach the sink to wipe it up.

I am quiet now, waiting for what happens next. Maman puts the fly into the dustbin and then holds on to the table with two hands, rocking as though there is sad music in the kitchen that only she can hear. The tomato sauce is spluttering in the pan behind her. Without saying anything else, she straightens up and takes her tears upstairs.

The darkness is in my stomach. This is what scares me most.

Telling Maman about the fly was a disaster, I say.

Yes, says Margot, you should have told her she was looking beautiful today.

That would have been better, I say.

Never mind, says Margot. I don't really like tomato sauce. Shall we have a picnic?

I hear the splash of the shower coming on upstairs. On the stove, spits of tomato sauce are dancing over the saucepan and on to the floor. Some of them are flying so high they are splattering the clothes on the airer. Our clothes, saucepans and frying pans, strings of garlic and chillies and onions, dried sausages, all hanging together out of reach on S-shaped hooks with pointed ends.

All getting very spotty with tomato. I get up from the table and turn off the gas.

Come on, Pea, says Margot. I'm hungry.

Outside the bright sunshine makes us squint. I have forgotten my hat and can already feel my hair heating up. Sometimes I wish it didn't get so hot here, but Maman said that French summers are much nicer than those in England, where she came from. She said that here at least you can always rely on the sun.

We stand in the courtyard and wonder where we will go today, although the answer has been the same for two summers, one winter and a birthday. Our choosing began when Maman came back from hospital last year. She had changed from fat to thin, but she didn't bring back a baby like she promised. She left it at the hospital, along with her happiness.

When Papa was at home things were still OK. He hugged Maman all the time and there were girl-shaped spaces in between their elbows and tummies that I could squeeze into and join in the cuddle. But when he was out working, Maman would tell us to just get out of the house and go play, and so we did. We play mostly in the low meadow, and sometimes on Windy Hill, the places that Maman used to take us on walks before the dead baby happened. Some days I still ask her to come along, but she prefers it indoors. Even though she started growing a new baby right away, it didn't put the happiness back.

Then Papa died. One day in spring, he was driving his tractor on a hill and he fell off it and was squashed. That was tragic, the priest at the church said so, but afterwards it was a catastrophe. Without Papa here there is never a very good time to be in the house, so every day we have to decide where to go.

* * *

Sunny side or shady side? says Margot, which is another way of asking the same question.

If we go around the sunny side of the house we can take the path down through the peach orchards and across the village road into the low meadow. If we go to the shady side, and around the back of the barn, we can cross the high pasture and go sit on Windy Hill.

Shady side, I say. I want to go and see the wing turbines.

The turbines are taller than houses. They stand over on another hill in two rows, like three-wing angels with their backs to the sea, watching over the villages and the meadows. They make the electricity that goes to our light switches, so at night when I'm in bed, even when everything else is dark, I know there is a little bit of light behind my door. That stops me being afraid. The darkness is lonely, the turbines stir it away. When I watch them turning, see that they are still there, everything slows down to the steady round and round and I forget about being upset.

Pea, scolds Margot, for goodness sake, it's midday. There is no shade on Windy Hill, we will burn up like toast and get sunstroke and melt.

I start to argue, but Margot interrupts me, which she does a lot.

Today I am the maman, she says, so you will do as you're told.

But we haven't been to Windy Hill for ages, I say.

Pea, look at you, you haven't even got a hat on. We're going to the low meadow and that's the end of it. Margot folds her arms. Besides, we can paddle, she adds, looking down at my yellow sandals.

The stream will be cold and my feet are hot. The stream will feel good. Margot knows this. Margot knows a lot of things before I even think of them.

Why are Maman's feet so dirty and not mine? I ask her.

Because she spends too much time indoors where the dirt is, says Margot.

There didn't used to be so much dirt.

No.

There didn't used to be so much indoors either.

Papa wouldn't have liked it.

I don't like it, I say.

Can you remember if Maman ever came paddling with us? Margot asks.

I can, I say. She definitely did. Her feet looked like big white fish under the ripples. Her toenails were painted pink and she waggled them in the water.

Yes, says Margot. Her feet are dirty now because she doesn't paddle enough. And also, my tummy is rumbling, we have to stop dawdling.

I'm thirsty, I say.

Come on then, says Margot.

To get a drink of water from the courtyard tap you have to kneel underneath it and the water runs down your neck and wets your clothes, but they dry fast in the sunshine.

We're going to need some bread, says Margot.

Sylvie, the breadlady, has left our baguettes on top of the letter-box as usual. There are two of them, hot as though they had just been baked and each with a little paper coat around its middle. Since Papa died we only eat one of the baguettes each day, but Sylvie still brings two. I put the hard ones in a box outside the front door and the peachman takes them for his pigs.

I break off the knob-ends of the bread, one for each of us, and we dig inside them for crumbs as we walk. On the way down through the orchard we look under the trees for peaches that have fallen off. There are plenty, more than we can hold. We both eat one, ripe and sweet, then I make an apron out of my still-damp dress to carry the rest.

Down in the low meadow, the ground is softer and there is plenty of shade. On the path down from the road, we skip around the brambles, checking for ripe blackberries, but they are all still green and red. Josette's donkeys meet us at the bottom of the path and we give them the crusty leftovers of our bread. Then we sit in a patch of dandelions under the alders and oaks close to the stream. Somewhere up in the trees a bird is drilling holes.

Woodpecker! says Margot.

That's an easy one, I laugh, with peach juice running down my chin.

Croo, croo, says another bird and I shout, Dove!

I usually win at this game. Maman knows all the bird calls and she used to teach me: cuckoo, crow, blackbird, seagull, song thrush . . . She taught me the feathers too. Birds leave their feathers lying around all the time, like presents. In the days when Maman sang and baked cakes we would come out together on treasure hunts, collecting feathers and flowers. Back at home we stuck them on to paper and Maman put them on the fridge with magnets, or pinned them to the walls.

Margot and I point our ears to the sky, listening for more birds, trying to untangle their calls. It is quite complicated and keeps us very busy until a long fat hornet arrives, hovering and buzzing around my face. I jump on to my feet. Margot becomes bossy again.

Come on, quickly, she says, now we must wash our hands and faces. She takes my sticky hand and leads me down to the stream.

We crouch down at the edge of the brown water and rinse our fingers in the reflections of trees, scattering half-made tadpole-frogs under the rocks.

The rocks look different, says Margot. What's wrong with them?

They're out of the water, I say. It's because it's summer.

I know about summer, of course, says Margot, and rain and snow and mountains, but it isn't just that they are out of the water. They have moved. Look.

Rocks don't move, I say. But I take a few steps backwards just in case. From further back I can see the pattern. The big rocks that were dotted around the stream before are now zigzagging from one side to the other, from the low meadow into the low pasture. They are making the water slow down, pool up against them and run off the sides. In the still water in the middle, pond skaters spin around in circles on the surface while silvery water boatmen and tiny fish glitter underneath.

Stepping stones! I shout. Let's go! And I rush to the water's edge, sticking out my arms ready to balance my way across.

Rocks that move, says Margot quietly.

Yes, I say. I step back again.

Margot is right. Something is wrong with rocks that move. I look at the stepping stones again. Seven big stones that look very heavy. Too heavy for children to carry.

It must have been a witch, I say.

Witches don't exist, says Margot.

On the other side of the stream there are evening primroses. I want to go and get them.

It was a witch, I say. Look at the flowers.

The flowers?

Witches do that, they put things you want in places you shouldn't go. They make houses out of cakes to catch you and then they put you in cages to fatten you up.

Flowers aren't cakes. What do you want the flowers for? says Margot.

For making Maman happy with.

Do you think they would make her happy?

Well, they're yellow, I say. I don't know. Maybe nothing will make her happy.

That's just silly, says Margot. There are more than a thousand things in the world and one of them must make Maman happy.

But how do we know which one?

Exactly! says Margot. This is our new challenge. We are going to use our cleverness to make Maman happy again. We will start by trying yellow flowers.

OK, I'll go and get some, I say. But then I stop again. No, I've changed my mind.

It wasn't a witch! says Margot.

I'm not going! If it wasn't a witch then who was it? I say. It could only have been a grownup, but grownups don't come down here. Even Josette just calls the donkeys when it's their feeding time and they go and meet her up by the fence.

No grownups at all? says Margot.

I think about it. The only grownup I've ever seen down here is the man who made the dragging footprints in the snow.

The first time we saw him I was four years old. Maman had just come home from the hospital and was staying in bed. Papa was spraying the peaches because he didn't know what else to do. That's what he said. We couldn't stay with Papa, and Maman was in a terrible mood, so we went to see if the donkeys were in a good one, which they were. We stayed all day in the low meadow, and late in the afternoon he came. We were sitting under the white mulberry tree, being doctors and nurses. The leaves are big and the tree also had hundreds of white berries. It makes a good hospital but was also useful for hiding. The branches hang very low, close to the ground, so we felt quite safe.

We peered out, watching the stranger like spies. The man was half-hopping as though he had a stone in his shoe, and a red dog was walking by his side. I wasn't happy about the man but I liked his dog. I could tell it was a kind one, staying with his person like that when he would probably rather have been chasing smells.

Just when I thought they were about to turn and go the dog barked three times, making me jump, and ran over to the mulberry tree. He came straight underneath and nosed us with his wet face. The dog was quite thin and slinky and friendly-looking. His tail was a flapping floppy brush. I wanted to pat the dog, but if it didn't go away I was sure the man would follow.

Shoo! I whispered, and waved my hands at it.

Buzz off! said Margot, making a cross face.

The dog stepped back from us, sniffing the air, but he didn't buzz off. Instead he had a snack, eating a few of the lowest mulberries, nipping them straight off the tree. The man's feet had been still all this time, just standing, pointing towards us, but not moving. Then he bent down to his shoe, maybe looking for the stone, and for a moment he seemed to be looking right at us. I stayed as still as a statue, and closed my eyes to a squint. The man squinted too. His face was very hairy, except above one ear where a big patch of hair was missing and the skin was red-brown like a chestnut. I held my breath, my heart thumping against my ribs.

But then he stood up again, his face was gone and he whistled for the dog, who nudged me one last time with his nose then ran back to the man's heel.

He was here last winter too when the snow came. I was following my footprints from the day before, trying to put my feet in them without making any new ones. Margot was lagging behind, stepping slowly and carefully on the new snow trying not to make prints. She's very good at that, better than me.

I saw them first: big fresh footprints with zigzag bottoms, half of them normal and half of them stretched and blurry. Next to them were a patter of paw prints, all heading down to the stream. I was examining them more closely when I heard the snow crunching ahead of me and when I looked up he was close, making the same pattern but coming back up the hill. Each step of his scrapy walk made a small pile of snow. The red dog was still at his feet but this time covered in a layer of frost like icing on a cake.

I stood still, watching them walk towards me. The man limped, his dog trotted, I thought about running away.

Don't worry, said Margot, he looks rather stupid. If he tries to kidnap us we will easily be able to trick him. Pull a fierce face, she said.

She said it really loud and I was sure that the man was going to do a big wicked laugh and say, Oh, do you really think so? But he didn't. I don't think he heard.

He came right up to us, smiling all the time, his face bristly with grey, his eyes dark and sparkly on the inside but wrinkled on the outside with two eyelids on each eye, one at the top and one at the bottom.

My bone was itching terribly; I remember because it was inside my two T-shirts and my jumper and my coat so I couldn't scratch it. There is a place on my arm where it was broken when I was a baby. Maman told me that, although you can't see anything on the skin. If I'm nervous, the bone inside itches like mad. As the man shuffled closer I thought I might have to take my clothes off, right there in the snow, just to rub at the burning itch. I was starting to unzip my coat when the man passed right by me.

He didn't stop, just nodded at us and kept going, following his own footsteps back up out of the meadow, his red dog taking a last look at us as they approached the road.

See, said Margot, he's terrified of us.

I grinned behind his shuffling back, proud and relieved.

That night I told Papa about the man. How his footprints were ragged, how his dog was always by his side like magic. I told him how we had scared him off with our best worst faces.

Papa frowned.

Pivoine, he said (because that is the other one of my names), children shouldn't go wandering in the meadows alone.

I laughed at him then, but he pulled me up on to his lap and stared me right in the eye with his serious face.

I mean it, Pea; please promise me you won't go down there alone.

I promise, I said, and snuggled into his arms.

I didn't tell Papa how the man touched my pink hat with his black glove as he passed.

## *Chapter 2*

These are the rules of hide and seek. First, you have to play in the right place. It's no use playing in the middle of the meadow, or near the donkeys' stable. If you do that it's too easy and soon you have to choose a different game. No, you need to have different places to hide. The other rule is that the person counting must not peek through their fingers. Not even slightly.

Me and Margot are looking for the right starting place. It is early morning, not too hot yet, and crickets crackle like popcorn around our feet as we go. When we get to the dirt-track crossroads we stop and look for the place where the big spider has made her web right across the path. We don't want to break it.

Here it is, stretched like laundry between tall blades of grass. The crickets are popping all about and some land on my arms and on my clothes. I never have time to touch them, though, before they spring right off again.

It is not long before one lands in the web. There it goes, a chubby little green one, kicking its long back legs and making the web swing like a hammock. The spider hurries over as we watch. She is big and fat and yellow like a stripy apricot. She cuts around the cricket and spins it in silk. Then she mends her web again. It goes very fast. We watch her finish all her jobs and go back to the middle of her web. She will catch lots of crickets and she will wrap them all up. I know because we have watched her now for three days. She is never hungry in the morning. Then, when the sun drops behind the trees on the banks of the stream, sending their shadows rolling out across the low meadow, we will pass her on our way home, and she will be eating her supper.

If we are lucky, when we get home, Maman will have had some sleep and we can have our supper too. Most nights the baby in Maman's tummy does not sleep, but does somersaults instead. This means Maman is awake too, because how could you sleep with someone doing their exercises inside you? In the mornings Maman is usually cross about everything. This morning she was in such a mood. She came downstairs at breakfast time and made coffee without saying a word. She took it back to her bedroom with a piece of toast. She will eat it in bed, with four pillows behind her, waiting for the baby to get tired, and then, I hope, she will sleep too.

Further down into the meadow we find the perfect spot to play. There are lots of different paths to take and trees and bales of hay to hide behind.

OK, says Margot. I'm going to hide first.

That means I am counting. I can count to over one hundred but for this game I only count to eleven. When I have finished – and I do not peek through my fingers, not even slightly – I look around. I can't see Margot, but I can hear her easily. She is hiding by the cherry tree in the corner of the meadow. There are no cherries on it now, but the rotten ones and lots of stones are scattered all around nearby. She is making too much noise because the grey donkey has followed her and is snuffling her for food. It tickles when they do that. I run over, laughing.

I found you! I sing, but she looks at me with her serious face as though she had never been hiding at all.

Welcome to the library, says Margot in a very important voice. Today we are only allowed to choose one book, and it was my turn. I have chosen this book. It is about skeletons.

She holds up the book. It is a pretend one, of course.

I know about skeletons. Once I went to a museum and saw dinosaur skeletons. They are like jigsaw puzzles for scientists. Scientists are people who do experiments, and jigsaws made of bones.

Are they dinosaur skeletons? I ask Margot.

The dinosaurs are dead, she says. They did used to exist, not like witches, but now they are all dead.

Why are they dead? I ask.

Please don't interrupt, says Margot. Everybody will be dead one day, but for now it's just the dinosaurs and Papa.

And the baby, I add.

Well, yes, and the baby, she says.

Did they have skeletons?

Yes, of course, everything has a skeleton, says Margot. Please concentrate.

So, she says, this is how you make a skeleton. When you get old you grow into a maman, and after that you get very old, with the wrinkles, then you die. Margot pauses.

Then what? I ask.

Then you stop talking and then you are a skeleton and then there is a big party with sandwiches, but not as much cake as at Christmas. And then you get born again like a baby and a policeman comes and pumps you up to be a grownup size.

I'm not sure if that is exactly right, but before I can ask Margot says, No more questions, thank you. And she shuts the book. I have to take the book back to the library before it closes, she says, looking at her watch.

Is it my turn to hide? I ask.

Oh, yes, that's just what I was thinking, she says, but I think she had forgotten all about hide and seek.

I have thought of a new and very good place to hide, though, so I have been waiting for my turn. Margot puts her hands over her eyes and starts to count. She is counting in French today. *Un, deux, trois . . .*

I run back up the path, jumping over the spider, and then, instead of following the path back up to the house, I turn left at the crossroads, as if I were going to go up to the village. As I charge around the corner I run smack into a man and both of us cry out.

It is him. He is big like a bear, bigger than a normal grownup, with grey-black hair and hairy legs covered in scratches. He is wearing shoes, rubber ones like Wellington boots, only not boots. His shoes are wet. He has a big nose with hair coming out of it like spiders' legs. His red dog is nowhere to be seen.

We stand and gape at each other, me looking up, him looking down. Then he takes the little grey cigarette from between his dry lips and squishes it under his foot. White smoke slithers like worms from the corner of his mouth.

You are Pivoine, he says slowly. I know your papa. He shakes his head as though he has sand in his hair. I knew him, he says. Sorry.

I am surprised that he knows any of my names but especially the one that belonged to Papa. Sometimes I am Peony to Maman, which is my real name in English. Papa said it in French, Pivoine, because he was born here. Both names mean the same thing, so I never minded, but it is funny to hear someone I don't know call me that. I don't know why I have the same name as a flower anyway, especially one that I have never seen. I am usually Pea. Pea is not a flower. It is a vegetable, actually.

My name is Pea, mostly, I say to the man. Who are you?

He has crouched down in front of me now and is staring right into my face as though he is about to scold me. My name is Claude, he says. Close up, the part of his head without hair is very ugly, and he smells of cigarette smoke, which makes me feel a bit sick.

Then my face is being licked.

Merlin! Stop! says Claude.

The dog has run over to say hello, but its face smells even worse than Claude's.

Merlin is a funny name for a dog, I say. Is it really magic?

Yes, in a way he is, says Claude, giving Merlin a stroke.

What are you doing down here alone? he asks. He is still staring right at me, and my bone is getting itchy, but his voice seems friendly.

We're playing hide and seek, I reply.

Are you hiding, or seeking?

I'm hiding.

Who's seeking? he asks.

I wonder where Margot is, but then she comes running up through the tall grass and is right by my side. So I am found, and the game is over.

I've got a good idea, I say to her. Let's put on a show!

Margot and I put on shows all the time and we are very good at it. Margot is best at dancing and I am best at singing.

Oh yes! Margot says. I will do some flamenco and you have to clap.

And I will sing a song about ladybirds, I tell Claude.

And you will watch us, we say to him.

Do you like our dresses? says Margot.

OK, he says, frowning a little and looking at me as though he expects me to start singing just like that.

Not here! I say. You have to go to the sitting place and we have to go on the stage. It's over there, come on!

Claude is a strange kind of grownup: he does as he is told. Merlin walks by his feet all the way down to the cherry tree, and when Claude sits down obediently Merlin sits next to him and opens his mouth a little so it looks like he is smiling.

I announce the show and introduce Margot. Ladies and gentlemen, please put your hands together for Margot, the amazing Spanish flamenco dancer!

She is not really Spanish, but we are pretending. I start to clap my hands like maracas and Claude watches.

Clap! I tell him. He tries, but to be honest he is not very good at it and he keeps looking around.

When Margot has finished she does a big bow and I clap and cheer. Claude claps too. Then Margot introduces me and I stand on the stage, feeling a bit nervous. The ladybird song is quite long and sometimes I get the words wrong so I have to do parts of it again. While I am still singing, Claude takes out a shiny green packet and starts to make a cigarette.

No smoking! shouts Margot, but he carries on anyway. So he doesn't always do as he is told.

When we have finished we do curtsies and bows and Claude does applause. Then he stands up slowly and says, Come on then, your maman will be wondering where you've got to.

She won't really, says Margot.

I can help you cross the road, he says.

We are very good at crossing the road, I tell him. I'm five and a half.

Well then, would you be so kind as to keep me company? Claude rubs the sweatiness off his head and wipes his hands on his trousers. Merlin licks his hand.

Of course, I say, because that is polite.

It is slow, walking with Claude. While he walks, Margot and I run up ahead, and back again. Sometimes we stop to look at beetles and flowers.

Have you got friends to play with, from the village? Claude asks when he catches us up. While he is waiting for the answer he is staring at me hard.

Margot is my friend, I say.

Yes, he says, but children from the village, from school?

I didn't go to school very much since Papa died, I say.

Why not? Were you poorly?

No, I wasn't poorly, I say. I was busy being friends with Maman.

Claude's red skin makes wrinkles on his forehead like waves on the seashore. I don't want to get into trouble. In September, I say, I am going to the big school and then I will go every day.

That's good, says Claude. Then you will have lots of friends. A little girl like you should have lots of friends.

The air is starting to cool and there is thunder in our tummies as we run back into the house. I bang the door, too excited to remember that Maman was in a bad temper. The house smells of pastry, making my mouth water, and I spot a quiche sitting on the table under a fly screen. Somehow a fly has got underneath and is buzzing about angrily, trapped inside. I let it out and the salty-sweet smell comes too. My fingers go quickly to the crust and break off a piece before I can stop them.

Margot waggles her own finger at me. That fly has been treading poo on that pie, she says.

I can't see any poo.

Margot raises her eyebrows. I can't see it either, she says, but flies have got very small feet.

So it must be very small bits of poo.

Yes, but it is still poo. Maybe different kinds of poo. Dog poo and cow poo. On that pie. You shouldn't eat it, Pea.

I stare at the crust in my fingers, golden and crumbly. I can't see any poo. The fly tries to settle on my hand and my fingers quickly push the pastry into my mouth.

Margot watches. Well?

Yum, I say.

Not pooey?

Not at all.

Can I have some too, then?

I break a second piece of the crust off, so that we are even, and we lick our lips. Then we dash into the living room to find Maman.

Maman is sitting sideways at the bureau, surrounded by lots of paper and files. Her feet are up on a stool and her cheeks are pink.

Maman, I say, we have a new friend!

She looks up and her shoulders sigh. Her hair is tied back off her face with a green scarf and her face has small drops of sweat running down the sides. She smells of lemons.

Where have you been? she asks.

Down in the low meadow, I tell her. And there was a great big spider catching crickets, and the apples are nearly ready to eat, and we made a new friend.

That's nice, Pea, she says, flipping through the pieces of paper on the desk. She sighs again and wipes her arm across her forehead. She starts to look hard at something up on one of the beams in the ceiling. It's such a mess, she says quietly.

I look around the room. I have left out some toy animals and my card game on the floor.

I'm really sorry, Maman, I say. I'll tidy them up right now.

Just for a moment her eyes begin to turn up in the corners and she starts to unfold her arms.

Have you eaten something? she says.

I think we are going to have a hug and I open out my arms, stepping closer. Bread, I say, and peaches. But just as I am close enough to touch her, her stomach jumps and she folds herself over it like pastry on a pie.

## *Chapter 3*

The sun is already high in the sky, but Maman is still in bed. Down in the kitchen we talk very quietly, in case she's sleeping.

It is day three of our challenge, says Margot. Today we are being helpful.

And also, we are not complaining, I say.

That's right, says Margot.

I spread jam on the bread and pour glasses of milk. When Papa was here, he would get up before we were awake, and the breakfast would already be on the table. In the summer he picked us peaches from the orchard and in the winter when we came downstairs there would be logs crackling in the fireplace and hot chocolate on the stove. Papa liked breakfast time a lot. He drank long slurps of milky coffee out of a big white bowl, and if we had croissants he would dunk them in, pushing the soggy bits into his mouth and fishing with his fingers for the buttery flakes left floating on the surface. But Papa is not here any more because we put him in the ground. He isn't ever coming back.

I wish Papa wasn't dead, I say. I don't think it's complaining if Maman can't hear me.

I know, Pea, says Margot. But people have to die to make room for the babies. If no one died then all the houses and beds would get full and there wouldn't be enough jam at breakfast time.

I think about it, hard.

But then why would the baby have died to make way for another baby? I ask.

Margot is quiet for a while. While she is thinking she sucks her hair. Finally she says, Maybe the new baby is better?

I think of the new baby in Maman's tummy, making her sad and keeping her awake all night. I doubt that this one will be good enough.

We eat slowly, licking jam off our fingers and trying to dunk the bread in the milk without making a mess. At last I hear the bed creak upstairs, and soon afterwards the toilet flushes.

I have laid out a place for Maman, a plate and a knife, a glass for juice and a napkin. I have put a mug by the kettle, but I haven't boiled the water. The milk is in the carton because I can't reach the pottery jug. I have put out bread, butter and two kinds of jam. Margot thinks she will choose cherry, I think apricot. We sit nicely at the table and wait.

Maman comes downstairs; she has put on a big yellow summer dress that gets to her belly and then floats around her legs like a cloud. Her hair is clipped up off her neck with a twinkling butterfly. Her feet are already filthy.

Good morning, I say, smiling my best smile. Margot smiles too, showing her teeth and batting her eyelashes.

Good morning, says Maman, heading straight for the apple juice. She drinks it fast and pours herself seconds. When she has drunk that too she pours a third glass and looks around at the breakfast things.

You've laid the table very nicely, she says, thank you. And she smiles at me.

Margot grins at me and parrots, Yes, Pea, you've laid the table very nicely!

My face feels hot and I try to stop my small smile from spreading into a big one.

You're welcome, I say.

Maman starts the kettle boiling and then sits down at the table.

Would you like me to pass the jam? I say.

Yes, please.

Cherry? I mumble. Or some delicious apricot?

Oh, some delicious apricot I think, please, Pea. Maman smiles again.

I pass it over, carefully, frightened of breaking her smile.

Say something nice, whispers Margot under her breath.

You're looking very beautiful this morning, Maman, I say.

Do you think so? she says. I don't feel very beautiful.

I'm not sure what the best answer is to this. Your dress is very pretty, I try.

Maman looks down at her dress as if she is surprised to find herself wearing it. Thank you, she says.

The kettle has boiled and she pushes the chair back as far as it will go, the feet scraping on the tiles. She stands slowly, heaving herself up with her arms. As she squeezes herself out of the gap between the chair and the table, her baby-belly knocks into the full glass of apple juice and it starts to topple.

I try to catch it but I am too far away and the apple juice spills all over the table. Maman watches it happen. Then the glass rolls towards her, towards the table edge. She does nothing, and it falls, bouncing once on the wooden chair then smashing on the floor. When I look up, Margot is already standing by the door. She waves her fingers, telling me to come too.

Maman is trapped between the chair and the table, and around her feet bright splinters of glass are twinkling, waiting for her to walk so they can stick themselves into her skin.

I'll get the dustpan and brush, I say. But Maman sits back down at the table and covers her face with her hands.

Pea, just go and play, she says. And mind the glass.

But I can . . .

Pea, she yells, just go!

We stand by the road, which is quite busy with cars, waiting for it to be safe to cross. Margot is counting the blue ones. There haven't been any yet.

The breakfast was good, she says.

The glass was bad, I say.

Glass is too breaky, says Margot.

Big bellies full of babies are too clumsy, I say.

We will try again, says Margot.

Maybe we could get the baby to come out, so Maman's belly isn't so clumsy?

Or get a new papa to clean up the glass? says Margot.

Or maybe both?

Yes, both would be good, says Margot. We should think about a plan.

How do you get babies out . . . I start to say, but Margot interrupts.

Here's one! she shouts.

Sylvie's car is coming towards us with the indicator flashing. It is telling us that when she gets to the signpost for our house she is going to turn up the path. She is bringing our bread. Her car is round and blue like the sky, and the backseats are full of baguettes, crammed together in brown paper sacks. She takes the bread to people who live too far away from the baker's. We wave, and she stops on the corner.

Hello! I say.

Hello. Are you OK? Sylvie's mouth is pink like a pig.

Yes, fine thank you.

Where's your maman?

In the kitchen, I say. She's sweeping up the glass.

Sylvie nods. What are you doing down here?

We're going to the low meadow, says Margot.

We are waiting to cross the road, I say.

Does your maman know? Sylvie is frowning as though we have done something wrong. Why do all the grownups ask us silly questions?

We look both ways and we listen and we never run, I say. Well, sometimes we run up to the road, and then we run after we have crossed the road, but not while we are crossing.

We do looking and listening, says Margot.

Right, says Sylvie, well, see you soon.

Yes, I say. Bye!

And Margot says, Sylvie, Papa is dead, so stop giving us so much bread.

Sylvie's eyebrows are still frowning, but her pink mouth smiles and says, Bye!

Claude and Merlin are already down in the low meadow, as if they had been waiting for us. Claude is sitting with his back against a tree trunk, smoking a cigarette. Stinky. Merlin is lying by his side, having his belly rubbed, two wet legs up in the air. As we skip down the path, Merlin barks and tugs at Claude's sleeve. I wave, and Merlin comes galloping over. Claude follows more clumsily behind and we meet halfway, in the middle of the apple orchard.

You shouldn't smoke cigarettes, I tell him, looking at my feet. They make you die.

Hello, Pea, he says. Down here on your own? Want some company?

I remember what Papa said.

I'm not alone, I say, pointing up at Margot, who has climbed up into an apple tree.

Claude looks over and smiles. Oh, hello, Margot, he calls. Then he looks back at me. I used to like climbing trees when I was a boy, he says. Can you do it too?

I'm not very good at it, I say.

Would you like me to teach you?

I'm not sure I would, but at that moment Margot clambers down, jumping the last part and doing a big bow. Your turn! she says.

I get my foot up into the part where all the smaller trunks open out like a hand. I pull myself up, so I am standing in the middle of the tree.

That part's easy, I say.

Good, says Claude. Now you have to choose a branch. So you need to think ahead. Which one looks the best – nice and strong, good footholds, somewhere to sit when you don't want to climb any more?

I see what he means. Some of the branches look good, but then they split very quickly and become thin and leafy. I choose a big fat one, and start to scrabble about on it. The leaves and the apples are in my way and I can't see where to put my foot. I am reaching up with my hands when I feel my foot rest against something firm at just the right height, and I push off against it. But when I try to move my foot on to the next spot it feels stuck. I look down to find that I am standing on Claude's big hand, his fingers still curled around my shoe.

You can let go now, I say.

From there it is easy and soon I am sitting on the branch, holding on tight and dangling my legs. My face is about the same height as Claude's, it's like being a grownup.

Don't fall! says Margot.

I hadn't thought about falling, but now I do, and I wobble. Oh!

Don't worry, says Claude, you're not going to fall. He peers at me. How is your maman? he asks.

Maman is sad, I say.

Because of your papa, says Claude. It isn't a question, but it's not the right answer either.

I think for a minute, twisting my fingers round in the leaves.

Maman is sad because the baby died, I say, because it wasn't good enough. She didn't want it to have to make way for the new one. I think she wanted to keep that one. And she is sad because the new one kicks her and keeps her awake and won't let her walk properly. And she's sad because there was a fly stuck to her foot and because her belly knocked over the juice and because she couldn't bend down to clean it up and because Papa isn't there to help her. And also she wanted to keep Papa, but he died.

It was a disaster, says Margot. Down near my feet, she is being a ballerina, twirling and jumping. Maybe she wants Claude to ask her about Maman, but he is asking me.

Stop interrupting me! I say. We are trying to make Maman happy but we have about a thousand things on our list so it is taking a long time, I tell Claude. But she likes it best when she is at home and we are not.

I'm sure that's not true, says Claude.

It is, definitely, I say. So we come here, or otherwise we go to Windy Hill. That way we are helping.

And it's fun, says Margot.

It's lots of fun, I say.

Do you know where we could get a new papa? asks Margot.

Windy Hill, says Claude, where's that?

Over the high pasture, I say, where you can see the wing turbines and the sea.

Ah, says Claude. He twists his mouth so it looks half sad and half happy. He has a very ugly face, but his eyes are kind. His hand comes out towards the branch, and I think he is going to touch my shoulder. Not to push me, but a sort of a pat, or a tiny hug. Probably it would be quite nice. But that's not what he does. He puts his hand on the tree branch and leans in a little bit. I can smell coffee on his lips.

Come on, he says, I've got something to show you.

Claude has led us down to the stream. He wants us to cross the stepping stones.

Do you know what is on the other side? I say.

Claude nods. I do, he says.

Do you know who put these stepping stones here?

Yes, says Claude, I do.

Was it witches?

No.

Was it you?

Claude smiles and looks up. Margot has already set off across the stones, holding her hands out like a tightrope walker. Merlin goes next, splashing through the pools of tadpoles.

Come on! says Margot.

I start to cross, wobbling as I go. By the third stone I am far from both sides, but the fourth one is not very flat and I'm not sure where to put my next foot.

I can't do it! I say.

Here, let me help, says Claude. He walks down into the water and holds out his hand.

You're getting your feet wet!

That's OK, says Claude, I have my waterproof shoes on, and anyway the water feels nice!

I put my small hand in his big one and soon my feet are safe on the other bank.

The low pasture is mostly field and not so many trees. The field is wide and tall, a sea of grass up over my head, coloured-in with flower-fish. There are no cows or sheep here now; they have gone on their summer holidays up the mountain. Only their poo is left behind.

Look at all the flowers! I say.

No donkeys, says Margot, no cows, no sheep. That's why.

We can pick a big bunch on the way home, I say. We can have all of the colours. But first, please can we see the surprise?

Claude nods.

Where is it? I ask him.

He points to the corner of the field.

Can you see anything? I ask Margot.

Margot shakes her head.

Come here, says Claude. He puts his hands under my arms and scoops me up above the grass. Look over in that corner, he says.

There is a big clump of trees. I can't see anything exciting about them. Just that some of the colours are not tree colours.

You should go and have a look, says Claude. Merlin will show you the way.

Let's go! says Margot, charging off, swish-swash-swish. I run after her, right into the long grass, sweeping it aside with my arms as I go. Merlin leaps along by my side.

The tree has a fat trunk that my arms do not fit around. There is a small wooden ladder leaning against it, fastened to the trunk with blue rope. Up in the leaves there are some smaller branches missing, cut away, and big planks of wood have been nailed there, with sides like a big wooden basket. A green and red blanket is hanging over the edge.

It's a nest, says Margot, for girls!

Can we climb up? I say.

Well, it's obvious we are supposed to, says Margot. This must be the surprise! And her fat bottom is in my face as she monkeys up into the tree. I follow close behind.

From the girl-nest, looking out into the low pasture I can see back across the sea of grass and over the stream into the meadow. I can see the top half of Claude, slowly following the rushed snake of crumpled grass that we made to get here. There are other snakes I can see from here too, other paths to our tree. Now I am a bird on a branch, seeing the people-places from up high. Everything looks strange and different and exciting.

I'm going to live here instead, I say.

Well, you could! Margot is flicking tea towels at me.

I could?

Yes, says Margot. Look at this!

On the wooden floor, the big checked blanket is spread out and laid for a picnic. Margot has already found a bottle of lemonade and some cake. We peel the other tea towels off bowls and plates and find more treasure. There is a baguette, crisps and cubes of cheese in shiny paper. There is no salad and no sandwiches, just party food. There are a few ants, but the baguette is too big for them to carry. I stuff a whole slice of cake into my mouth.

Hello up there! says Claude.

I look out over the uppy-edge and down at Claude. I chew and swallow quickly. It's a girl-nest! I shout back down.

Claude puts on the biggest smile I have ever seen him wear. His face goes even more spicy-red.

Do you like it, Pea? he says. The words are soft in his mouth, like goodnights used to be from Maman and Papa. Just before they would say 'I love you' and '*Je t'aime*'.

It's brilliant! I say. Are we having a party?

Is it your birthday? says Margot.

Yes, it's Merlin's birthday, says Claude.

How old is he?

He's eleven.

That's not even grownup.

Well, it's quite old for a dog.

Happy birthday, Merlin! says Margot.

Who's coming to the party? I say.

Just you, Margot, Merlin and me.

Merlin flops down under the tree with a grunt.

Ah, says Claude, Merlin thinks he would like to stay down here.

Well of course he does, says Margot, dogs can't climb trees.

If it's his birthday he should be able to do what he wants, I say.

I think I'll stay down here with him, says Claude. Let me just come up and get our plates.

There isn't really that much room up here anyway; I am not sure Claude would fit. When his face appears at the top of the ladder, Margot says, Hello, Mister Claude, what would you like from our café?

Would you like some wine, Mister Claude? I say.

Yes please, he says, and I pass him a cup. Could I have birthday cake for Merlin and me, also? Oh, and a bowl for Merlin's water.

There you are, Mister Claude, enjoy your lunch, I say, passing him plastic plates and laughing. Claude really is a funny grownup.

Claude disappears again, and soon after the smell of cigarette smoke comes up from under the tree. I don't really mind it today. The cake has cherries in and now I am not so hungry I pick them out and eat them first. When my tummy is so full that I can't eat one more cherry I climb down the ladder and sit next to Merlin in the shade. Merlin is having his belly rubbed and making small happy noises.

Claude, I say, you made the girl-nest, didn't you?

I did, he says.

And the stepping stones to get here?

Those too.

For us?

For you. Claude looks up at me. His fingers go too far across Merlin's belly and touch my knee and it tickles.

Why did you make us a girl-nest? I say.

Claude shrugs and keeps stroking Merlin. The scratchy tips of his fingers brush my skin, back and forth. Every little girl needs a secret, he says.

## *Chapter 4*

Today is Wednesday, and on Wednesdays we go to the market. Well, in fact the market comes to us.

We walk together down to the village road, on the lane, not through the peaches. Maman walks ahead, leaning back as she goes down the hill, walking so fast that her hair can't keep up. The air is warm and wet and the hurrying makes me sweaty. Maman looks up at the white sky and rushes on. When we reach the road she pauses to catch her breath, which is coming in short huffs.

I used to love market day. We would spend all morning winding around the stalls, touching the carved wooden toys, hiding in the racks of bright patchwork trousers. We would dilly and dally by the stalls that let you taste things: honey, fruit juice, olives and jam. We would even sometimes have our lunch there, sitting outside in the sun. Every Wednesday morning in the village was like a party. But now we just do our shopping, we don't speak to anyone, and we go home.

I wonder, whispers Margot, if we just crossed over here, would she notice we'd gone?

I wonder too. The gate we climb to get into the low meadow is just across the road. The donkeys are hanging their heads over it and grinning at us. The brown one pushes his nose forward and does a noisy *hee-haw*! They are pleased to see us.

Come on, let's go, says Margot. She takes my hand and we look and listen, ready to cross the road.

But Maman has got her breath back. She grabs my other hand and sets off again, turning right, towards the village. Margot and I are pulled along behind her like ducklings in a row. On the crumbly tarmac we have to stick close to the side because it is narrow and cars come too fast.

There is only one house between our lane and where the village begins, and it is far back from the road. You can just see the red roof tiles peeking through between gaps in the trees. As we pass along the garden wall we peer in, wondering who lives there. Every now and then I can taste the sweetness of jasmine, but the flowers are hidden. We run our fingers along the rough stones. Skinny brown lizards bake themselves in the cracks. When they see our hands creeping closer they blink their shiny black eyes and skitter away.

You can hear and smell the market a long time before you get there. Chattering grownups and laughing children, dogs barking and paella cooking – the smells and sounds all pour up the street to meet us. By the time we get there the village square is dancing with colours. Lots of people are going from stand to stand, the ones who carry baskets are shopping, and there are others just having a look. Some people are sitting outside the café under the plane trees, drinking teeny cups of coffee or glasses of beer. They don't seem very worried by the clouds. I recognise some faces that are here every week, but others are new.

In summertime the market is bigger and full of people who are here on their holidays. It's easy to tell who is who. The people that were born here move slowly, when they move at all. They are brown-skinned, and smile at each other and say hello. They stop and chat in the middle of crowds, while the holiday people hurry around, turning red in the sun and snapping at each other. Sometimes it seems that there are two markets, both happening at the same time, one for normal people doing their shopping, and one for the others, having a holiday. We all mix up together in the market but we are as separate as apples and oranges in a bowl.

Maman came here on holiday too, once upon a time. She said she was looking for peace and quiet. But instead she found Papa and stayed for ever. Whenever Maman told me about meeting Papa – and I made her tell me about it a lot – she would turn pink and smile so hard that tears squeezed out. Even before he died. Papa was her handsome prince, she said.

Maman is pushing through the crowds belly first. She has her hands on it, so no one bumps the baby, but it looks as though someone has tied a string to her belly button and is pulling her along. As she marches through them, people step away from her, making a bubble of air around us like a cage.

There are some children from my old nursery school. I wave at them as I am tugged past and shout, *Coucou!* But they don't wave back. They start to laugh.

Papa was an orange but we are apples, I say.

You know why you are super-clever? says Margot.

I'm not.

You are.

Why?

Because you can speak all the languages and they can only speak one.

I can't speak all the languages, I say. What about Spanish?

Well then most of the languages.

We have come to a corner where a man is roasting chickens on spits. The air is full of roasting flavours and the corner is blocked by people huddling by the stand just to taste the chicken smell, even if they aren't going to buy one. We have never bought one of these chickens but I am sure I know how delicious it would be. I slow down, letting the saltiness fill my mouth and my ears eat up the sizzling sound. Maman grabs me by the hand and pulls me away.

As we turn the corner, there is Claude. He is standing with Merlin at the butcher's van. The butcher is wrapping up meat in white paper parcels. Merlin is staring at it, then he sniffs the air and turns his head my way. When he sees us he barks a loud hello and wags his flappy tail.

Claude turns too and looks over in our direction then says something to Merlin. He looks at Maman, then at me and Margot, then back at Maman. He smiles half a smile. He looks like he wants to be friendly but thinks Maman might bite him. With the head she has on her today I am afraid she might.

He needn't worry, because Maman doesn't see him at all; she is following her list. As we pass by him I look up. He is turning back to the butcher to pay for his sausages, but not before winking at Margot and me.

At the market we have a routine. It means we do the same things every week. We get our meat first and it goes in the bottom of the basket. Then we go to the vegetable stall and we buy something green, depending on the weather. In the summer that means courgettes and artichokes, green beans and peas in pods. After that we go to Marcel the fruit man under his stripy yellow awning. He is quite fat with white hair and a red face and an apron covered in seeds and juice. And he has one gold tooth. His wife is there too. She is thin and happy-looking and doesn't say much. As Marcel juggles plums into brown paper bags, for weighing, she is arranging the fruit and bringing out new trays of things from the back of a white van.

While Maman is choosing between different kinds of plums and apricots, round tomatoes on vines or the ones that look like small red pumpkins, we stand in the queue – there is always a queue. Margot decides on one kind of fruit and does counting; she can count all the numbers, which is clever but quickly becomes boring. What's worse, if someone buys some of whatever she is counting she has to start again. I just like to press my nose close to the fruit displays to breathe in the warm, ripe smells. Marcel always notices me and comes to tell me how beautiful I am.

Today there is a cantaloupe cut open on top of the others, green on the outside but orange on the inside. I can smell the honey-sweetness from far away. I put my face so close to it I could reach out and catch the juice on my tongue. My nose is tweaked.

Hello, green-eyes, Marcel says, how are your curls today? Hey, Dolly (he calls me that, but it's not a good nickname: I am not a dolly at all, I am a five-years-old girl). Hey, Dolly, what would you like from Marcel today? Usually he gives me apricots or slices of peach and a pinch on the cheek. Today Marcel hands me a nectarine, which I share with Margot. Marcel laughs and says, You'd better get home, Dolly, there's going to be a storm.

When Maman has chosen, he changes his voice to a more special one and says to her, Hello, *Madame*, how are you today? Then he nods at her belly and says, Can't be long now!

Maman, as usual these days, does a smile that is not a smile and says, Hello. She looks up at the sky, which is getting dark.

After fruit we buy green olives, scooped into a clean jar that Maman pulls out from her basket. Then we go for cheese, usually goat's cheese because that was what Papa always asked for, and then to the baker's for tomorrow's croissants. When Maman was cheerful she would buy us a treat to share, a pain au chocolat or a brioche, but today we just get the croissants and hurry away.

Come on, says Maman, let's get a drink before we go home.

Ooh yes, says Margot, I would like a glass of lemonade, please, with an ice cube and a pink straw.

But that's not what Maman means. In the middle of the village square is a fountain where pigeons take their baths in the pools at the base. All around its sides, dark metal fish spurt water out of their mouths and we catch it in ours, Maman too. The holiday people look at us strangely, as though we are savages to drink the water, but you can tell that they would like to join in. Maman splashes it on to her face and neck and I copy her. The cool water feels perfect against my summer skin.

As we go back up the lane to the house, Maman is huffing and puffing. She has one hand on her basket and the other on her back. Every few steps she is swapping hands. Now it is Margot and I who are leading the way and Maman who is trailing behind. Even without the sun, the day is turning very hot and we are all sweating. About halfway up, Maman stops and just sits down on the path. She takes off her shoes and rubs her feet which are big and very pink. She breathes like this: her-hoo, her-hoo, her-hoo.

It takes us a long time to get her home, and when we walk into the kitchen, Maman puts down the basket and drops into a chair. I get her a cold drink from the fridge and then lay out everything on the table for our market-day lunch: bread and butter with salt on, slices of tomatoes, cheese and olives. Maman drinks her drink and watches me without smiling. She is holding her head up with one hand, her elbow on the table.

I'm sorry, Pea, she says at last. I think I'm going to go and have a lie-down. I watch her drag herself upstairs without eating a bite.

Shall we eat, or go and play? says Margot.

Both, I say grumpily. First, lunch. I've been hungry ever since the chickens.

I make two plates of food, with all our favourite things. I put more salt on the bread than I should and leave off the cheese. I find a bottle of fizzy drink in the pantry and manage to get it open. I eat my tomato like an apple, getting the juice all over my dress, and I use my fingers for the olives, licking off the oil and going back into the jar for more without washing my hands. When we have finished eating I leave the food uncovered and we go out to play without clearing the plates.

Children from the village used to come here all the time, to play in the fields. They made dens, and tree houses, and the big ones sometimes left bottles and litter. Our barn has its back turned to the fields, with one round eye looking out to the high pasture and the wing turbines. Around the edges of our courtyard we have a lot of fruit trees: a small bundle of apple trees that maybe once were an orchard, two pomegranate trees, a fig tree and a quince tree next to each other, an olive tree on its own and a great big cherry tree.

The fruit game started with the quince tree. The quinces are no good at all to eat, and anyway the tree is sick and all the fruit goes brown and bobbled. The summer when I was three years old some boys from the village picked all the quinces from the tree and threw them at the back of the barn, trying to score goals through the ox-eye. Most of the fruits rotted around the bottom of the barn, only a few got in. Papa found them near his tractor and laughed. Funny game, he said.

In autumn they started on the pomegranates. We don't pick many to eat or sell; they usually just burst open on the tree. Then the magpies peck at the jewels inside until the fruits fall off and smash. The boys had got better at the fruit game and a lot of the pomegranates went through the hole. The ones that didn't exploded on the wall, the seeds making a glittery red carpet by the barn. Papa grumbled as he swept up the mess.

The next spring the boys took cherries off the tree, all the ones they could reach. The fruit was too good to waste so they ate the cherries then tried with the stones, either throwing them or spitting. But the stones were no good for that so they started using the unripe apples. It was just after Maman came home from the hospital, which was bad luck for the boys because Papa exploded.

Enough is enough! he shouted at them. I had never heard him shout before, not once.

We eat those apples, he said. They are not toys, and neither is my barn. Go and find something useful to do with your week-ends, and if I ever catch you taking my peaches I will really give you something to be sorry for.

The boys never came back, so last year's pomegranates fell off the trees as usual and there were plenty of cherries on the tree that I could knock off with the mop. But it had been nice to have other children up here even if they weren't my friends. Sometimes now the fruit looks lonely.

Margot, I say, I have the darkness and it's cloudy. We can go to Windy Hill. I don't say it like a question because I am not feeling in a very good mood.

That's OK, says Margot, and takes my hand.

On Windy Hill there are pine trees and poplar trees, fig trees and oaks. It smells of salt, herbs and animals' skin and now, in summer, it smells like the earth is cooking. There are gorse bushes with yellow flowers that look like purses and smell like coconut. In between the big boulders there is lavender and rosemary, which you can chew if you are hungry.

Today there is a strong breeze that feels delicious in my hair and I stand for a while letting myself be blown and staring out at the turbines. The ground is hard and stony here and not comfortable to sit on. Even in spring, when the poplar trees throw off swirling balls of fluff that make a soft white carpet on the hill, when you would think it would be nice to sit down on it, the stones come through and leave purple-red bruises on your legs.

Out behind the wing turbines you can usually see the sea if you squint a little bit. If you use your imagination you can even see pink flamingos wading through the *étangs* on stick-legs, grazing the salty water for their food. If you come here early in the mornings you can see the sunrise, turning everything from grey to rosy.

Nothing is rosy now, though. Not blue either. The sky is low-down swirls of grey and the air is warm and heavy. We can't stay too long, I say.

We haven't seen good clouds for ages, says Margot. Let's see what there is.

So even though these ones are dark and low and not very pretty, I unstick my eyes from the turbines and start to name them.

Elephant, dragonfly, house, I say.

Sausage, robot, knickers, says Margot.

Then she begins on the clouds right above her, tilting her face up so far she nearly falls over backwards.

Oh! Lie on your back, she says.

No, it'll hurt!

Go on, just try, she says. And she lies down in the scrubby dirt.

I lie down beside her, our feet touching and the ground digging into my back, and we stare up at the gloomy sky.

By lying like this the clouds blowing fast overhead don't look like animals any more, but monsters. In the distance there is a rumbling of very quiet thunder which makes it even worse. We lie here scaring ourselves until a giant purple-black cloud sails up, making its shadow right over us and bringing a cold wind with it that whips up the dust, sharp on to my face. But I am busy thinking. There is a strange mistiness under the cloud, as though parts of it are breaking away and flying off in the wind. I am trying to figure out what it is doing when a piece of the sky hits me between the eyes.

To begin with I think the boys have come back and are throwing peach stones at us, until I see the chunk of ice at my feet, which is unusual. I sit up and shout, Hey! But no one is there. A second one hits the top of my head, and then another smacks me on the back. Now big lumps of ice are falling all around. It starts off as a pattering, but quickly becomes a smashing and a clattering of icy stones, bouncing off the rocky hill, and my less rocky head. Where they hit my bare arms and legs it stings and burns.

Come on! says Margot, pointing at a big fir tree nearby. We dash under the umbrella of branches, pressing ourselves up against the trunk. The branches are thick and spread wide from the trunk but the ice is coming in sideways and snapping around my feet.

The sky suddenly lights up in a big flash, a crack of thunder booms and I can't help my tears.

Don't worry, says Margot, it won't last long.

I don't like it.

It will go past soon, Margot says. You saw how hard the wind is blowing.

But the sky is dark all around and so many hailstones are falling so fast that I can't see anything beyond the tree.

Margot, I want Maman, I cry.

Hang on, Pea.

There is another flash of bright white light and a smashing like cymbals by my ears. I think about climbing up into the tree, but there are no footholds, the needles are spiky and blowing in the wind. I hug myself against it closer, pressing one ear to the scratchy bark and covering the other with my hand. Margot presses up behind me. She starts to sing.

I hear thunder! I hear thunder! Hark, don't you? Hark, don't you? Pitter patter raindrops, pitter patter . . . she stops without finishing the song.

Through the thinning shower of ice, a shadow appears on the path. It is moving quickly towards us, with one glowing white eye and a black coat flapping in the wind. It's a storm-witch! I scream. But it keeps on coming and I don't know what to do. I keep screaming as it gets closer and closer. Then I see. It is not a witch at all, but Claude, holding a coat over his head and staggering towards us, fast.

What are you doing here? I shout, because Claude belongs to the meadow not Windy Hill. But he doesn't answer. He grabs my arm hard, pulling me away from the tree and under his coat-roof. Through panting breaths he says, Go!

The thunder seems to be all around now, the skies growling angrily as we stumble through the pelting ice across the high pasture and down a dirt track. But it is not the one that leads to our house.

It's the wrong way! I shout, but Claude says nothing.

We are moving too fast for me to shout in his ear. I am holding on to Claude's T-shirt and being sort of dragged along. I am not at all happy, but before I have a chance to concentrate properly on what I would rather be doing we are arriving at a big stone house. I recognise it – it is the one we saw this morning from the road. Claude is not taking us to the house, though, but towards a barn next to it. As he rattles the latch on the big wooden door, another crack of thunder shakes my feet and the sky lights up as though someone has lifted its lid off. At last the door swings open and I am shoved inside. I stand at the entrance feeling dizzy and ready to cry again.

Are you OK? Claude asks.

We nod, miserably. Although Claude is a grownup, he doesn't seem to know what to do next. For a minute he is just standing there, panting like a dog. The hailstones are thumping down on the roof and on the wooden shutters where the windows would be. Claude throws the raincoat down on to the stone floor of the barn and turns to close the door.

Have you got any towels? I ask him.

He keeps his back to me and doesn't answer. Then he turns and stares hard.

Could we have some towels, please? I ask again.

Claude looks around. Right at the back of the barn are some bales of hay stacked up against the wall.

Sit down over there, Pea, he says. I'll find something. And he goes back out into the storm, slamming the door behind him.

The hay smells fusty and is scratchy on my bare legs. I tuck them up under my wet dress and wrap my arms around myself, shivering.

Let's have a look around, while he's gone, says Margot.

I daren't, I say. What if he comes back? He told us to sit here.

Not me, just you, she says. I'm not scared. And she hops down from the hay to go exploring. I follow her with my eyes.

Against one wall there is a big pile of logs, stacked neatly in rows. Margot sniffs at them, but I can smell them from here. They smell like just the firewood we have at home, which is chopped-up oak trees. By the door where we came in there are two sacks of dog food, some paint tins with drippy lids, white and yellow, and a stack of black buckets. Margot looks in the buckets and shrugs. Empty.

On the other wall there is an old *armoire* by the shuttered window and lots of tools hung up on nails, just like Papa has at home: saws and knives, spades and rakes and hammers.

The hay takes up half of the other wall, and then in the space that is left, not far from where I am sitting, is a corner cluttered with big things that wouldn't hang up on nails. Margot stops by the corner and points.

Look, Pea! Look!

There is a wheelbarrow, a ladder, some ropes and tarpaulins and right at the back there are two shiny little red bikes.

## *Chapter 5*

Can we ride on them? The bikes have taken my mind off the bruises coming up on my neck and back.

Claude, who has just walked back through the barn door holding towels, looks over at the bikes.

Ah, he says. Listen, we'd need to ask your maman first. He passes me a towel and I wrap it around me. He drapes another one over my head so I look like I'm getting married.

She won't mind, says Margot.

Really, Maman won't mind at all as long as we don't bother her, I add.

Claude scowls at the bikes. He crouches down and brings his rained-on head close.

These things have to be done properly, he says. His voice sounds like the rumble is coming up from his tummy. These are very special bikes, you know. I don't share them with just anybody who asks. He winks at me. Claude winks a lot. He's very funny.

But they're too little for you, says Margot.

And also, there are two of them and only one of you.

A very good point, says Claude. Can you ride a bike?

I don't know, I admit.

I bet you could if you tried, he says. You look like the kind of girl who'd be particularly clever at bike-riding. Maybe I'll teach you. Claude frowns slightly. But not today.

Why not today?

You're all wet. You'd make the handlebars go rusty.

Merlin has come into the barn, maybe to see what the fuss is all about, and he trots over. I am wrapped in the towels, but my dress is still wet and I'm cold. I hug Merlin up against me. His tail thumps against the bale of hay. It feels cosier now. The banging on the roof has stopped and there is just a dripping noise. A bird chirrups outside the window. A blackbird, I think.

Claude scratches his head. His hair is slicked back, showing his ugly part.

Claude, what is wrong with your head?

Claude looks very surprised, as though he just saw himself in a mirror for the first time. His hand goes up to touch where the hair isn't.

Didn't you know? I say.

Well, yes, says Claude. But you're the first person who ever asked me about it.

Really?

Really.

The problem with a lot of people, says Margot, is that they don't notice the important things.

Does it hurt? I say.

Not now, no, says Claude.

So how did it get like that?

A tiger bit me, he says.

That's not true. You don't get tigers in France, says Margot.

Are there tigers in France? I ask Claude.

It escaped from a zoo, he says.

Wow! we say.

It bit my leg too; I was quite lucky to get away alive.

That's right, says Margot. You should always beware of tigers. And lions too.

And bears, I add, and snakes.

All excellent advice, says Claude.

I am going to tell him about some more ferocious animals, but my words turn into a big, wide-mouth yawn. I snuggle down on my hay bale, my arm draped over Merlin. Sunlight sloshes through the windows, brightening my thoughts and warming me into sleepiness. I fly up into my head to play with my thoughts.

When I wake up I have another towel on top of me like a blanket. Merlin is still here, but he is lying down on the floor, snoring. Margot has found a thin piece of rope which she is using to skip with. She is completely dry.

Claude has a rag and is standing by the *armoire* polishing a big knife shaped like a banana, his fingers moving in tiny circles on the metal. He seems to be concentrating hard, rubbing the same spot over and over as though there is a stain on it he can't get off. But the knife is shiny-clean. A sunbeam slants in through the shutters and glints off the edge of the blade. Summer has come back while I slept.

I'm awake, I say.

Merlin wakes up and barks a friendly sort of bark.

Sixty-six, sixty-seven, sixty-eight, says Margot. She even counts when she is skipping.

Claude looks up at me. Did you have a nice sleep?

I nod, feeling a bit shy. What's that for? I ask.

Claude swaps the knife into his other hand and swishes it through a dusty sunbeam. It's for hacking through the jungle when you're looking for elephants, he says.

Oh, I say.

When I am an elephant, Margot says, you will never catch me. I'm too fast for you.

And when I am a tiger, I say, I won't bite you.

You won't? says Claude.

Probably not.

Claude smiles crookedly and says, Listen, I want to tell you a story. He puts the knife back on its nail and his cleaning rag in a drawer. Then he comes over to the hay bales and sits down beside me. He is damp and smells like bath-time. Margot comes over and sits on the floor at his feet, next to Merlin. We like stories.

Once upon a time, says Claude, there was a little boy called Gaston, who liked very much to have adventures. One day, this little boy was out on a hill, when a storm came over, with thunder and lightning. Lots of it.

Just like us, today! I say.

What happened? says Margot.

What do you think he did? Claude asks.

We shake our heads and shrug.

Well, first of all, because he was very scared, he went and sheltered from the storm under a great big oak tree. But then, while he was there he remembered what his papa had once taught him. Claude pauses.

What? I ask.

His papa had said, Gaston, if you are ever caught in a storm you must never, ever shelter under a tree. Claude looks up at me. Never, ever, he says, slowly.

Why? Margot and I ask, both at the same time.

Because the lightning is looking for tall things to hit, says Claude.

I wonder why the lightning doesn't like tall things, but Claude carries on.

So Gaston plucked up all his courage – that means braveness – and he got out from under the tree and he ran all the way home in the thunder and the lightning and the rain. When he got home he was very wet, but he was safe.

That's a silly story, says Margot.

I kick her feet and scowl at her. Sometimes she says very rude things, even to grownups. She gets up and goes to skulk around the bikes.

I haven't finished, says Claude. Do you know what that boy found, when he went up to the hill the next day?

No, I say.

He found the big oak tree had been struck by lightning, and there was nothing left of it but a small black stump. It was still smoking.

I make the surprised O with my mouth, although I am not really that surprised. It was the kind of story that grownups tell children to complicate a thing when they could just tell you the thing itself, much faster.

Is that a true story? I ask.

It must be, says Claude. And it should tell you that you have to be clever about looking after yourself. Do you promise me you'll be careful? He sounds like Papa and I feel the music of his words tugging inside me.

OK, I say. We'll be careful.

Claude looks at his watch. Well, Pea, the storm has passed; your maman will be worried about you so you and Margot had better get home. He takes his banana knife off the nail and opens the barn door with a creak, letting the warm day find us again.

After you, he says.

Outside is sweet and grassy. The clouds are far in the distance and above us blue skies have made the garden colourful again. In between the barn and the house are rows of tomatoes, peas and yellow courgettes growing on canes. There is a square patch of soil dotted with bright-green lettuce-mops and floppy-leaved pink radishes. I don't really like radishes much, they sting my tongue, but they are one of the nicest coloured of the vegetables.

Can we see the garden? I ask.

Why not? says Claude. Follow me, and stay on the path.

We walk slowly in amongst the vegetables. My dress is clammy against my legs and my feet sink into the wet soil. As we go, Claude pulls out small weeds with the tips of his fingers and pinches tiny insects off the tomatoes with the hand that is not holding the banana knife. He lets a ladybird crawl on to his finger and passes it to me, the ladybird using his fingernail as a bridge between our hands.

Can I see? says Margot, sidling up close. She starts to count the spots. One, two, three, four, five. Easy, she says.

I turn to her and she watches the ladybird crawl up my arm, the little hairs like a tiny insect-sized forest.

She's my friend, says Claude. She eats bad bugs.

She's beautiful, I say.

That's her name, says Claude. *Belle la coccinelle*. He smiles.

It rhymes! I say.

Put her back when you've had enough, says Claude, I need her for my plants.

So I let her walk off my finger on to the tomato vine. We walk further down into the garden. But walking is quite boring and Margot and I start to run off ahead. We are really fast, we are like leopards through the grass. Soon we get to a clump of oleanders growing around a square wall.

Oleanders look nice, says Margot, but in fact they are dangerous and will poison you to death.

I know, I say.

So don't even touch them!

Can the smell poison you?

Margot shrugs. Probably, if you smell enough of it.

We find a gap in the bushes where we don't have to touch the leaves or the flowers, and try to investigate. The wall is just too high for us to peer in, even on tiptoes, but I manage to hoick myself up so my legs are dangling down and I am half leaning in, looking over the rim. It doesn't smell so good. Inside it is full of black-green water, with a cloud of mosquitoes buzzing above. I rock forward and back. Margot is smaller than me and she can't quite get up to have a look.

Come on, I say, jump yourself up. There is a pool in there. I don't want to swim in it, though.

What kind of pool? asks Margot, still clambering against the wall and scrabbling with her feet, but not managing to see in. Is it like a drinking bowl for elephants?

Mind your toes, I say.

Then, No! yells Claude and the loudness of his voice makes me let go and wobble scarily. I twist off wall and stand my feet back down on the wet grass and look at him. He is coming fast towards us. One hand is reaching out and the other one has still got his banana knife, glinty-sharp. My bone is itching. I scratch at the skin that covers it, watching the red lines turn white and then dark red again. Not looking at Claude. Merlin's nose arrives at my feet.

That's. Dangerous, Claude says to my face. He is crouched down, his spit is getting on me.

I don't like being shouted at. I scowl at him and stare my eyes hard so that the tears can't get out.

Are there elephants in your garden? Margot asks.

Claude's face is an ugly big plum. Stay away from there, he says in his rumble-voice. You could drown.

Sorry, I say quietly. Is it where the elephants drink?

Elephants? says Claude.

The elephants you hunt. With your banana knife.

Ah. Claude breathes a big breath. No, there aren't any elephants here. No tigers either. But sometimes in summer my garden does look like a jungle, so the knife is still useful. Claude scratches at the cuts on his legs. I'm sorry I shouted at you. Now, he says, before you get into any more trouble today, I think it's time you got home. If you go back up that path it will take you up to where I found you earlier, and the tree which may or may not still be there now . . .

Margot starts to jump on the spot and I know what she is thinking.

No, Margot, I say, we cannot go and check.

Huh. Margot folds her arms.

If you go this way, Claude says, pointing down through a patchwork of grass, marigolds and roses, you will get to the road, and over to the meadow.

And if you go this way – he points up behind the well to a high hedge – on the other side you will find the irrigation canal, which

I think you are big enough to jump across, and on the other side is your papa's peach orchard. You can get home fastest that way.

It looks quite spiky, I say.

Here. Claude shows us a perfect, girl-sized gap. Go on, he says.

Goodbye, we shout, and jump over the stream of water, laughing as we run back up through the orchard.

The kitchen table is tidy, everything put away, washed and wiped.

I forgot about the challenge, didn't I? I say. Maman will definitely not be happy. I'm going to be punished for the mess.

Shall we play in our room? says Margot.

I'd rather get told off quickly, I say.

We'd better find her then. Guess where she is? Margot is grinning.

I put up my finger. Me! Me!

Yes, Peony?

In her bedroom! I say.

Not a bad guess, says Margot. Let's go and see.

We still walk quietly upstairs, in case she is asleep. Maman's bedroom door is ajar, so I push it a little bit and peep around into the room. It is shady, with just a straight of light coming through a crack in the shutters. Fairies are flying around in the glow.

Maman is in her bed with her dress on. She is lying on her side facing me. She is fast asleep and so beautiful, like a queen. It makes me think of Papa. He used to call her 'the queen of my heart' which sounds like a song, and sometimes they called me Princess. Looking at Maman on her bed, I wonder if it is true. This could be our hilltop castle, built of gold and stone, looking out over our kingdom, away from everybody else. Kings and queens and princesses don't have to speak to normal people, only to fairies and talking cats.

Are you a queen? I whisper.

Is this your tower? says Margot.

Did a witch put a spell on you? I say.

Maman does not answer, just snores a little bit. The fan blows ripples in her yellow dress. The fan is brown, but has three turning blades, just like the white wing turbines. I imagine how wonderful it would be to fall asleep watching it turn, turn, turn.

The telephone rings. Once. Twice. I wonder, should I answer it? Maman will not be pleased. Or should I leave it (it will wake her up and she will not be pleased)?

Answer the phone, says Margot. It's giving me a headache.

Or you could answer it! I snap. But then I run fast to pick it up.

Hello?

Hello, says Mami Lafont, is your mother there?

I make my yucky-food face at Margot and she makes one back. I try not to giggle. Mami Lafont is my grandma. She lives on the other side of the village with Tante Brigitte. Before Papa died, if she phoned, she would always want to talk to Papa. Now she calls for Maman but it's usually me that answers the phone. Mami Lafont is not very friendly and she does not like to chat. Her hands are thin and bony like a witch's, and usually cold even in the summer. She doesn't seem to like children much. Whenever we used to go to her house with Papa, there was nothing to play with and she never had any good biscuits. I am not pleased that Papa is dead, but it is good that we never go there any more.

Papa told me that when he was little, he and Tante Brigitte and Mami Lafont and Papi Lafont, who died a long time ago, used to all live up here in our house. Then it was Papi who rode on the tractor and Papa helping him out. But that was a very long time ago, in the olden days. I wonder if Mami Lafont was nicer then, and if Papi called her the queen of his heart. Maybe she had a dead baby too, or maybe all the mamans turn cross one day.

Hello, Mami Lafont, I say. Maman's asleep at the moment.

And so who is looking after you? Mami Lafont asks.

Margot's here, I say.

What? Mami Lafont sounds cross.

We're fine, I say.

Fine? Well could you tell your mother to call me? Tell her it can't wait. Tell her I won't go away.

I ponder for a moment because this is confusing. Where would Mami Lafont be going away to, and why has she decided not to? Holidays, perhaps? I will ask Margot later.

Pardon? I say.

Just tell her to call me, please, she says.

I imagine saying this to Maman. I imagine Maman's face. Yuckier than mine and Margot's.

I'll try, I say.

Right, she says. Goodbye. Then she says, in a new voice, singsong and soft, Oh, have you had lunch?

Mami Lafont, I say, it was market day. We bought olives and cheese and bread and . . .

OK, OK, says Mami Lafont. That's enough.

I blow her a kiss down the phone, but she has already hung up.

Maman appears at the top of the stairs looking bleary and crumpled.

Who was that? she says.

It was Mami Lafont, I say. She wants you to . . .

Peony, where have you been? Maman sounds like a dog barking. She is scowling at my dress. I look down and realise that although Margot skipped her dress dry, I fell asleep and mine is still wet.

Margot smiles and sticks out her tongue at me.

There was a storm, I say to Maman. It's OK, we got out of it quickly. And we didn't go under any trees and get burned up by lightning. I'm sorry about making a mess and not tidying it up. Mami Lafont says can you call her and please can I go and get changed?

After I stop talking there is a long wait. Then Maman sighs. Why don't you change straight into your pyjamas? she says. It's nearly bedtime anyway. I'll make us some supper.

When I come back downstairs, Maman has laid out a picnic, not in the kitchen but the living room, on the coffee table. There is green salad, cold sausages, crisps and soft cheese, and Maman has put a grownups film on to watch. Maman will watch the film until it makes her cry, then some more until her eyelids start to slip. I won't understand the film and I won't cry. Instead I will watch Maman out of the side of my eye, counting her freckles. Margot will sit in a corner and pretend to read a book. She knows the stories by heart from when Maman and Papa used to read to us. But she can't really read. Except for a few words like PEONY and LAIT and STOP.

Maman sits on the sofa, with her feet up on a stool and her plate balanced on top of her belly like a hat. I sit beside her, just the tiniest amount of cool space between our warmnesses. It feels like nothing and everything.

# *Chapter 6*

I wake with a shout, because I thought someone had just turned on the lights. But it is black night in my room. So I must have dreamt it. I am snuggling back down when a huge boom makes my door rattle. I am afraid of the dark and I am afraid of thunder so I am very afraid of thunder at night. The rain is pattering hard on the roof. I try to think about the rain. It is like people clapping, as though the clouds have done something clever. Or maybe for me and Margot after one of our shows. Or maybe the swallows have put shoes on and are dancing on our roof. I can see them in little blue clogs, tap-dancing on the tiles, and it makes me smile. I get under the sheet and try to fall back asleep again, but every time I do I start to dream bad dreams. I am up on Windy Hill under a tree. I am holding tight to the trunk and the lightning is reaching down with clawed white skeleton hands to shake the tree. I'm trying to hold on but my arms are slipping. A storm-witch with Claude's face comes screaming at me through the darkness, but when I take his hand it is a bony, witchy hand and I am lifted up into the stormy sky. I try to pull away from her and she lets go, but then I am falling into the storm clouds. I wake up before I find out what happens next. I am glad about that and I decide to stay awake for a while. I scratch at my arm and lie listening to the rain, raining itself out. Every time the lightning flashes I jump a little, but then I count like Papa taught me until the thunder comes. One (hippopotamus), two (hippopotamus), three (hippopotamus). You can't just say hippo or it doesn't work. Every time there are more hippopotamuses between the lightning and the thunder, which is good.

But I need a wee, which is not good. If I want to go to the toilet I have to put my feet down out of bed and on to the dark floor, if it is still there. If it is not then I will fall somewhere. I try not to think about it. Also, even if it is still there I don't know what is under my bed. I try not to think about that, too, but the not thinking about it makes me think about it more.

I decide to do a plan. If I manage to get to the corridor, the light will be left on for me, which is good, but the house will be empty and quiet, except for the creaks and snaps. The floor of the corridor is made of wood and it bounces when you walk on it. Right outside my room, on the other side of the wall to my bed, there is a creaky bit. When Maman goes to the toilet in the night I hear the creak and I wait for the flush. I am always a bit afraid until the flush comes, until I know that no monsters could be standing outside my room.

I lie in bed with my legs twisted in a knot, and my hands tight between them, holding in my wee, listening to the dripping outside the window and remembering about when things were nicer. What was best was that Maman was my best friend. Maman used to like it that way. She always held my hand, unless my hands were busy mixing up cakes or planting flowers. She used to call me Sweet Pea, which is a flower not a vegetable. Every night she would do my shower for me, soaping my back and washing my hair. Then she would read me a storybook and tuck me in with kisses. Later she always came back to tuck me in again. She would tiptoe over to my bed and kiss me on the head and call me beautiful. As she went she'd whisper, I love you. Every night, even if I was awake I used to pretend to be asleep. Now I wish that I had kissed her back and said, I love you too. I don't even remember the last time she kissed me, because I never knew I had to.

I can't hold it any longer, and I have not been able to pluck my courage like Gaston, so the wee escapes in hotness down my legs. Maman is going to be mad. And now the tears start to come too. The warm water comes from everywhere inside me and the wetness starts to fill the bed like a boat with a leak.

Margot, I whisper. But she doesn't reply.

Margot!

Not a peep. She will probably tease me if I wake her up just because I'm scared of the dark, or because I have wet my bed because I am afraid of the dark. Margot isn't afraid of anything. So I wait here in the hot blackness of my room, holding my breath. The window is open a little and while I am not breathing I hear the *croooo-ak* of the frogs and the *trrrrp* of the crickets. There must be about more than a hundred frogs outside, and nearly as many crickets. Then I hear the rushing out and in of air as I can't hold it any longer. I do this until the puddle in the bed goes cold and my spotty pyjamas stick to my legs.

Margot's voice is soft in the dark. Pea? Are you OK?

I need a wee, I tell her.

Go to the loo, she says.

Is the floor still there? I ask. Can you check?

Of course the floor is still there, Margot says.

Just in case?

Margot tuts, but I see her shadow move and her legs come out until she is standing by her bed. She does not fall down into the kitchen.

There, she says.

Thank you, I whisper. I look around the room carefully. I take some deep breaths, and then jump out of bed as fast as I can and run to the door and into the corridor. I am breathing hard but it is OK. The corridor is strange, small and quiet, like it is asleep too. In the bathroom I take off my pyjamas and put them in the laundry basket. I wash my legs with a flannel and get dried.

Maman's room is dark too. I leave the door open so I can see the floor. She is on top of her sheet and has forgotten to take off her knickers. She has her back to me and the fan is blowing air across her, making a few long hairs flutter about her head. The windows are wide open and she has the same sounds as I have in my room. I go closer. She is curled up like a cat in her basket. Under her tummy, she has rested the baby on a lot of pillows.

I climb ever so quietly on to the bed and cuddle up to her back. I am trying not to wake her up, but I do. She turns her head to look at me, and then she sits up, puffing a lot, and lies back down facing me. Her belly is big in between us, her face too far away. She puts the pillows back under her tummy, and pulls the sheet up over us both.

Pea, she whispers sleepily.

I love you, Maman, I say back.

Her hand takes mine and she holds it, a little bit too hard. She shakes as though she is laughing, and squeezes tighter.

I lie up against her belly pillows, my knees touching Maman's, my face close to her breasts. When I was a baby I had milk from her breasts, but I can't remember that. I smell the soap on Maman's skin and try not to fall asleep, but I am so tired and she is warm and soft.

I am either asleep dreaming or awake or nearly awake but with my eyes closed when something thumps me hard in the chest. For a moment I am not sure where I am, but then I remember that I am curled up against Maman's belly. I wonder if I dreamt it, but then it happens again and I jump. It is the baby kicking me. It wants me to leave it alone. I am not cuddled up to Maman's belly after all, but to the bossy baby inside it. Not soft but hard, not friendly, not fun.

You are not polite, I whisper.

The baby doesn't say anything.

It is not kind to kick people, I say.

The baby belly kicks me again.

I do not want to keep getting kicked, but Maman's hand is resting on my shoulder and I will stay here being kicked all night if I have to. Once it was me that was inside her, curled up safe and warm against her skin, but on the inside. For a long time. Everywhere she went she took me with her. I think that I would have loved that, and even though I don't really remember, I'm sure I didn't kick Maman's insides like this baby does.

It's all your fault, I say. It's all your fault.

I look up at the fan to try and feel nice but it is spinning too fast, blurry in the darkness. Maman fidgets and turns over again. She has to sit up to do it. She doesn't say anything, just lets go of my shoulder, sits up, lies down. Her bottom nudges up against my knees. Then she groans and turns back again. The bed rocks and creaks. It seems like it is hard work, as though her belly is heavier than a bag of shopping.

Pea, says Maman, with her eyes open, you have to go back to bed now please. I can't get comfortable with you here.

I can move over to the other side of the bed, I suggest. Outside the window the last of the raindrops are dripping off the roof.

She shakes her head. Pea, I'm too hot, I can't breathe; the baby won't keep still, I'm tired. Please, go back to your room.

I breathe in her skin one last time and climb down slowly.

I leave my door open so there is a bit of light, and take my pillow from the wet end of my bed and put it at the other. If I don't lie straight, but curl up like Maman, then I can make it so all of me is on a dry part.

It's still too dark, though, in the room and inside me. Before I can stop myself I am fighting with my face. Pressing my hand against my mouth. Screwing my eyes tight and sniffing to stop tears coming out of my nose.

Hey, Pea, whispers Margot, what's up?

Nothing, I say.

It can't be nothing if you're crying.

I'm just a bit fed up, I say.

Hmph, says Margot. This house has enough grumpy people in it without you starting.

I'm not grumpy, I say. I don't like the dark. I sniff again, and the sniffing is annoying me, so I just let the tears roll out of my eyes. I still try not to cry with my mouth.

Dark? laughs Margot. Pea, it's not dark at all. It's a beautiful night.

What are you talking about? I say. Go back to sleep.

But she doesn't. Margot sits up in bed, crossing her legs and putting her hands on her hips. My eyes are getting used to the dark and I can see her grinning like the Cheshire Cat in *Alice*.

I know something you don't know, she says.

No you don't, I say. That's impossible.

Yes, I do. Look out of the window, Pea, she says. There's a rainbow.

A rainbow? Margot, it's night-time.

Yes, she says. Look outside, can't you see the night rainbow?

I am not afraid of the floor any more. I tiptoe over to the open window and peer through the half-shut shutters. A full fat moon makes white rings in the after-storm air. The black sky is shiny-fresh as though it had been rinsed and the stars are scrubbed bright.

See, it's so beautiful, says Margot, even better than a day rainbow. The colours are more sparkly at night.

And I stand and I look, and there it is. A night rainbow, curving up over the barn, seven colours glittering against the black sky.

Can I keep it? I say.

And Margot says, It's yours.

## *Chapter 7*

Today we are going to run everywhere, says Margot, standing by my side at the open window.

I was hoping the night rainbow was still there, but it has gone. Over the barn there is nothing but blue sky.

What do you expect? says Margot. It's the daytime.

The air is fresher. It is still hot, but in a nice way, as though the storm put the sticky summer in a washing machine, sloshed it about and hung it out to dry. It does feel like a good day for running.

You should wear your green dress, I say, to match with me. My green dress is cheerful and has pockets on the front. There are yellow daisies sewn on to the dress as though they were growing up out of the pockets.

I have a good idea for breakfast, says Margot.

What is it?

Something green and sticky, she says, puffing out her cheeks and boggling her eyes at me.

Yuck! I say, although I know the answer really.

Don't forget the mop! says Margot.

We gallop downstairs, out of the house and round the barn to the fruit trees. I stop at the chicken coop, because the chickens are walking slow circles in the shade, holding out their wings and clucking quietly. They look like they are dancing.

I grab a handful of sage stalks and stick them down the back of my knickers.

I'm a chicken! I say. Watch me!

Margot giggles as I stick out my elbows and do the chicken dance. She thinks it's the best joke ever. She laughs and laughs. The more Margot laughs, the sillier I make my dance. I jiggle my bottom and my feathers shake.

Actually, says Margot, the chickens don't look very happy.

It's true, their dance is not a funny one like mine, it is a little bit sad.

Shall we go and see if there are any eggs? says Margot.

I think about it. We are not supposed to go in to the chickens without Maman, but maybe she has forgotten about them lately.

Yes, I say, come on.

The chickens wake up a bit when we go through into the coop. They gather around my feet; they think I have brought them some food. There are no eggs there. Also they haven't got a drink of water.

The chickens need us to look after them now, I say.

Yes. They can share our breakfast, says Margot.

It is hard work getting figs off the tree with the mop; I only manage to get three before I am tired and cross and give up. We sit sharing them under the tree's honey sweetness, leaves like hands making fingery shadows on our bare legs. Our figs are green and the skins are quite thick, so we eat out the seedy pink flesh from the inside and save the skins for the chickens.

When we have fed the chickens and given them some water, making them very happy, we run out across the high pasture. Our feet make a flattened trail through the tall grass, up and over to Windy Hill.

I'm sure, says Margot, not at all out of breath, that the lightning will have burned away the big fir tree.

I don't think so, I say.

But as we get closer I am still disappointed to see the tree standing there. It would have been exciting to think that Claude had saved our lives and that the tree had been sizzled away by the lightning.

Maybe it is just a little bit burned, says Margot. We'll have to inspect it.

We walk around the trunk, peering at the bark. It is not even slightly burned, I say.

That is true, says Margot. This tree had a lucky escape. Look at this, though!

Margot is pointing to the bark of the tree. I didn't notice it very much in the storm, but the bark is unusual – it is peeling off in handprint-sized scabs. Each flake looks like a tortoise shell: shiny, with lots of rings inside each other and under the cracks scuttle hundreds of little red and black *gendarmes*.

It's the police, says Margot. They have come to do an investigation too!

It takes a lot of them, I say. But I suppose they are only small. I watch them hurrying about. It's funny how the police got called after insects, I say.

And also, why do the people-kind not wear the right-colour uniforms?

I don't know, I say. Red is much nicer than blue.

Yes, says Margot. You would think the grownups would notice things like that.

Grownups don't notice as much as we do, I say.

I expect there's a bank robbery, says Margot.

At the insect bank, I say, but I'm not laughing. The *gendarmes* are interesting, but I've had enough of this tree. I want to watch the wing turbines.

The wing turbines are turning slowly. The wings don't go round together, they aren't in tune at all. It looks as though they are all being blown by different winds. I count across to my favourite. My favourite is number five, because that is my number, the same as my age. Margot has number four just next to mine. I pick one of the wings and watch it turn. When it points straight up I breathe in, then once it has done a full turn I breathe out again. I wait until it is pointing up to breathe in again and I carry on like this. It feels very sleepy, standing up, looking at the wing turbine, thinking about breathing, listening to the sound of it coming in and out of my nose.

Then I wonder, what would happen if I stopped breathing now? Would the turbine stop turning? So when the blade points up to twelve o'clock again I don't breathe out, I just hold it. To start with nothing happens, but then there is a burning in my throat, a pushing forward into my mouth like there is darkness trapped inside me trying to get out. I don't like it at all and I let the breath escape in a rush. After a while breathing with the turbine again I decide to try the other way, so I breathe out, and then don't let myself breathe in. There is a boiling inside of me, almost straight away, and my head starts to thump, my face tingling.

Hey, says Margot.

But I shake my head.

Pea! she says. You have forgotten to breathe!

I shake my head harder and she nods hers very hard back. I shake and she nods and I shake and she nods until my mouth opens itself all on its own and the air is sucked in. I think it is very strange that we breathe without even thinking about it, and that we can't stop it and start it like we can with other things. I wonder, since it's so hard to stop breathing, how people manage to do it until they die.

In between me and the turbines, Margot has started cartwheeling.

Come on! she says. This is very good exercise and it's also very impressive.

It is impressive, I say. And I join in. The ground makes dents in my palms, but the turning over part makes up for it. We are angels' wings, turning over and over, on the top of our own hill. When we stop we are smiling and puffed out. I sit and look out towards the *étangs*. The sunshine is painting white splashes on the blue water.

Do you think she is going to be hiding for ever? I ask Margot.

Maybe, maybe not, Margot says. She cocks her head to the side which usually means she is going to say something interesting.

I think, she says, that it will depend on the baby.

I take a stick and start to write my name in the dirt. I make a big 'P' and then stop.

P is for peacock, says Margot.

No, I say. P is for me, I'm just not sure which one.

E, says Margot. I draw the E, scraping the stony ground to get the corners straight. After that the A is the right thing to do. Then I write Margot, then I draw a spider with zigzag teeth. The baby will be quite small, I say. I'm not sure it will be able to help us much.

No. But maybe the baby has got Maman's happiness, says Margot. Maybe the happiness wasn't left at the hospital but it stayed in her tummy?

Or maybe when the baby is born it will be my turn with Maman again?

Could be, says Margot. Or could be not.

You know what we really need? I say.

A papa, she replies.

I still don't know where to get one from. This is a chewy thought, so I look at the angels some more and ask them in my head if they have any ideas.

Margot appears in front of my face. Would you like a *bonbon*? she says.

Oh, yes please, I say.

Margot gives me a handful of purple seeds. I chew them. They are a bit gristly but the flavour is very nice. As I chew I scratch at the ground some more with my stick. The soil here is sandy-coloured on top, but underneath it's the same red-brown as Merlin. It is warm like Merlin too, but not as flappy. I would like to see him now. And Claude.

Margot, I say, shall we go to Claude's house and see if he wants to come and play?

He's a grownup, Pea, she says.

Papa was a grownup, I say, and he used to play with us.

Yes, but Papa was a papa. It's not the same when you're not a papa. You aren't so interested in children and you like to talk to grownups and to meet ladies. Not girls, she says. Not normally.

I'm bored of normally, I say. And anyway, Claude is interested.

Well we can't go to his house, says Margot. It's in the rules.

What rules? I say.

The Rules! Margot replies.

Can you remind me? I say.

Margot stands up straight. Here are The Rules, she says.

1. Don't go down to the low meadow on your own.
2. Don't lick your fingers then put them back in the olive jar.
3. Boys have to wear brown, grey and blue and girls have to wear the beautiful colours.
4. You don't ask grownups to come out to play.
5. Only do the things that make Maman happy.

I wonder if she's out of bed yet, I say. And then I spit out the lavender because it tastes scratchy in my mouth, and stare back up at my turbine.

I bet Sylvie's brought the bread, says Margot.

I don't say anything.

I bet it's warm and crunchy on the outside, and soft and crumby on the inside.

I smile a little bit. It's time for our second breakfast.

We are sitting by the letterbox – still two baguettes – with tummies full of bread, listening to the quiet of the house. A tiny aeroplane leaves a long cottonwool trail across the sky. I try to imagine the people on the plane, with their suitcases and sunglasses. Maybe they are the coming ones, and we will see them next week at the market. Or maybe they are the going ones, with red noses and homesickness.

Come on, says Margot, I'm going to teach you a game.

Here?

No, in the orchard. Come on! she says. It's our running day, so run!

We race round the sunny side of the house and off into the orchards. Margot is very fast and I can't keep up.

Boo! She jumps out at me from behind a tree.

Boo! I say back, just because.

OK, says Margot, now this game is complicated so you have to listen carefully.

I'm too busy for complicated games, I say. We'll do it later.

Don't be silly, says Margot. Listen. First, she says, you have to put everything upside down, like this. And then she folds in half, putting her hands on the ground, and looks backwards and upwards between her knees. Then, she says, we have to race, like crabs.

You try it, she says.

I bend down and put my eyes between my knees. Up in the sky are the red balls of peaches in amongst the green teardrop leaves. The peaches look wrong and it's not just the upside-downness of them. There are shadows and black dots. I unfold myself to have a look.

The peaches are covered in holes as though someone had been shooting at them. Thick lines of ants are marching up and down the trees and into the peaches. They are stealing our fruit, one ant-bite at a time.

Pea, you have to concentrate, says Margot. Race! So I do the crab thing again and we scuttle about between the trees, making ourselves dizzy and sometimes squashing some of the ants.

Scrunch-unch-unch up the path, a bumping of tyres is coming our way. A white truck stops by the side of the track and the man who buys the peaches steps out. He isn't wearing a shirt or a hat. His skin is brown and he has hairy nipples. He has a belt on his trousers.

This is the peachman. Every few days he comes to pick our peaches. Last year he collected them together with Papa, on hot afternoons without their shirts on. Afterwards they would sit in the shade and drink pastis, which is not for little girls, and Maman would take them olives. These days the peachman just comes to the door and gives us some money, then takes the peaches away to sell. Maman makes me answer the door; she doesn't want to be disturbed.

The peachman has left the car running, with the door open and the radio on, but it is nothing we can dance to, just people talking about boring things. He unties a stepladder from the roof and walks into the orchard.

We crab over to where he is, and look at him upside down from between our legs, his head floating like a grey cloud in the blue sky.

Hello, I say.

How are you? says Margot.

The peachman does not answer straight away, but pulls off a few more of the fruits. Normally he picks out the ripe peaches and sets them in careful rows in wooden crates. Today he is just picking off all the ones with holes, which is most of them, and throwing them on to the crates in a heap. It's ruined, he says.

What happened to the peaches? I say.

The hailstones happened, he says.

Are they all broken? I ask.

Margot stares at him upside down and opens her eyes wide and white. I giggle.

Where's your maman? the peachman says.

I don't know, I tell him. Can we come and see your pigs?

With your maman?

No, just me and Margot.

No, he says. Get your maman to bring you some time. Tell her she's welcome. Amaury would have wanted an eye kept on her.

His smile is confusing. I don't like him any more, says Margot.

I don't either.

Come on, Margot says, and we stand up and run away without saying goodbye.

Why would the peachman want to keep an eye on Maman? I say.

Maman is a grownup, says Margot. He's being silly.

Do you think Maman would take me to see his pigs? I ask.

Pea, says Margot, don't ask silly questions. We have more interesting things to think about.

Like what?

As we get to the path, the talking people on the radio remind me that the car door is open.

Should we take his car for a drive? says Margot.

I think about it. There are good reasons to do it, like it would be fun. But also there are good reasons not to do it, like I don't know the way to the beach, and also Maman would be furious. But I am also cross that Maman wouldn't take us to see the pigs, and cross with the peachman too.

Just to pretend then? says Margot, smiling.

We climb in. The metal burns my fingers and the leather seat scalds my legs. Even the keys, jangly under the steering wheel, are burny.

Ow! Ow! I say.

I try to put my seatbelt on but it is hot too. I have the wheel and the two sticks, Margot is the passenger. My legs don't quite reach the pedals, but almost.

I'd like to go to a restaurant, Margot says.

Of course, *Madame*, I say. Which one?

One that makes lamb chops and chips and ice-cream, she says. And lemonade.

And so that is what we do, until the restaurant gets too hot and we are all sweaty and we need to find some cool.

We go around the back of the house. Our plan is to pick up the rest of the baguettes on the way to the kitchen door and take them inside. We get the bread, but before we make it into the courtyard I hear the screams.

The barn door is wide open. Maman is standing by the door with a crate of peaches. She is throwing them at someone inside the barn who I can't see, but mostly she is hitting the tractor. The arrows on its big black tyres point down into a muddy mess of splattered peach. Maman is screaming and crying like she is cross and scared and sad all at the same time. Like she is a little girl, not like a grownup.

Maman's not very good at throwing, says Margot. I'm glad I'm not the tractor. She smiles at me like it's a funny thing, Maman and the peaches, but my laugh is lost.

I don't say anything. I have dropped the bread and I am scratching my arm. My fingernails make white scrapes on the brown skin, then pink ones, and now the blood is starting to come. But the blood doesn't stop the itch. The itch is on the inside. It's worse than ever. Maman sometimes shouts, but I've never seen her this angry. I suck at the blood, bite at the scratches. Maybe I can chew the itch away.

Pea, says Margot, don't. She takes my hand. I don't mind about the blood, she says.

Damn you! Damn you! Maman is shouting. She has peach in her hair and wasps are flying around her. Her legs are wide apart and her shadow is stretched long across the courtyard. It makes her look like a witch. We stand at the edges of the courtyard where it becomes the soil. We have nowhere else to look. Margot looks through her fingers. I look from underneath my fringe. We hold hands and stare.

One, says Margot, two, three . . .

Maman bends down to the crate and scoops up more of the hailstorm peaches. The holes are still black and bubbly with ants. She throws another one, hard. Flying ants, flying peach, but I don't even see where it lands because almost as soon as it lifts off out of her hand, Maman cries, Oh! and drops the rest of the fruit, grabbing at her belly. She doubles over and everything stops.

Oh! Ohhh! she moans. But she does not move. Then, very clumsily, she starts to lower herself into the dirt by the barn. She looks like a camel going from standing to lying down. A heavy sideways flopping down into the dust. The wasps buzz around the peaches and Margot and I start to run.

I'm sorry, I'm sorry, she is saying. And then, Ohhh. Then again, I'm sorry, I'm sorry, please don't . . .

Are you OK, Maman? I am shouting before I even get to her, just so she knows I am there. I can't help myself; she seems hurt and maybe she was stung by a wasp and I could fetch something for her. But Maman is wrapped over her belly and breathing hard.

No! she says.

Maman? It's me.

It's OK, Pea. It's . . .

But it really does not look OK. It looks like Maman has been hurt, maybe shot, or had a spell put on her. Wasps zoom around us as we sit together on the peachy soil.

Did you get shot? I say.

No, says Maman. It's the baby.

Did it kick you? Worse than usual?

But Maman is not talking. She has got on to her hands and knees, the way she used to when she came with us to find flowers and feathers. She is arching her back like a big-bellied cat and her eyes are closed. Waaoooooooooh! she says.

Margot and I look at each other. Maman does a lot of strange behaviour but now she is a camel and a cat and a wolf. She is an angry peach-thrower. Then I remember to be frightened of what is in the barn with the tractor. I look over past the swung-open doors, but it is quiet in there. I wish Claude was here.

Who's there? I whisper.

You'd better come out or we'll throw the rest of these peaches at you, shouts Margot, and we can throw much better than Maman!

Still nothing moves.

And we're better at hide and seek than you, Margot adds. She tosses her head. She's really too bossy to be scared of anything.

Who's in the barn, Maman? I say. Did they shoot you?

Don't be silly, says Margot. When people shoot each other the guns do a big bang, like this: BANG! She points her fingers and shoots me. She's right; it can't be a shooter.

And don't tell me that you think a witch has put a spell on her because witches Do Not Exist, she says, making the face that says 'When will you learn?' Bossy girl.

The howling has stopped. Maman is doing her blowing breathing: her-hoo, her-hoo, her-hoo. She opens her eyes, looking around frownily, as though she isn't sure where she is any more.

There's no one in the barn, she says, through puffs.

Who were you shouting at, then? I ask. Her face tightens up and I understand it was the wrong thing to say. I scratch at my arm and look to see where the peaches are. In any case if she starts to throw them at me I can run very fast, and she won't be able to catch me because she is too fat and full of baby.

Nobody, says Maman. Just the tractor.

Margot and I look at the tractor. It is very peachy.

Tractors don't have ears, says Margot. It wouldn't have heard you.

It's OK, says Maman. Let's go inside. As though it had been waiting for her command, the wind swoops around the barn and into our hair, blowing off the hot sun. It reminds me of a story Papa used to tell me, about the sun and the wind having a competition to blow off a man's coat. But we don't have coats. Our dresses ruffle as we wait for Maman to get up off the floor. I am worried she might not be able to do it, but she does. She leans on me a little bit but I am too small and she is too heavy. Her hand touches the blood on my arm and she pulls it back quickly.

What did you do to your arm?

Nothing, I . . .

It doesn't look like nothing, she says, standing straight at last, one hand on her back, one twisting my arm so she can look at the bleeding.

That hurts! I say. Maman stares at the bleeding scrapes.

It was a tiger that did it! says Margot.

It was itching, I say. I'm sorry.

Itching?

She is frowning again. Before, when we were all happy, I noticed the lines Maman has at the corners of her eyes and I wanted to know what they were and why I didn't have any. Maman told me that every time you smile, a very tiny bit of the smile stays stuck to your face, so as you get older and older your face starts to show all the tiny bits of all your smiles and you look like you are smiling all the time, even when you are just thinking about what to have for breakfast. She said, also, that if you frown a lot then the frowns stick to your face instead. That way, when you are old you have a very frowny face and look cross all the time and people are scared of you. There is a lady like that who we sometimes see when we are doing our shopping. At first I thought she was a witch, because she is ugly and looks like she is scowling at you all the time. But Maman said she probably wasn't, she just did a lot of scowling when she was younger and so now even if she is thinking 'what a beautiful little girl' her face is saying 'Ugly! Ugly!'

Maman, I say, don't make the frowny face. I want you to stay beautiful when you are older and not look like the scowling lady at the shop.

Maman sighs. She drops my arm and rubs at her belly, through her dress. She rocks back and forth, heel toe, heel toe.

I'm sorry your arm was itching, she says. I'm sorry I scared you. But try not to scratch it. Please. Her hands move round to her back again. I need a sit-down, she says. Shall we go inside?

Maman's legs are not hard enough. They wobble as we walk together back to the house. She holds my hand, tight, and we walk slowly. A cough from behind the barn makes me jump, and I hear the soft sound of raggedy footsteps moving away. I smile, and squeeze Maman's hand to let her know we're all right.

Outside I could feel my skin starting to burn and my head getting dizzy. The cool kitchen feels better already. I blink away the white spots as my eyes get used to the shadiness. Maman turns on the light, letting go of my hand. She was holding it so tight, though, that it feels as though her fingers are still there.

Would you like a drink? I ask her.

It's OK, she says. She turns her back to us, starting up the stairs slowly, her legs shaking with every step.

I think she forgot to put her skeleton in, says Margot.

I'm going to lie down, Maman whispers.

You're all sticky, I say.

She turns and looks at me with dark eyes.

Perhaps a shower would make you feel better, I add.

Oh . . . yes, she agrees.

Margot smiles at me. Just in time, she says.

Pea, says Maman.

Yes?

Don't go out. Stay here for a while.

OK, Maman, I say.

Just until I'm asleep, she says.

Now what are we going to do? I say, when she has gone and the shower is running upstairs.

Well, says Margot, with crafty-bright eyes, I have a very good idea.

## *Chapter 8*

Our house is big up and down and side to side and front to back. There are a lot of rooms before you even count the barn and they all smell different. When you come in from the courtyard, you are in the kitchen. That is where most things happen and it smells of our family. Papa's best boots are by the door. Sometimes I put them on when Maman is asleep, and walk around the kitchen floor being Papa. Afterwards my feet smell like Papa too and I have to sit and smell my toes. Papa also has some tractor-driving boots. They are hidden upstairs in a sadness box in Maman's bedroom. I am not supposed to know this, but I do.

From the kitchen you can either go into the living room, where we sit down in soft places, and I have toys and there is the television and the desk, or you can take the stairs up to where our bedrooms and bathrooms are. Maman's bedroom smells of Maman. Papa's smell was one of the first things to follow him away.

My bedroom is yellow and smells of nothing at all unless I open the windows. Then it smells of outside. I don't know what it smells like in the baby's room because the door is closed to keep the remembering shut-in.

Also, from the kitchen which actually has a lot of doors, you can go into the pantry, which is painted white and doesn't have glass in the windows, only wire netting. The pantry smells of cheese. There is another door that goes to the summer rooms. They are down some stairs and are quite dark and smell of gone-bad fruit. They are colder than the upstairs bedrooms which is bad in winter but good in summer. But all our things are in our bedrooms and so that is where we always sleep, in the summers and in the winters. Sometimes I go to the summer rooms just to see if anything is different. It never is.

From the kitchen you can also go into the laundry room. It is called the *buanderie* and smells of soap powder and has a door to the downstairs toilet, which is not interesting, except that it has a toilet-roll holder shaped like a wide-mouthed frog, and purple violets on the white wall tiles. From the downstairs toilet there is another door, which is always locked. This door is brown underneath, but has been painted over. The paint is peeling away in shiny flakes like sage leaves. The handle is old and feels greasy. I know that this door leads to the cellar, and children are not allowed down there. In any case I cannot reach the lock.

Things go down into the cellar and we don't see them for a long time. Things come up from the cellar to surprise us. At Christmas, Papa comes up from the cellar with tinsel and baubles and a small stable with a manger and sheep. When Maman and Papa were happy, they would bring bottles of wine up at night-time, dusty and smelling like not-washed hair. Papa would wipe them carefully, then pull the cork out, *ploc*. They would sit next to each other, at the kitchen table, twizzling their grownup glasses and wrapping their feet together when they thought I wasn't looking. One day, after the baby died, everything from the baby's room disappeared and was swallowed by the cellar.

The sun is high above the courtyard now and baking hot. Maman is asleep or trying to be asleep in her room, with all her peach juice washed away and there are no more animal sounds. There is not going to be lunch today, so I get a drink of milk. Milk is great because it is good for thirstiness and hungriness at the same time, and because I can reach it out of the fridge. Then I go to the toilet.

Margot is already there and she is leaning against the violet tiles wearing a great big smile.

My good idea has got even better, she says, while I do a wee.

What is it? But then she doesn't even need to tell me because I see for myself.

See? *Génial!* she says. Shall we?

I nod. *Génial!* I whisper.

The door is propped open by a cardboard box. The light has been left on and a metal staircase like one of Maman's long curls twists down into the fusty cellar smells. Margot goes first and I follow. I forget to flush the toilet.

The staircase makes a clanging noise as we go down. I try to walk more softly, on cat paws, but you can still hear a soft clank with every step. Margot gets bored and pushes to the front. She leads the way down fast, not paying any attention to her feet at all. As we go deeper into the cellar the air gets cold and salty. The coolness is a very nice surprise. I didn't know you could find anywhere this cool at midday in August.

The cellar is enormous, and very quiet. There are no windows, no outside noises. No birds, or crickets, nothing. There are cobwebs and corners. The walls are grey and unfriendly. There are boxes stacked high, and big black bags bulging in rows.

Shall we open some? says Margot. But I can already feel my heartbeat thumping on my chest like banging on a door.

I look up; above my head must be the toilet, the kitchen, the pantry, the living room, everything. What if it just falls down?

It won't fall down, says Margot.

I tiptoe around a corner and the cellar is different again. There are two gigantic wooden barrels, lying on their sides, with holes in the front big enough to crawl through.

I will if you will, says Margot.

Through the cobwebs? I say. Yuck.

Grey cobwebs like curtains drape from the ceiling to the top of the barrels and then down to the concrete floor. The cellar smells horrible.

Margot is poking around a pile of shoeboxes. Some of them have names that I cannot read, but one of them, right on top, is labelled just 'OLD'. The lid lifts off easily, it is not taped down. The box is only half full. Inside paper photographs are stacked neatly. The top one is a baby in a yellow laundry basket. It is awake and looking right at me. The baby is wearing a little yellow dress, but it doesn't come far enough down. You can see its nappy, and its fat baby legs sticking out like chubby scissors. It has not very much orange hair, stuck up in funny points, and green eyes, with bits of blue and brown like a kaleidoscope. Like Maman.

I hold the photo for a while, then put it to one side and look at the others. There are more baby pictures, and pictures of Maman on her own looking happy. In one photo Maman is standing under dark clouds by a lake, rain is coming in sideways at her and her hair is blowing the same way as the rain, a few strands of it plastered across her face. Her hair is the only colourful thing in the photograph. She is wearing a big black coat and she looks angry.

The last picture I pick up makes me want to cry, because it looks really lonely. Maman is standing on top of a hill I don't recognise. Beside her is a bench, and behind her is a clump of houses, with black walls and grey rooftops. There is a factory, with smoke coming out of two tall chimneys, and a sort of pylon on a hill, with a big wheel perched on the top. A few starlings are walking on the muddy grass near her feet. Maman's face is white and thin, but her cheeks are wind-red. She has a baby, wrapped up warm and held tight against her chest so you can only see its back and sausage legs. I suppose it is the orange-hair baby from the first picture, but in winter. Maman is looking away, staring hard at the houses, the factory and the smoke.

I look at the photo for a long time, trying to figure it out.

Let me see, says Margot, peering over my shoulder.

That's Maman, she says. I wonder who the baby is.

Me too. Does it look like us?

Neither of us really, says Margot. Maybe it's someone else's baby.

Where is she standing?

I don't think it's near here. Perhaps she's on holiday?

What's the big wheel thing?

I don't know.

Then we stop talking so we can think. We cannot ask Maman any of these questions without her knowing we have been down in the cellar where children are not allowed. Also, I remember that the door we cannot open is only kept ajar by a box, and that no one knows we are here. The cellar seems creepy now, and dark with secrets.

We'd better tidy up, I say. But I don't put the lonely photo back. I am glad that I chose my cheerful green dress this morning. I plant the photo in with a daisy; maybe it will make it less lonely.

* * *

Even though every step up the air gets a little bit hotter, it also gets fresher and more colourful. We walk out of the house and back into the bright heat. It is coming up off the courtyard slabs and down out of the sky. It is making my hair bother the back of my neck. Last summer Maman used to tie my hair up into plaits, before she put my hat on. But I'm not big enough to do that on my own, so even though I try to stuff it up inside my hat, hot strands keep falling down again, tickly and annoying. My neck is too hot and very itchy. We need to get into the shade, fast.

I'm bored of running, says Margot. So shall we decide to fly to the meadow today?

Oh, yes! I agree.

I pick up the baguettes that I dropped earlier and we stick out our arms like aeroplanes and speed as fast as we can, all the way down the path. Crossing the road is sticky, our sandals coming up with black bottoms from its meltiness. Then we are over the gate, and just hot and fast-flying legs all the way down to the water.

Claude is down by the stream. He is throwing a stick all the way over it to the other side and Merlin is racing to fetch it. As he splashes through the water his fringes are getting soaked, which he seems to like. Every time Merlin runs back to Claude with the stick, Claude crouches down and smiles at Merlin, ruffling his ears. As we get closer, still quite a long way off, Merlin lifts up his nose and sniffs the air. He can smell us coming. He starts to bark his hellos. Claude looks up and spots us.

Run! he shouts. Come on, run!

We laugh and start chasing down the field, Merlin running towards us, wet and wagging. When we reach Claude we are puffed out but very happy and it is hard to stop. He sees that we are going to tumble into him and drops his cigarette, lifting out his hands palms forwards. I charge straight into them and his fingers close around my arms. He is laughing, his eyes and his ugly face crinkled up. Smoke still trickles from the edge of his mouth. The skin on his fingers is rough against my arms and it reminds me of Papa. I straighten up, feeling as though a wave has come right over me, washing all my happiness off and sucking it back into the sea. Claude seems to feel it too and he uncurls his fingers and holds his breath. Merlin slaps my legs with his tail.

So, how is Pea today? says Claude.

Fine, I say.

And Margot?

Margot is fine too, I say, because this is my conversation. And how are you?

*Impeccable*, says Claude. I roll the word around on my tongue, it is a new one. *AmPeKarBleu*. Lovely.

Look what I found, he says, pointing into the grass. There are little brown mushrooms hiding in amongst the green.

Can we eat them? Margot and I say together. Mushrooms are delicious. We could make sandwiches.

No, says Claude. You can't eat anything you find down here.

But I like mushrooms, says Margot.

I really like mushrooms, I say. And I'm hungry.

Again! says Margot.

I'm always hungry.

Well, says Claude, maybe in the autumn we will go out together and find lots of mushrooms, and we will take them down to the pharmacy to see which ones are good.

Don't you know? I say.

I do and I don't, says Claude.

What does that mean? Margot asks.

Here, look at this one, says Claude. He has a wet stick in his hand and he pokes at a big white snowball in the grass. A puff of smoke comes out of it, like magic.

Wow!

Puffball, says Claude. And no eating those either.

I am going to add it to my list of 'Don't Dos', says Margot. But it's getting very long now; I need more paper, please.

Where have they all come from, so quickly? I ask.

The toadstools? says Claude. The storm brought them. Speaking of which, are you all dry now?

Margot fluffs her hair up to show him and I do the same.

The peaches are broken, I say.

Broken?

They have holes in them. The ants are eating them.

Ah, he says. And, Oh. And, So that's why . . .

Last night there was a night rainbow, I say.

I saw it first, says Margot.

A night rainbow?

Yes! I say. Have you ever seen one?

I didn't know you could have night rainbows, says Claude.

You can, I say. There was one right outside our house and it had all the colours, just like in the daytime. I saw it. It was like magic, it was . . . I stop, because Claude is staring at me with that look again. As though he can see through me and behind me there is something that is making him smile.

What? I say.

Pea, says Claude, I believe you.

Oh.

Um, how is your maman today? he says.

I heard you, I say.

You heard me?

You know how Maman is; you were there when she was throwing the peaches.

Claude's face is flat with surprise. Ah, he says. You heard me.

Yes, I say. Your feet have a special sound because of the tiger-bite walk that you do. Can I have a go at throwing the stick?

Of course, says Claude. I just . . .

I pick up the stick, slimy with dog spit, and throw it as hard as I can. It bounces on the ground right by my toes and almost hits my face coming back up again.

*Oh la la!* says Claude. Here, let me show you. He crouches down behind me with one knee on the floor, and he holds my wrists from behind. A bit too hard but I don't say anything.

Hey! says Claude, turning my arm so he can see the old scabs and the new scratches. What happened here?

I don't know, I say.

You don't know? Did you fall over? Did somebody hurt you? You need some antiseptic on that.

I don't know, I say. Maman said it was broken when I was a baby.

Broken? Claude runs one finger over the pink skin and the bobbly red scabs. But this? he says, where it was bleeding.

It stings. I snatch my arm away. It itches, I say. I was scratching it.

Don't scratch it, says Claude. You'll make it worse.

Can I throw the stick now? I say.

OK, he says. First, look where you want the stick to go. So, remember that rainbow you were telling me about?

Yes . . .

Now you have to imagine the stick is going to make the same shape, from here to there. Can you see the rainbow?

I can, it's easy. Yes, I say.

Show me the shape with your finger.

I draw the rainbow in the sky.

Great, says Claude, so now you throw the stick up the rainbow like you were trying to reach the very top. He pulls my wrist down and back. Are you ready? Off you go.

He lets go of my wrist and I fling the stick forwards with a grunt. It goes a bit further than before, but not very much. Merlin pounces on it and takes it back to Claude.

Margot laughs. You sounded like a pig! she says.

That's not funny, I say.

Hmmm, let's try again, says Claude, handing me back the stick. This time, take your time, and keep imagining the rainbow. His fingers close around my wrist again.

Can you let go of my wrist please? I say. I want to do it by myself.

The fingers uncurl and I feel a breeze on my back as Claude moves away from me. I look out across the meadow, then I close my eyes. I paint a full high rainbow in the sky of my mind and I let the stick fly up out of my fingers. When I open my eyes the stick is high in the air and still going up. Then it turns and starts to tumble down, curving towards the ground.

*Impeccable!* says Margot.

Very good! says Claude.

I smile proudly. Can I do it again?

Claude shakes his head. I think we should stop now, he says. Merlin is getting tired.

Merlin has got the stick, but he has not brought it back. He has taken it into the stream, where he is lying on his belly, chewing it.

Do you want to go over to the girl-nest? asks Claude. There's a snack there and some water.

Yes please! we shout.

Claude, what are you? I ask as we walk.

Claude looks at me strangely. I don't know what you mean, he says.

Well, what do you do?

I used to be a *gendarme*, he says. Now I just look after my garden. And I like to make things.

Why haven't you got a proper job?

Are you too old? says Margot.

Not too old, says Claude. But a bit broken.

Because of the tiger, says Margot.

Ah yes, I say. The tiger.

Claude shivers. He looks like he is going to cry. That's right, he says. The tiger.

Don't be sad, I say. The tiger is probably dead now.

Claude screws up his mouth.

Also, I say, why don't you live in a proper family? With four people, or three people, or a man and a lady? Where are your children, Claude?

Claude chews his tongue, so I can tell he has something important to say. He reaches out for my hand, not grabbing at it, but putting his palm forward, emptily. I put my own inside it and he closes his fingers, one at a time. Pea, he says, you know, sometimes there are some questions that can make grownups sad. It's OK to ask them, but it has to be OK to not answer them too. I wish I had my own little girls and my own lady. But I don't.

At least you have us, I say.

Yes. That is a thing that makes me very happy, says Claude. As we arrive at the tree he leans back against it with a big sigh. Merlin flops down at his feet.

Go and have a look, says Claude, pointing up to the girl-nest. See if there is anything you'd like.

We scramble up the ladder to see what there is up there. A paper bag with the top corners twisted into cat ears. Inside are brioche and pain au chocolat, doughnuts and apple turnovers. One, two, three, four! counts Margot.

I'm only going to eat one, I say, and save the rest for later.

Happy, happy, happy! We make Claude happy! sings Margot.

But not Maman, yet, I say. My fingers find the lonely picture in my pocket.

Do you like them? Claude shouts up.

Oh yes! we shout back.

Would you like one? I wave the bag out over the edge.

No thank you, they're for you. Claude is smiling again.

Claude, I say, if I tell you something do you promise not to tell Maman?

Hmmm, says Claude. Well I can't promise that. It depends, is it going to be something like you have made your maman a birthday present, or something like you are running away to join the circus?

The circus? I say.

Never mind, says Claude. Yes, tell me, what is it?

We went somewhere in the house today where the secrets live, I say. The door was open.

You should be careful with opening doors to secrets, says Claude. Sometimes secrets are secrets because that's the best way.

I found a photo, I say, and I take it out from behind the daisy and have another look. It still looks lonely.

It's Maman, I say, but she is in a lonely place. Do you know where it could be? I lean over the uppy-bit, holding the photo out for him to see.

Don't reach out too far, says Claude, and he stretches up his arm. I let the photo flutter down into his fingers.

I watch Claude, looking at the photograph. His thinking makes his face move – his lips pout and twist, his eyebrows frown and lift up. After a long time he breathes a big breath and lets it come out of his nose.

It's a lonely photo, isn't it? I say. Did it make you feel sad?

It does look lonely, says Claude. Your maman looks beautiful, though, don't you think?

Maman is very beautiful, I say. She is the most beautiful person in the world. She is probably a queen.

Maybe this was England, says Claude.

But then what about the baby?

Well that must be . . . Claude's face stops moving in the middle of his sentence, like it was frozen. Then it makes a kind smile. I don't know, he says, but I bet they have babies in England too.

Come on, he says, we'd better tidy up the wrappers.

Claude helps us back over the stepping stones, first me, slowly, then Margot, all quick and bouncy.

Now, he says, see how fast you two can run home. I bet your maman has had a nice rest by now and she'll be looking forward to seeing you.

We're flying now, not running, says Margot.

We always fly on Thursday afternoons, I say.

OK, Claude smiles. Fly home, little birds, I'll see you tomorrow.

## *Chapter 9*

A row of dark blue swallows sit on the telephone wire that goes between the house and the barn, under the blue, blue sky. These are the summer babies, all thin and wobbly and not as polished as the grownups. The mother bird is with them. She keeps leaving the wire and flies in big circles, whizzing past the blue shutters of our house, past the cherry tree and the eaves of the barn where they were born. Their nests are right by the big scar where the earthquake shook the stones apart in the olden days.

I am watching them lying on my belly, looking into a puddle, where upside-down trees drop into a deep well of blue. At the bottom of the well a fat dappled morning-moon has just a small sliver shaved off one side. When the mother bird gets to the point of the barn roof, with the witch-catcher tile, she keeps going up, high into the space between the two buildings, and comes back down to sit on the wire again. Margot, I say, if there are no witches then why have we got the witch-catcher tile?

Those birds don't want to fly, says Margot. They want to be back in their nest.

You don't know, do you? I say, rolling over and looking up at the realness of the reflection, at the red tile that sits on the point of the roof like a crown. The tile is for catching witches, I say, and it was put there by grownups. So grownups must think there are witches.

Well, Maman says there are not.

Maybe Maman is wrong, I say.

The mother swallow is twittering at her children. Come on, I think she is saying, flying is easy. But her children edge from side to side on the wire, cocking their heads and looking nervous. They're not sure they can do it, so I start to feel scared that they can't too. I remember them as tiny baby birds when they just hatched. From my window I could just see their small fluffy grey heads and yellow beaks poking out of the mud nest. They yelled for their food. As they grew bigger there was less room, but they still huddled up, a nest full of shiny feathers and bright eyes, and their mother still put food in their open mouths. She doesn't do that any more. They have to do it for themselves.

You should be able to choose when you want to fly, I say.

Yes, Margot agrees.

Fly, fly, sings the mother bird, edging up beside them and chittering. She is helping them. If they had fingers instead of wings I imagine them all holding hands.

It's sad that birds can't hold hands, I say.

They can't even hug, says Margot.

What do you think they do instead?

They just snuggle up together in their nest.

That sounds nice too, I say.

Then something seems to scare them, and they all lift off the wire together, flashes of white and blue. The mother leads them on the tour of our courtyard, and they follow her. They have remembered that they can do it after all. The wire bounces as they land, one, two, three, four . . . and five. Brothers and sisters, all together. Something brushes against my legs and I jump. But it's only a cat-visitor. He rubs up against me, silky against my skin, and purrs, but he is not looking at me, he is looking at the baby swallows.

He's waiting for one of them to fall, says Margot.

They don't fall, I say, they're birds. Birds fly.

Not always, says Margot.

That's not right, I say. Birds don't fall over while they're flying. I look at the cat. He is still staring at the swallows.

They won't fall! I say.

The father bird arrives on the wire, bigger and even more glossy. He sits at one end of the baby birds and the mother bird sits at the other. I look at the swallow family on the wire and start to feel the darkness dripping into me out of nowhere.

It seems best, I say, if a family has the maman and the papa.

It's twice as many people as just a maman, says Margot. But mamans are still best.

I put my fingers into the pocket of my dress, which I have chosen again today, and feel the edges of the lonely photo. Papa loved me, I say. He used to pick me up and swing me about.

Maman loved you too, says Margot. You used to bake cakes and pies and biscuits shaped like stars.

That was before the baby died, I say. Papa tickled me, used to let me ride on his tractor.

Maman is the most beautiful, says Margot.

Papa had big hands and a splendid smile, I say.

Maman let you help with the laundry, says Margot, even when you dropped things on the grass.

I remember that, I say. Maman floofed the clothes and put them on the line, and I passed the pegs.

And Maman used to sing to you, says Margot.

We sang together, I say.

You knew all the songs, says Margot. Children's ones and grownups' ones. French ones and English ones.

But then the baby died, I say, and took her voice away.

Right, that's quite enough of this, Pea, says Margot. You are being grumpy and it's boring!

She throws herself on top of me, squashing all the air out. Her face is right on top of mine, her nose pressing my own nose and her eyes so close that I can't see her at all, just a smudge of colour. Come on, she says, we are going to do some science.

If you go around the side of our house, on the sunniest side that looks out over the mountains, everything is very wild. There grass is seedy and scratchy and there are lots of nettles. There are also big thistles, taller than me, with beautiful hairy purple flowers that you can't pick because the spiky leaves stick out too far to reach over. You can find a lot of insects there all the time: ladybirds and *punaises* and *gendarmes*. There is a big tree that has purple blossom on it in long dangly bunches, where you can see all the butterflies. We don't normally play there, because it is right in the sunshine, and because of all the stingy-ness, but today we are out of bed early and it is not too sunny yet.

So, we are going to do the science, says Margot, and we are looking for specimens.

Alive ones?

No, we are not allowed to take alive ones from nature, only plants and things that are dead but not smelly.

I have got a magnifying glass, I say.

Yes, and I have got a stethoscope, says Margot. So let's go.

A black and white swallowtail butterfly is sitting on the purple flowers drinking the nectar. There is a peacock butterfly too, and a brown and orange one that I don't recognise. They are all alive, though, so they are good to look at but not good specimens. I decide that down on the ground is a better place to search. Soon I find a butterfly wing. It is very fragile and a creamy-white colour, like milk. The rest of the butterfly is not with it. It either dropped off, maybe, or perhaps the butterfly got eaten but not the wing. I put it on to a big flat stone while we find some more things. Margot finds a white feather, using her stethoscope, and then we find a crispy little yellow thing, a bit like a ball. I poke it with a stick. Nothing moves. When I look closer, through my magnifying glass, I can see that there are lots of empty spaces in it.

It looks a bit like a wasps' nest, says Margot.

They would be very tiny wasps, I say.

I didn't say it was a wasps' nest, she says, just that it looks like one.

It does, I say.

It is a very good specimen, she says.

What do you think made it? I ask.

Well, says Margot, fastening up her white scientist coat. I would say that this specimen was made by very small wasps or another kind of very small insect.

I put the tiny nest together with the feather and the wing very gently into my pocket and keep my hand pressed over the opening so they don't fall out. We will take these specimens to the girl-nest, I say, where they will be safe.

Claude must have already been down to the girl-nest because there is a new bottle of water and a red tin with pictures of biscuits on it. Pink ones and yellow ones and brown. It is hard to open. I have to put my fingers under the corners and try to pull the lid off. It is stiff and stuck and I am getting annoyed, and then all of a sudden the lid flies off and the biscuits tumble out of their places and some land on the green and red blanket and others in my lap.

The girl-nest is clean, says Margot.

I thought so, I say.

We eat some of the escaped biscuits and then put the lid back on, but less pressed-down. I start to empty my pocket. I get out the photo of Maman and the baby. Then I take the butterfly wing and the nest for very small insects and the feather. I hold them all together in my cupped hands. Four kinds of things that are treasure. I decide that I will bring things here to our nest and I will make a collection. Then when it is too hot to go to Windy Hill I can come here and like my collection, and it will make me feel better. I will keep everything in the biscuit tin, next to the pink and yellow and brown biscuits, and then when we have eaten all the biscuits it will just be for treasure, and no one will look in the tin because it has pictures of biscuits on, and not pictures of photos and feathers and wings.

We did good science this morning, says Margot. And I have decided that our challenge has to be sciency as well.

Making Maman happy? How is that sciency?

Science is about solving puzzles, of course. With our brains. We need to do more brain-thinking.

OK, I say. How?

Well, Maman is happy mostly when we don't make a noise, says Margot, and when we do make her breakfast.

Yes but only if things don't get broken.

Yes. And we know some things that make her sad.

Yes, I say, like dead flies, Papa's tractor and everything being a mess.

Right then. We can't stop flies dying, or move the tractor, but we can do cleaning up.

Margot, I say, you really are an excellent scientist.

I am full of excitement about this idea, so we quickly have one more biscuit each and climb down the ladder.

We bump into Claude and Merlin on the other side of the stream.

Hello, I say, but we are just going home to make Maman happy.

Hello, says Claude. That's OK, we were just popping down to see if you had found your biscuits.

Yes thank you! And the tin is good too.

Claude smiles. I'm glad.

Merlin winds around me, wagging his tail and lifting his head to be stroked.

Merlin is really lovely, I say.

He really is, says Claude. I love him a lot. And he crouches down to give Merlin a big cuddle. When I see Claude's arms all wrapped around Merlin, and Merlin happy at being loved, I feel a strange sort of sad.

We really do have to hurry now, says Margot. We have work to do.

## *Chapter 10*

We are working especially hard this afternoon. We are cleaning and tidying. I have taken a cloth from the kitchen and a dustpan and brush. I have swept the doorstep and I have washed the windows in the back door with water from the courtyard tap. Now I am sweeping the courtyard while Margot hoovers the air. We are making it very clean and nice. Once we have finished this part we will do the peachy barn and the tractor, even though I am scared of the wasps. The courtyard is hard work, though, because the dustpan and brush are small and the courtyard is quite big. Also because my hat keeps falling off.

That's it, I say, I'll just leave it off, it's a stupid hat anyway.

If you don't put your hat on in sunny weather you will die, says Margot, turning off her hoover.

Well how can I keep it on and do the cleaning? This house is a mess! I say.

You will have to use your head, says Margot, and I laugh. Margot makes up good jokes. Except for the knock-knock jokes that she is rubbish at.

The scorpion is in the shade of a big pink rock. He is almost black, except some yellow legs, and he is shiny and low to the ground. I don't notice him until I sweep him out with the leaves and he starts to run.

Look, says Margot, it's another specimen.

It's an alive specimen, though, I say.

Well yes, so you can't have him in your treasure chest, says Margot, obviously. But still, we could keep him – like a pet.

We could put a lead on him, I say, and take him for walks like a dog. I am only joking when I say this, because I know about scorpions. I know that if they sting you it hurts a lot and sometimes it means you have to go to the hospital. I know not to touch. So I get an empty jamjar from the box of glass for recycling, which like everything at the moment is overflowing. The jar has no lid, but it is much taller than the scorpion, and slidy, so I'm sure he won't be able to climb the sides. I take a stick and poke the scorpion into the jar. He skitters about trying to climb up the glass walls, his pincers waving, his tail curled over his back like a sausage hook. I'm still a little bit scared he's going to get out and sting me but I can see that I was right; the jar is too slippy and he has to stay in the bottom and be looked at. I'm glad that scorpions can't fly.

Let's keep him by my bed, I say. Do you know what scorpions eat?

I will have a look on the internet, says Margot.

Margot sits down at a rock, which she has made into her computer, and looks on the internet about scorpion food.

Hmmmm, she says, hmmm, aha, aha, right.

So what do scorpions eat? I ask.

Cheese, says Margot.

We are halfway upstairs when Maman appears at the bathroom door. She stands at the top of the stairs, a big dark shadow.

What have you got? she says.

I look at the jamjar in my hands: the little black scorpion still trying to climb up the slippery glass insides, his sting up over his back and the small piece of cheese which he has not eaten. I daren't put it behind my back in case I tip it and the scorpion gets on to my arm.

Nothing, I say, looking her in the eye.

Peony, what's in the jar?

Oh it's just . . . I just found it by the rocks, I'm going to look after it. I've given it some cheese.

Maman starts coming down the stairs. Now the stairs are crowded, and there is no way past Maman and her belly. I hold my hands around the jar, trying to hide the scorpion. He is skittering at the sides, only the glass between his sting and my palm.

I look down through the banisters to the kitchen floor. I cannot throw the jar, it would smash, and there would be a scorpion in the kitchen. Both very bad. I look up at Maman, nearly here. I look behind at Margot, who just shrugs and looks back at me. I am trapped in the middle with my scorpion, who is now seeming like quite a bad idea.

Maman is trying to see into the jar. Cheese, she says. Is it a mouse?

No.

A spider? she says, coming down another step and peering.

Not a spider.

Peony, she snaps, what have you got in the . . .

Her hand is reaching out to take the jar. I am holding it tight. I am scared of dropping it but it is slippery and I am also scared of putting my fingers inside to hold it better, although the scorpion is still now, flat to the glass bottom. Raindrops of sweat drip down from my neck past my heart and make a paddling pool in my belly button.

. . . jar, she says. She is leaning forward down the stairs, past her belly, one hand holding the handrail and the other reaching for the jar, her fingers pressing around mine, looking for spaces where mine aren't. She tugs, and I let go of the jar.

As Maman brings it up to her face, the scorpion jumps, lifting his pincers and his tail again, ready to fight.

Oh! Maman screams and drops the jar.

The jar bounces on the step between our pairs of bare feet, then falls another two steps and bounces again. I turn to watch it, to see the glass shatter, to see what happens to the scorpion. But the jar does not break. Instead it bounces on every step, *toc, toc, toc,* and ends up on the kitchen tiles on its side.

I think of the scorpion escaping; Maman would be even madder than she is already going to be. I start to run back downstairs, to try and keep it in, but after two steps I feel the sting, then the burning on the side of my foot.

Oh, Maman, it's there! On the stairs! Oh it stung me! Maman! I cry.

The scorpion has run to the corner of the stairs.

I get down to the kitchen and climb up on to the bench. Pulling my feet up behind me.

Maman! Get it! It's on the stair!

Which step, Peony? Which step? Maman daren't come down the stairs. Her feet are bare and she can't see the scorpion. Her belly is in the way.

Maman! It stung me, Maman! Please, it hurts!

My foot is already starting to go red and swell up. The kitchen feels like winter. The darkness in my stomach is spreading out into my arms and legs.

Maman has gone from the stairs.

Wait there! she is shouting. I'm coming, hang on. At the top of the stairs, Maman is wearing Papa's tractor-driving boots and carrying a bottle of shampoo and a fat green syringe. She stomps down the stairs heavily, watching her feet as she goes. She stops, and starts thwacking at the stairs with the shampoo bottle, and stamping with one foot. I don't think the scorpion will be alive when she is done.

Margot has her arms around me on the bench. I squeeze my eyes shut, it is black as night behind my eyes but with sparkles of colour and flashes of white. My foot is burning and I squeeze tighter and tighter. Margot is rocking me.

Don't worry, she says, it hurts, but you'll be OK.

I am trembling in the dark, trying to think about being cuddled, but only thinking about my foot hurting more and more. Then the arms lift me up and it is not Margot any more it is Maman, and she carries me outside into the light. I cling to her side, trying to sit on her hip but her belly getting in the way and me slipping further and further down as she stomps across the courtyard in Papa's boots. She puts me on the table and looks at my foot.

Hush, Pea, it'll be OK, she says, I'll fix it.

It hurts! I cry.

I know, she says, hang on. And she takes the big green syringe and puts it over the sting on my foot and when she pulls up the inside part my foot pulls up too, making a white bubble of my body inside the clear plastic end-part. Then I see drops of blood being sucked out of me and I think I am going to be sick.

Wait here, says Maman.

I sit curled on the table, looking out past the barn and wishing I could see the wing turbines.

Then, The witches are coming! Margot shouts.

Where? Where? I scream, looking around. Everything looks normal but the witches could come up out of the shadows at any moment, and I am sitting on the table, easy to spot.

The witches are everywhere! They're real, after all! Margot is laughing.

Stop it! I scream. Stop it!

Maybe you are going to die, says Margot. She has started peering at me curiously. Scorpions are very dangerous, she says. And she laughs some more.

Go away, Margot, I say. I don't want you any more.

When Maman comes back I am curled in a ball, sobbing. Maman unpeels me like an orange. She has a towel full of ice cubes. She presses it against my foot and one kind of hurt pushes away the other.

Am I going to die? I ask.

Don't say that, Pea, Maman says.

I'm scared, Maman. Can you tell me a story?

Maman sits down in a plastic chair, which creaks as she fits her bottom into it, and holds the ice against my foot.

Once upon a time, says Maman.

I don't want a made-up story, I say. I want a 'When I was a little girl' story. Those ones are always the cuddliest.

When I was a little girl, says Maman, there weren't any scorpions.

Were there spiders? I ask.

Well, yes, spiders and bees and wasps, but no scorpions.

What else did you have? Margot wants to know.

Did you live near the mountains, like us?

No, not really. Just a town. Not far from the countryside, though.

What about the sea?

We were quite far from the sea too.

Were there meadows to play in?

No meadows, Pea, but we had a garden, with a swing.

Oh.

What did you do in the summer? I ask.

Maman is thinking, rolling the icy towel back and forth on my foot and rubbing her feet together. Her hair is a long wet snake down her back.

I played in the garden, and at friends' houses. Our houses were all next to each other in a long row, just streets full of houses. The front gardens were joined by pavements, but the back gardens were joined by snickets, like footpaths. We used to climb over the back fences into each other's gardens. We had paddling pools – yours is yellow but mine was green – although in summer it did rain a lot. We would call on each other to go out and play. If one of us had money we would go to a shop and buy ice-lollies. Other days my mummy would pack me a picnic. Some days, if we were really, really lucky, we would get in the car and drive to the seaside.

Maman's face is empty, as though she is far away from here.

Our seaside?

No, a long way away. A different seaside. A different sea.

There's more than one sea?

Maman smiles. Well, she says, kind of.

Were there flamingos, I say, and *moules-frites*?

There were donkeys to ride on, she says, and the sea was so cold. And there was rock to eat . . .

You ate rocks? I say.

Not rocks, rock, she says. It's a kind of *bonbon* stick. And my granddad would sit in a deckchair and make us all sunhats out of hankies.

You can't make hats out of hankies!

You could then.

That was a long, long time ago, I say.

Yes, says Maman, it really was. Her belly jumps and she curls over it. Pea, she says.

Yes?

Don't do anything stupid like that again. I've got enough to worry about. I need you to be a big girl.

I suddenly feel sad again, and a little bit sick in my throat. Sorry, I say.

Maman gets up slowly. Are you thirsty? she says, and I nod.

Does it hurt a lot? says Margot, when Maman is inside fetching drinks.

I scowl at her. Yes, it really hurts a lot, I say.

Do you think we have to go and play now or can we stay here today?

I hope we can stay here, I say. I don't feel like playing. Maybe we can do a colouring-in.

What about Claude? He'll wonder where we are.

You could go and tell him? I look down at Margot, sitting cross-legged on the paving. Maman didn't notice all our cleaning, I say.

She was just busy with you because of the scorpion, says Margot.

Margot, why were you so horrible to me when I was upset?

Horrible? says Margot. I was not. You must have imagined it.

## *Chapter 11*

The bedroom door creaks open and Maman fills the space with herself, soapy-smelling and with wet hair.

Come on, she says, hurry up and get ready, we're going out. Then she slides into the room and pushes the shutters back so the hot outside smells fly in to wake us, and the cockerel's crow agrees that it's time.

Come on, don't just sit there, get up! Up, up, up! says Maman, as she swings her belly out through the door. I stare after her.

Where are we going? says Margot.

I don't know, I say, it's not market day. Maybe to the shops, or to the doctor's?

It's very early for shops, says Margot.

Mami Lafont's?

I doubt it. Margot rolls her eyes round in her head.

The cemetery to see Papa?

Margot shakes her head. It doesn't feel like that.

No, I agree. But how do we know what to wear?

We could just choose our favourites? says Margot. But my green dress is really dirty now, I had it on for two whole days.

I have a better idea, I say. We will wear something yellow. For the challenge.

Oh, yes, says Margot.

In fact, I don't have a yellow dress, or a yellow skirt, or any yellow trousers. But I have got a yellow T-shirt. The neck is a bit tight going over my head, but I manage. And I find some yellow knickers.

What are you going to wear on the bottom?

Nothing. It will spoil my colour scheme.

I think it will spoil Maman's mood if you try to go out only in knickers. What about colours that match with yellow?

Which ones?

Margot shrugs. Pink?

So I find my pink trousers, the same colour as strawberry yoghurt, and put those on.

Very nice, says Margot.

The radio is playing down in the kitchen, where the table is laid for breakfast. A big checked bag sits on the kitchen floor with things falling out of it: towels and bottled water, plastic boxes with food inside, sunhats and suncream.

Are we going on a picnic? I ask.

We're going to the seaside, Maman says.

Now? This morning?

Yes, if you hurry up. Maman has red eyes, but she is smiling. She is wearing trousers, rolled up at the bottoms, and flip-flops with a big red jewel sitting on top of each foot. She is drinking from a glass of water, covered in sparkling drops on the outside.

We hurry our breakfast, I tidy the table and Maman wipes it. Then we close and lock the door behind us and climb into the car that we hardly ever use. Today it is *canicule*. That means it is mostly a day for swimming or lying down in the shade. It is too hot for anything else. The car door handle burns my hand and I snatch it back again. Inside it is steamy and unbearable, and the smell of car is very strong. We wind down the windows as we set off, letting in the cooler outside air. The car drinks it up thirstily.

The drive to the seaside is all downhill, and Maman drives slowly. She is sitting far back from the steering wheel, because of her belly. Her arms stretch over the top of it. Every now and then her belly jumps and so does Maman, and the car swerves, making me jump too. On the drive to the beach I sing songs. Sometimes Maman joins in for a chorus. She is in a very good mood today. Margot catches my eye and I can tell she is thinking the same thing. I wonder what it is that has made her cheerful. It must have been the cleaning. While I am thinking about this I stare out of the window, watch us pass through the village. We cross a big road by a bridge and I look down to see the traffic speeding underneath us: lorries and caravans and cars. I wonder where they are all going, so fast and so many. When we get to the other side, which smells like Windy Hill only saltier, we turn so that the *étangs* are out of my window, dotted with clumps of moss and yellow grass. Seagulls swoop over them making shadows on the rippling water. I stare hard looking for the flamingos but there are none to be seen. I look at the trees instead. The trees down here are all bent sideways, leaning over because the Tramuntana, that's our wind, has been blowing them hard all their lives. It makes me feel a bit sad for the trees. I think they deserve a rest.

Maman has gone quiet.

Are you OK? I ask.

Me? says Maman. I'm OK. Nearly there.

When the *étangs* turn to beaches we turn off and park the car. I can see the sea now, waiting for me to jump in and splash and swim. I want to run straight on to the beach and flop into the water, but instead I walk slowly beside Maman. As soon as the path down to the beach becomes sandy we take off our shoes, dangling them along as we let the sand scratch off the inland dirt from our feet.

We get to a big square of decking with thatched umbrellas and sun-hammocks.

I'm going to sit here, says Maman, putting down the bag. You go and play. She waggles her fingers over towards the sea.

Do you want to build a sandcastle? I say.

No, you go build one. Go and have fun.

Do you want to paddle, then?

Peony! she snaps.

Margot shakes her head at me and takes my hand. The beach is dotted with bellies and bottoms and towels and bags with the sea twinkling at the other side. We set out over the obstacle course, across the hot sand.

At the water's edge, my bottom is getting very sandy. The waves swoosh in and out, little white pups that lap my toes. I circle my good foot in the soupy sand and keep the stung one, which is big and red, in the cold water. I have dug a big hole with my hands, and Margot is sitting in it. From here we can see Maman. She is still sitting in the shade at the beach café, reading a book. She hasn't moved since we arrived. Instead, people who we don't know at all are fussing around her, bringing her drinks and cushions. Earlier she sent one of the café people down here with ice-cream, vanilla flavour. I wonder again if she isn't really a queen. She definitely looks like a queen, with her treasure between her toes. I have treasure too – a small pile of seashells, white and pink, and some of them with grey-pink glossy insides. Earlier I built a very big sandcastle with the sand out of the hole, and my seashells were its decorations. But the white sparkles on the water are getting brighter now that the sun is higher in the sky. More of the holiday people are starting to crowd on to the beach and I know we will have to go soon. So I am collecting all my shells up to take to the biscuit tin in the girl-nest.

I feel sad, I say.

Sad about the seaside? Margot asks.

No, not sad about the seaside.

What then?

Oh, nothing, I say.

No, but what? says Margot.

Well, I say, the seaside is nice; Maman is just there, here with us on the beach and she's smiling. The water feels nice on my toes. I can still feel the ice-cream in my tummy, a bit colder than the rest of me, which tickles in a nice way. So I feel sad.

Ah, says Margot, that's the kind of sadness you get when you're happy.

Really?

Really.

So am I happy? I ask.

Yes, says Margot, of course you are.

On the way home I sit on the other side of the car so I can watch the *étangs* again.

I am hungry, says Margot.

Me too.

Even the wind through the windows isn't enough to make the heat better now. Maman's skin is red and she has sweat.

Suddenly, there they are, the flamingos! Some just standing still close to the water, their necks curled backwards, lying over their wings, looking at each other over their shoulders. Some wading and dipping their hooked black beaks into the water. One flaps his wings, the underneath bits surprisingly black and red.

When I'm a flamingo, says Margot, I will paddle all day long.

When I'm a flamingo, I say, I will fly low over the water looking at the sparkles.

When I'm a flamingo? says Maman, and laughs as though we were making jokes.

As we turn away from the water, up on the hillside the wing turbines are turning, moving almost but not exactly in time like the children last year in our nursery-school play. They look smaller from here, but still peaceful. The hills look different too; the rocky parts shine, nearly white in the sunlight, which makes them seem friendlier than the dark green in between.

We pass a hut, where a lady is sitting on a chair. Behind her is a big pile of watermelons. One is cut open showing the dark pink middle all freckled with seeds and it looks extremely refreshing.

Oh, can we? I say, before I have had a chance to think about it. Can we get a watermelon?

Maman huffs. Don't you think that's enough treats for one day, Peony? she snaps. Are you never satisfied?

Pea, honestly! whispers Margot, and I close my eyes for the rest of the journey.

I do planning. When we get home, I think, Maman will go upstairs for a sleep, and Margot and I will rush down to the low meadow to tell Claude about our morning. Claude will want to look at all my seashells and ask about how deep the hole was that I dug (very) and how beautiful my sandcastle was (very beautiful). We will tell him how our challenge is working and that to make

Maman happy we have to do some more cleaning. Merlin will lick my hand and Claude will be proud.

Claude is sitting under the mulberry tree with Merlin. Merlin stands up when he hears us. Hello, Pea, Claude says. How are you today?

I am fine, I say.

And how is my little Margot?

Margot is pretending to be shy, so I say, Margot is fine too. And how are you?

This is how it is every day now. He says, How are you? And I say, Fine. He always asks if Margot is fine too and she doesn't answer and I answer for her. But then when we ask Claude how he is he always tells us something different. Today he says, I have the peach! Which is funny and makes us laugh.

Where? I say.

Where what?

Where is your peach?

Claude laughs too. It's here, he says, and points behind his ear. Claude is funny.

Guess where we have been! I say.

Claude shakes his head. No idea, he says, but it looks like you had fun.

Margot is miming the sea and making a shooshing noise, like the waves.

I'll give you a clue, I say. Somewhere beginning with 'S'.

The Sahara? says Claude. Sausages?

Sausages is not a place, I laugh.

Claude reaches over and brushes sand from my leg. Are you sure it's not the Sahara, he says, you are certainly very sandy. He makes all the 'S' sounds hissy, like a snake.

Well, he says, I would say the beach, but that doesn't begin with 'S' . . .

The seaside! I shout. And Margot says, But actually that's cheating, because seaside is in English.

That's great, says Claude. But his face isn't happy.

Don't you like the seaside? I say.

I used to love it. Claude stops talking because Merlin has interrupted him by nudging his hand with his nose, and licking at his palm as though it were an ice-cream. Claude ruffles the long red hairs on Merlin's neck and says, Thank you, I know.

Merlin can speak! says Margot.

What is Merlin saying? I ask Claude.

Ah, Merlin likes the beach too, says Claude, but not in the summer. Too hot and too many people.

It's really hot today.

Yes, it's the *canicule*, says Claude.

I know, says Margot.

It'll be gone soon. Claude pats Merlin's neck. Merlin will be pleased about that too, won't you, boy? Merlin yawns. Did you know that *canicule* means 'little dog'? Claude says.

Merlin is a big dog, not a little dog, says Margot.

Do little dogs get very hot? I say.

Claude smiles his scrunchy-faced smile. Is your maman feeling better?

I think today she had a good day. I wish it were always like that.

It's a good sign, says Claude.

It's because I cleaned the courtyard and Margot hoovered the air.

I see. And what about you? Are you doing OK?

We're fine, thank you, I say.

Claude smiles.

What?

You remind me of someone, he says.

Do you want to come with us next time? I say.

I can't, says Claude.

I wish you could.

You wish a lot of things, don't you? Do you want to go and find lucky clovers to make them come true? Claude asks.

Oh yes, we do! we shout, and we start to run down to the clover patch, but I soon stop and slow down because my leg is still hurting.

Hey! says Claude, noticing me. What happened there?

I look down at my fat foot.

You're limping, he says.

Just like you, says Margot. You are the pirate twins.

What happened?

You're limping too, I say, what happened to you?

You first, says Claude.

I was stung by a scorpion, I say.

Truly?

Truly.

Where?

On the kitchen stairs. It got out of the jar.

Oh, Pea, why did you have a scorpion in a jar?

I don't want him to tell me off.

Margot put it there, I say.

I did not! says Margot.

Yes she did, I say. Margot scowls hard at me but I think she knows why I don't want to make Claude cross and she shuts up, scuffing the grass with the toes of her pink sandals.

And why did Margot put the scorpion in the jar? says Claude.

I can't remember.

Where is it now?

Maman killed it with Papa's boots and a shampoo bottle.

Did she? Claude's eyebrows are up.

So what happened to you? I say. It wasn't really a tiger, was it?

I was hit by a car, says Claude.

You should Stop, Look and Listen, says Margot.

Were you crossing the road? I say. Didn't you look?

Well, actually no, I was driving a car, and another car hit our car. It was going too fast.

Did you have to go to hospital?

Oh yes, for a long time.

For injections?

Claude laughs. Lots of injections, yes. And also they had to mend the broken parts of me.

But now you're mended.

Mostly.

Where are your still-broken parts?

Claude looks miserable.

Stop asking questions, whispers Margot, loudly.

Sorry, I say.

It's OK, says Claude, it's not your fault. It's just a sad question for me.

Is it because your leg still walks funny? I say.

No, that doesn't make me sad, says Claude.

Is it because you have got the funny bald bit on your head? says Margot.

Is it because you can only hear us when we shout? I say.

Are you keeping a list of all my broken parts? says Claude with a twisty smile.

I shake my head. No, I say, I'm not very good at writing. The letters always come out inside out.

We stop walking, we have got to the clover patch, and we all sit down in the green.

I can't hear very well at all, says Claude, that's true, but Merlin does a lot of my listening for me.

Can he answer the telephone? says Margot.

My heart still hurts too, says Claude, to the grass.

How does Merlin pick up the telephone with his paws? I ask.

Claude frowns; he looks confused. We don't talk to people on the telephone, he says.

Does Merlin speak French?

Well, he doesn't speak, he just listens. Like when he hears you coming he barks so I know you're there, or if we are crossing the road, or if there is a knock at my door – although usually there isn't.

And now, when I'm talking? I ask.

I can hear you a little, but mostly I'm watching your mouth make the words.

Margot sticks her fingers in her ears and says, Go on then, say something! I put my hands over my ears too, and we watch Claude's mouth, waiting to see what the words look like when you can't hear.

His mouth moves but there are no letter shapes or word shapes just opens and closeds.

It doesn't work, I say, disappointed.

You have to get used to it, says Claude.

I look at his ear, shiny and bent. Wouldn't it be easier to just mend your ear? I say.

You can't mend everything that gets broken, says Claude.

Like a broken heart, says Margot, who has been reading about Rapunzel, who lived in a tower but before that she was a baby and her maman gave her away to a wicked witch to pay for some lettuces, but it gave her a broken heart.

Is your heart broken? I ask.

It was, says Claude. Hospitals don't have anything for that. But some things get better by themselves eventually.

Claude rummages in his bag and offers me a drink of water from his bottle. I drink in big gulps.

Margot? he asks.

Margot shakes her head.

Margot likes milk, not water, I say. And sometimes lemonade. But thank you.

Claude looks down into the clover then reaches and picks one stem with four perfect leaves. He hands it to me.

Here, he says, you can make a wish on this.

He reaches down again. I'll get one for you too, Margot, he says.

I stare at the clover. I wish tha . . .

Shhh! says Claude. If you tell me it won't come true.

Claude, I say, will my foot stay limpy like yours now, for ever, until I am old like you?

Definitely not. You'll be all mended ready for school. Have you got any new school shoes yet?

I shake my head.

Probably after the baby is born, says Claude.

Margot is standing on one leg.

What are you doing? I say. There's nothing wrong with your leg!

That's right, says Margot. My legs are better than yours.

But what are you doing?

I'm a flamingo, she says. And I could stand like this for a hundred years.

## *Chapter 12*

I wake up hungry, thirsty and already sweating. I can tell it is very early because the sky is just waking up but it's already too hot to stay in bed. My bed sheet is on the floor where I kicked it off in the night, my pyjamas on top of it. I open the window to let a little bit of air in before the sun gets too high.

It's still little dog, I say to Margot.

Hot dogs, she replies, and we laugh at her joke. I go on to my hands and knees and start panting and yapping, but then I remember Maman asleep in bed and get up again.

We should do some more cleaning today, I say.

OK, says Margot. Get dressed then.

But I hear Sylvie's car outside and run straight downstairs to say hello and get the bread.

Good morning! I say.

Good morning, Pivoine, says Sylvie. Her mouth is pink with lipstick, which makes it look jagged at the edges like a monster because the lipstick has gone into all the wrinkles. She hands me the two baguettes and I bite the end off one.

Did you forget something? she says.

Thank you, I say.

Well yes, thank you, she says but also . . .

Do we have to pay you today? I ask. I wonder if there is some of the money from the peachman somewhere in the kitchen.

No, not today. But, Pivoine, where are your clothes?

Oh, I haven't got dressed yet. I'll do it after breakfast, I say.

I turn on the tap and crouch beside it, cupping my hands and drinking from the cold-water lake, already overflowing.

Pivoine, that's not very well mannered, says Sylvie.

You're a lady, I say. So it doesn't matter if I haven't got my clothes on.

I mean drinking from the tap. We drink from cups.

So do we, I say, but I can't reach the kitchen tap.

Where's your maman?

She's in bed, I say. Why do people keep asking the same questions? I wonder. Maman is tired, I say, because the baby does exercises all night and . . .

Sylvie interrupts. What did you do to your foot? she says, squatting down next to my big red ankle.

A scorpion did it.

A scorpion?

It was my fault; I had it in a jar.

Your maman let you put a scorpion in a jar?

Maman didn't know, she was in bed.

Does your maman ever get out of bed? Could you go and get her, please?

No, I can't wake her up.

Sylvie looks surprised. You can't wake her up? Did you try?

No. But she will wake up later. When the baby wakes up.

The baby?

I think Sylvie is a little bit stupid, whispers Margot.

Shhh! I say. And to Sylvie, The baby in her tummy.

Oh, says Sylvie.

The new one, I tell her, just in case she hasn't understood. Not the dead one.

Sylvie's lipstick mouth opens but no words come out for a long time. Eventually she says, Are you OK?

We're fine, thank you, I say. How are you?

I mean just you? I'm sure your maman can take care of herself.

We're fine.

Are you hungry?

I was, I say, but I have the bread now.

Maybe I should knock on the door, speak to your maman?

No! I shout it, and then am sorry. Sorry, I say. But please don't. Maman doesn't like being woken up.

Then can you take a message?

Sylvie puts down a third baguette.

It's TOO MANY, says Margot.

In case you're hungry later, says Sylvie. Now, why don't you go and put on some clothes? And tell your maman . . . actually never mind.

OK, I say. Bye!

Good morning, Maman says, walking out barefoot into the courtyard.

I'm sorry, I say. Did we wake you up?

No, that's OK. I think the baby liked the seaside. We didn't have a lot of gymnastics last night.

Say something nice. Margot is right behind me, hissing into my ear.

I liked the seaside too, Maman, I say. Thank you for taking us.

You're welcome, Pea. Now I have a job for you.

Really?

Yes, really. I am going to make a salad, so you have two jobs to do.

What are they?

The first job is to go and find me some mint, about two handfuls. You know what mint looks like, don't you?

Yes, of course I do!

Good. Next, if you look in the pantry you will find the big bag of peas that we bought at the market. I need you to pop all the pods and put the peas into the colander. You can give the pod parts to the chickens. Can you do all that?

Yes I can, I say.

But first, she says, go and put some clothes on, and a hat.

Yes, Maman.

And, Pea?

Yes?

Don't eat all the peas, Pea.

Maman is smiling as she goes back into the house to get her coffee.

The picked mint is on the table and the colander is half full of fresh, sweet little peas. We were just getting to the end of the paper bag of pea pods when Mami Lafont's car came up the path.

Maman doesn't speak the right language for here, at least not very much of it. Now she stands at the kitchen door, blocking it like a sentry and being cross in funny French. She is shouting at Mami Lafont. They both stand with their arms folded over their chests and I half expect them to run at each other any minute now and bump tummies. Mami Lafont's doesn't have a baby in it, but it is still quite fat. Margot and I have been sent inside, so we are sitting on the stairs, watching them argue.

You cannot just walk into my house! says Maman in her cross voice.

Your house? says Mami Lafont. This has never been your house.

I was Amaury's wife, says Maman, in everything but name. Don't you try and take that from me.

He deserved better than you, says Mami Lafont. It comes spitting out of her mouth like sour apple.

Leave me alone. Don't you think I have enough to think about right now? Maman is shouting now.

Better now, Mami Lafont says, than trying to move when you've got a newborn. Why don't you just go back home? You don't belong here, can't you see?

What do you know about where I belong? This is my home, you stupid woman, says Maman. This is our home.

Let's go upstairs, Margot says to me.

This is a good idea for two reasons. Firstly Maman seems really angry, and it will be better if we are not there to get under her feet when she has finished having her argument, and secondly because if we lean out of the window we can see better. We hurry upstairs and open the shutters.

You can't even look after yourself, Mami is saying. And what's that mess in the barn? The place is full of rotten fruit, wasps and ants everywhere, Amaury's tractor covered in the stuff. Are you crazy?

I want you to leave, now. Maman's voice is flat.

Brigitte is getting married. We will need the farm, Mami Lafont carries on. It's much too big for you. All those empty rooms going to waste.

And where am I supposed to go? I know you don't care about Peony and me, but do you want to make your grandchild homeless?

I don't have a grandchild. Mami is smiling the smile of someone who doesn't want her photo taken.

What do you think this is? Maman is pointing at her belly.

Well, says Mami Lafont, that's to be seen. But what are you going to do with the farm? You can't farm it. When the money in the bank runs out then what?

We will find a way, says Maman. It's none of your business.

Joanna, says Mami Lafont, what kind of mother are you anyway? That child is running wild. She drinks from the tap outside like a savage. She hasn't had a haircut in months. You're not even feeding her properly.

How would you know how I bring up my daughter? says Maman. You're never around to see.

There are eyes and ears everywhere in this village, says Mami.

Eyes and ears everywhere! says Margot.

In the trees! I say.

On the walls! says Margot.

In the sky, I say. Flying around with the birds. Then I hear Maman say, Ow! And I lean a little further to check that she's OK, but then Mami Lafont notices me and looks up. She waggles her bony finger at me.

And just to prove my point, says Mami, that child is going to fall out of the window if you are not careful.

Maman steps out into the courtyard, making Mami Lafont move backwards. She is holding her belly again, bent over a bit, and her face is white. She cricks her neck to see me.

Peony!

Sorry, I say, and slither backwards off the window ledge and back into my room. I stand by the window, trying to stretch my hearing so I don't miss anything. Maman has started shouting in English now, which is very strange because Mami Lafont doesn't speak English at all.

I can't do this, she says. Get away from me. Get away!

It goes quiet. After a minute I hear the engine rattle on Mami Lafont's car, and the front door slams. My heart thumps. Whump, whump inside my T-shirt. I hear bare feet slap slowly up the stairs and another door bang shut. Then there is no noise in the house at all, but the argument words are still bouncing around in my head.

Well, fancy that, says Margot.

What? I say.

Tante Brigitte is getting married! says Margot. We are going to be bridesmaids.

There are shouted words and lots of questions heavy on my insides like pebbles in my tummy. But every step away from the house I feel lighter, and we walk straight down the path to make it go faster. Margot is not interested in the argument, only in weddings.

What sort of dresses shall we have? asks Margot.

Why are they cross with each other? I say.

I think we should have flowers too, lots of different colours.

Why did Mami say she has no grandchildren? Has she forgotten about us?

Sometimes when you are a bridesmaid you get a present, says Margot.

Present? What kind of a present?

It depends what you wish for, she says. So come on, we have got to find some more lucky leaves. We need to do our wishes quickly before the grownups do all their wrong decisions. We can get one for every wish we have to have. Come on, hurry up.

We go as fast as we can with my still-sore foot, down past the donkeys, and tumble down into the patch of clover where we fall on to our tummies, nose to nose with the flowers. Margot checks every stalk. She runs her fingers through the patch of clover, one by one by one. She is very delicate with the leaves, skimming her fingertips through them; they hardly move. Margot is good at this game. But today she is not doing a good job. It's like a needle in a haystack, she says.

We look for a long time but don't find a single wish. I am starting to worry that my bridesmaid's dress will be blue or another awful colour, or that my present will be something I don't like, like socks, or exercise books with lined pages.

OK, come on, Pea, says Margot, it's not our day for wishes. But I've got something to show you.

What is it? I say.

You'll have to wait and see.

Tell me!

I haven't decided yet, but it's good . . .

So we skip further down towards the stream.

Here! she shouts at last.

What is it?

This, says Margot, holding her head up high and sweeping her hand around, showing me a tree stump and a fallen silver birch tree, some grass and a patch of dandelions. This is where the fairies live.

Really? Fairies? What are they like?

Come and have a look, says Margot. The fairies are small, like small daisies. They have yellow dresses or green dresses so you can't see them so well. That is called camouflage and it is to stop them getting eaten by bigger creatures like spiders and lizards. But also it means you have to be careful where you tread here. It would be best not to walk on this part at all. Also, she says, they are extremely beautiful. They have red hair that falls like a curtain down their backs and they have eyes like mini-kaleidoscopes, blue and green and sparkling. They are kind and they cook good things and they are always smiling.

Do they sing? I ask.

They sing all the time, says Margot. Can't you hear them?

I can hear cuckoos and doves and sparrows. There is even a golden oriole. I have never seen one of those, because they are shy, but I know what song they sing because Maman told me. I can't hear any fairies, though.

OK, says Margot, hold out your hands. She has her hands closed together like a box, like she has something inside for me.

I hold mine out, together, so she can give it to me.

Here, says Margot, as she empties her hands into mine. A fairy. Be gentle!

I close my hands. I can feel the fairy against my palms, light and ticklish and white.

She wants to come and stay in the girl-nest, says Margot.

Really?

Yes, she's a nest-fairy. She's been waiting for it for a long time.

It is very hard to cross the stepping stones with my hands cupped together, even though my hands haven't got anything to do with my feet.

Can't she ride on my shoulders? I ask, but Margot says no. So I decide to walk through the stream like Claude does and get my sandals soaked in the cold water. I will have to hide them from

Maman until they are all dried out. It feels so good on my hot feet, though, and I now wonder why we bother with stepping stones at all.

I am very busy organising the girl-nest. The fairy has got a new bed in the biscuit tin, which is where she would like to live, and I have made room for it by moving around some of the specimens and treasures. Also we have done some wiping and tidying up of leaves, so the nest is spick and span, now that we have a visitor. I am sitting doing some thinking about the argument at our house this morning, when there is a rustling below and I peep out over the top. Merlin is sitting in the shade, wagging his tail. Every wag makes a swooshing noise; he would be no good at hide and seek.

Hello, Merlin! I shout. There's a fairy come to live in our nest! I can't see Claude. Claude! I shout down.

Yes, Pea? he answers and he wiggles his feet, which were camouflaged in the grass. He must have snuck up very quietly. Claude would be very good at hide and seek. Have you got a mami? I say, to his feet.

Claude laughs. Merlin turns three times, like a magic spell, then flops down on to the grass by Claude's feet with a sigh.

A mami? says Claude, Not any more, my little flea. She died a long time ago. But I had two once upon a time.

How do you know if you have a real mami? I shout.

A real one? Well, she is the maman of your maman, or the maman of your papa. Often she makes jam, and wears an apron. Claude shifts so I can see all of him properly. He is smiling. And usually they like to give you lots of kisses. Why do you ask?

Oh, I say. I have only got one mami and I'm not even sure if she is a real one.

Claude sucks hard on his cigarette and drops it on to the grass. The last of the smoke sails up to the girl-nest and I breathe it in. I have started to like the smell of Claude's smoke.

Does she make jam? he says.

Yes, I say. Because she definitely does; I have seen it in her kitchen in pots with the wrong labels on. But she doesn't give me lots of kisses.

Would you like her to give you more kisses?

I think about it, and shake my head. No, I say. Because her hands are quite witchy and she doesn't have any good biscuits.

Well then it's OK, says Claude. She is definitely a mami and the kissing thing doesn't matter. I'm sure she has an apron, because they all do.

Why do we kiss people? I say.

Claude laughs. *Ooh-la!* he says.

Yes, why? says Margot.

Well, we kiss people when we like them, says Claude, and to say hello and goodbye.

So why doesn't Mami kiss us?

Maybe she doesn't like kissing?

What about you? Do you like kissing?

Claude's eyes go big and he opens his mouth but no sound comes out, just like Sylvie. It looks funny so I practise doing it too, but my face doesn't feel comfortable that way.

So, Claude says, tell me more about this fairy you have?

He hasn't heard you, says Margot. It's his funny head.

Yes, I say, and I climb out of the girl-nest because I want an answer to my important question.

Claude is watching my sandals slip on the ladder coming down.

How did your shoes get wet? he says.

She was carrying the fairy, says Margot, so she couldn't balance on the stepping stones.

I didn't want to drop the fairy in the river, I say.

Claude nods, as though he understands, but I'm not sure if he thinks that collecting fairies and walking through rivers in sandals is naughty or not.

I only collected one, I say, and I show Claude how you have to walk with your hands closed up like a box, and how if you try to do that on stepping stones – I pretend there are stepping stones in the long grass – it makes you more wobbly.

Well, says Claude, you take care in that river. It's slippery. The stepping stones are best. Maybe you should put the fairy in a bag next time.

That is a very good idea, says Margot.

I didn't think of that, I say.

Anyway, says Margot, we came down to ask you about the kissing.

Oh yes, I say. I sit down and lean against Merlin, who is very hot. So why don't you kiss us to say hello or goodbye or that you like us?

Don't you like us? says Margot.

We like you, I say.

Claude pulls his knees up and shuffles his back against the tree, like an itchy bear.

I do like you, he says. I think you are very clever and funny and kind and nice. But it is not nice for a grownup to kiss children when their parents are not there. It is a rule.

But Maman is never here.

No, he says, and that is why.

What about if we blow kisses? I say.

Yes, says Claude, we can do that.

But even though it was my idea this doesn't make me happy. A blown kiss is not like a proper kiss. Hugs and kisses should be hugs and kisses, not breaths of air. I am tired of breaths of air and not enough hugs and kisses. It surprises me, my crossness, blowing up inside me like a black balloon until I want to shout out loud. But I don't want to upset Claude and Merlin. So I decide to disappear myself.

Did you know, if you wave your hands really, really fast, they stop being seen? They are going so fast they are invisible. I wonder if this would work with a whole person. I stand up and I start to wave my hands, my arms, jiggle my head, faster and faster. I start to run, faster, faster through the long grass away from Claude and back towards Maman but I hope that I can just disappear somewhere along the way.

Margot and I sit at the kitchen table. I didn't disappear on the way home, and eventually I got out of puff from the fast running so we stopped to pick flowers. We have brought back pockets full of daisies and clover for Maman, and we are arranging them around the edge of a plate. She can eat her supper off it when she wakes up. We are too hungry to wait, though, so we sit at the table eating the bread, which is quite hard, but we have put both kinds of jam on it and so it's sort of crunchy-sticky good. I am spooning on some more jam – because that is the best part – but not looking what I am doing. I am just letting my eyes move around the kitchen, through the dusty light and the cool dark shadows, over the dirty floors at the bottom and the spotty tomato clothes above our heads. It is because I am doing this instead of looking at the jam that I see the little checked curtain twitch. The curtain is drawn across the part under the sink where Maman keeps cleaning things. We are not supposed to touch them, but sometimes, if I have spilled something, I can get a cloth and something which has flowers on the front but makes my eyes water and I can clean it up before she knows. But cleaning products are not supposed to move and make curtains twitch. I jump up, scraping the bench on the tiles, and the curtain twitches again. Something small and dark rushes fast as lightning along the wall.

It makes me jump, but then I see it properly just as it slips through the crack between the wall and the pantry door. A little brown mouse, with whiskers and a tail and everything.

Let's catch it! says Margot. We can keep it as a pet.

Do you remember the scorpion? I say. Sometimes, Margot, you can be very irresponsible.

But mice don't sting, she says.

What would we feed it on?

We could try bread, says Margot.

So I break off a piece of my bread and jam and put it down next to the pantry. I hope Maman won't notice, I say.

Just then, Maman starts to scream. My insides turn somersaults. I think that perhaps this is what it feels like for Maman when the baby is doing exercises. I think this very quickly because mostly I am scared that Maman is screaming. Then I think she is in the kitchen watching me and is cross that I am feeding the mouse. But then she screams again.

Amaury! Amaury! Her voice is upstairs and loud and frightened.

My heart thuds. She's shouting for Papa, I whisper.

I know, says Margot.

Do you think she's forgotten that he's dead? I say.

I doubt that, says Margot.

Maybe it's a different Amaury she wants, I say.

Or a nightmare, says Margot.

Yes, that could be it, I say.

Amaury! Maman shouts again.

We should go and help her, says Margot.

I'm scared.

We'll hold hands, come on.

So we climb the stairs, holding hands, and tiptoe down the corridor. We go over the creak, and quietly push open the bedroom door.

Maman is curled on her side in a pile of pillows, her hair is sweaty and pushed back off her face. Her face is wet but I don't know if it is crying or sweat. The fan is turned off and the air feels wet like bath-time in winter. Maman's eyes are screwed tight, one fist pressed up against her forehead and the other arm wrapped round her belly.

Amaury! she shouts again, making us jump.

I want to run away, but Margot pulls me by the hand close to the bed. Maman's belly is rolling in waves like the sea.

Maman, I whisper.

No! she groans.

Maman, it's me, Pea. Papa's dead.

No!

Maman?

You need to speak up, says Margot.

Maman! I say in my loudest voice that is not shouting, and I grab her hand and squeeze it tight.

Then the wail comes. It is like the wolf-wail she did the day she threw peaches at the tractor.

Maman, I scream. Wake up!

Maman's body jerks. Her arms fly up into the air and she cries out as though she is falling. But then her eyes open. At first they are black, but then black shrinks away and the colour comes back and she looks at me as though she wonders what I am doing in her house.

I . . . she says.

I don't say anything.

It's . . .

We stand side by side, waiting to know if it was good or bad, what we did.

Maman puts her legs over the side of the bed and makes her body sit up. Her belly is nearly touching her knees. She looks around the bedroom. Her clothes are mostly on the floor. There are some coffee cups and some plates with toast crumbs on.

If you would like, I say, there is a special plate for your supper. It has daisies on.

Maman stares at me and now she doesn't say anything. Her face is screwed into a question mark, but I don't know the answer. She looks around her room again.

Are you looking for Papa I say, because . . .

Can you turn the fan on for me on the way out, she says.

## *Chapter 13*

It is barely light, but I was woken up by a commotion outside, and now there is a noise in the kitchen. I creep down in my pyjamas to see if the mouse is back. But it is not the mouse, it is Maman. Maman has killed one of the chickens. She is sitting at the kitchen table, her legs wide apart, her hands covered in blood. She leans forward over the wooden chopping block, cutting the chicken into the right shape with a big pair of black-handled scissors. The scissors tug through the skin and crunch through the bones. Crunch. Snap. And under her breath she is muttering something.

Don't you tell me about how to raise my children, she says. Don't you come here with nothing but threats and bad intentions. Just you wait and see.

Crunch. Snap.

Good morning, Maman, I whisper.

She looks up. Good morning, she says, and looks away again. Her apron has blood smears on it.

Margot and I sit ourselves silently at the table and pretend to make rockets out of toilet-paper tubes, but really we are watching what Maman is doing. Her bloody hands have small pieces of dead chicken on them and every now and then she pulls out a feather or two. The other feathers are already in the bin beside her. Chicken feathers are not very interesting really. This part, with the blood and the cutting, this is the bad part. But I know what comes next. Later Maman will roast this chicken for our lunch and that will be the good part. We will eat it with some tomatoes and bread and it will taste good. The bones will be boiled for soup or rice. Even in summer Maman makes soup, but usually it is with courgettes or tomatoes and we eat it cold out of the fridge with green onions chopped on to the top. I am pleased that the long sleep was good for Maman and that she is up early and going to cook us something delicious. But we cannot eat breakfast because the table is busy with feathers and chicken insides.

Maman, I say, is it OK if I go and have my shower until it's time for breakfast?

Maman doesn't turn. Yes, OK, she says. Just don't make a mess.

Looking at her sitting at the kitchen table with all the red and the feathers, I wonder how much mess I could make with a shower and a bar of soap, but I don't argue.

By the time I come back down to the kitchen, cooled by the water and smelling of fruit, the feathers and the feet and the face with the beak is all put away and the lying-down cooking chicken is covered with oil and salt and pepper, ready to roast. Maman is clean and is drinking coffee.

Maman?

Yes, Pea?

You really are very beautiful, I say.

Maman smiles. Thank you, she says.

Maman and I are waiting for the bread to arrive so we can have breakfast, says Margot. And as if she had heard her, Sylvie's car crunches up to the house. Maman gets slowly to her feet and goes out. We follow.

Good morning, says Maman. But she is not smiling.

Good morning, Sylvie replies. She looks at Maman, then down at me, clean out of the shower and smelling of fruit, then back at Maman. Her face is surprised to see Maman, I can tell. How are you, *Madame*? she says.

Maman is still not smiling. You can leave the bread at the bottom of the path from now on, she says.

Sylvie hands me the baguettes. Two. At the bottom of the path? she says.

That will be fine. Maman is counting out coins from her red purse.

Don't you think, says Sylvie, I mean, wouldn't it be easier for you, in the state you're in, if . . .

Sylvie's pink lipstick mouth is making a tight scrunched-up knot and her eyebrows are down in the middle. She is scared of Maman. But still she is arguing with her, which is a big mistake. Maman holds out her hand with the coins in so that Sylvie has to come towards her to take them. Sylvie is stretching her arm forward so she doesn't have to get too close, as though she is taking a bone from a dog.

The state I'm in? says Maman.

It can't be long, says Sylvie, making a happy face. At least there's that.

At least there's that? says Maman, like a parrot. At least there's that? She is getting extremely angry.

This is going to be a disaster, says Margot.

I'm sorry, I didn't mean . . . Sylvie sighs. I just thought it must be hard. Young children are tiring when you're pregnant. Mine are all grown up but I still remember. I just meant well. She snatches the coins out of Maman's hand and steps backwards.

Meaning well means trying to be helpful. It doesn't mean sticking your nose in where it's not wanted. Maman says this in a very quiet voice, like a growl, and now all in English. She is pointing at the tip of her nose while she is growling. Sylvie looks confused.

I don't understand, she says.

That's right, says Maman, still in English. You don't understand a thing.

Sylvie looks at Maman, and then at me, and she shakes her head. I smile at her, just a small, sorry smile. Maman is being very impolite today and her idea about the bread is a silly one. Now I will have to fetch the bread from down by the road before I can eat it. Sylvie makes her mouth into a straight. It isn't a real smile but you can tell that she is trying. She gets into her car and slams the door. She has another look at me out of her window. I am just standing still with the bread, looking back at her. I haven't eaten any. My hair is drying in the sunshine, growing curls. Maman is standing next to me, with her arms folded together resting on the top of her belly. All of our toes are in a line.

Nice to see you have some clothes on today, Pivoine, says Sylvie, and she drives away.

After breakfast, Maman takes herself back to her room. I'm tired, she says.

OK, I say, although it isn't really.

Why do you think Maman was angry with Sylvie? I say.

She always leaves too much bread, says Margot. It's such a waste.

She said she'd been sticking her nose into it, I say.

Yes, says Margot. And that is very unhygienic.

And also quite peculiar, I say.

Never mind, says Margot. Hey, Pea, I've got a very good idea. Then she whispers it into my ear and it is a very good idea indeed. Especially after what Mami Lafont said. We take the things that we need from the kitchen to play our game and then we go quietly back up to our room and close the door.

Me first! says Margot.

I hand her the big black-handled scissors and she snip-snips them in the air. They shine softly in the triangle of light coming in through the shutters.

Great! she says. Then she holds up a big chunk of her hair, pulling it around in front of her eyes so she can see where to cut, and closes the scissors on it with a snick.

I can't reach properly, she says. You do it.

I take back the scissors. They feel snippy, and the cutting feels definitely good. I snip at her hair, just as if I were a real hairdresser, chatting to her about anything that comes to my head. When I have finished she has very short hair, but it is beautiful, not like a princess but maybe a pop star. Then it is my turn.

Margot takes the scissors and says, Now, *Madame*, what will you be having today?

I will have it nice and short, I say. And a tiara, please.

When it is all done I look at all the cut-offs and scatterings. I'm not sure how to tidy them up so I push all of it except one perfect curl under my pillow. I put the scissors under there too for safekeeping.

I am going to take this one up to the girl-nest, I tell Margot, showing her my curl.

Margot looks down at my pillow. I wonder if we'll come back and find we are very rich because the hair fairy has been?

I doubt there is a hair fairy. If there were then everyone would be very rich, just cutting off one piece of hair at a time.

But what if there is?

We decide it is better to only leave a little under the pillow for the hair fairy as an experiment, and the rest under the rug. Then if she comes tonight we will leave a little out every night and soon we will have enough money to buy Maman a really nice present.

What do you think she would like? I ask Margot.

Maybe a puppy? she says.

Maybe. Or some pink lipstick with glittery bits?

Like Sylvie? I don't think so.

Or a yellow hat to match her yellow dress.

Or some more cushions and pillows for her bed?

I close my hand around my one last curl. Come on, let's go.

We are trying not to giggle very loudly.

While he is hunting for us, Claude's hand keeps reaching down to have a scratch. In the hairy gap between the top of his socks and the bottom of his shorts, I can see the criss-cross of cuts on his legs.

Don't scratch them! hisses Margot and I shush her.

Claude is underneath the tree where the girl-nest is. He is looking upwards, and looking left and right for us; he is being very noisy.

Where do you think they are? he says to Merlin. Merlin wags his tail, swooshy through the air.

Not over here . . . Claude shakes his head. Not over there . . . Maybe they're not here today.

I poke my head out and shout BOO!

Claude doesn't jump, but he laughs. Hello, Pea, he says.

Boo! says Margot.

Hello, Margot, says Claude, squinting up at the tree and waving in the wrong direction. How are you both today?

I am fine and Margot is fine. Are you fine?

I am fine, yes. I see you had a haircut, he says.

It is because of the challenge, I say. Mami Lafont was cross with Maman because I haven't had a haircut. But Maman is busy. So I have done it myself with the chicken scissors. It's a surprise.

And the tiara is because she is a princess, says Margot.

You've scratched your legs, I say.

Again, says Claude. But tell me more about the scissors.

We just borrowed them, I say.

We were extremely careful, says Margot.

Hmm, says Claude. And where are they now? Have you got them up there with you?

They're under my pillow.

Don't you think your maman will be worried when she finds them missing?

I don't think she will notice.

And if she does?

Claude is right. Maman worries a lot and if she can't find the scissors or me she will probably worry about the trouble we could be getting into together.

OK, I say, climbing down out of the nest. I will go and put them back.

Good girl, says Claude.

It is the roast chicken that makes me forget. When we get in the house is quiet, but the chicken can't have been out of the oven very long because the whole kitchen smells of butter and tarragon.

The chicken pieces are in a china bowl under a fly screen. My tummy thunders so loudly I think it might wake Maman up. So I get out two plates, and we help ourselves to some of the meat. We eat it with our fingers and it is salty and delicious. Afterwards I take the bones and bits of fat out to the courtyard for any cat-visitors, so they will fill up their tummies on that and not wait for baby swallows to fall out of the sky.

In the middle of the night, in the dark, I realise that my head is very uncomfortable. At first I think that the hair fairy has been and that there is a pile of coins under my bed. But it is not that. The chicken scissors are still under my pillow where I left them with all the hair. I think about taking them back to the kitchen. I think about the emptiness of the night-time house outside my bedroom door. I think about what Claude said about Maman worrying, but since she has been in bed all afternoon I think she can't have noticed. I think it would be best if I keep the scissors under my pillow until the morning.

I wake up on the floor. I have fallen out of bed, although I don't remember doing it. Margot is laughing at me. She has already got her clothes on and she is wearing a red dress with a silver belt and a silver tiara.

I am the Queen of Amazonia, she says, and I say, Good morning.

Let us have breakfast, says the Queen of Amazonia. I have prepared cake and watermelon and chocolate spread.

That sounds delicious, I say.

The cake and watermelon and chocolate spread is pretend. But we do have some jam. We run down to the path to get the bread.

This is extremely inconvenient, says the Queen of Amazonia.

I'm sorry, I say. It's because Sylvie doesn't speak English. And because she's scared of Maman.

It's like we are in the zoo, says Margot, who is Margot again (but still wearing a tiara).

It is a bit, I say, although I'm not sure I understand.

Like when you have to throw the meat to the tigers so they don't bite you. Sylvie has to throw the bread to us so that she doesn't get attacked by Maman, who is ferocious. Except if she threw the bread it would break and get dirty and Maman would be more cross.

So she has to leave it down here on the signpost, I say.

Exactly, says Margot, and she looks pleased with herself.

Like a zoo, I say. If it's a zoo then I am the unicorn.

They don't exist, says Margot.

Like dinosaurs?

Like witches.

Oh.

Well then I'm a giraffe.

I'm a kangaroo, says Margot, and she bounces away up the hill.

Back at the house, we sit on the step to the courtyard and we eat without talking. There are sparrows in the eaves somewhere, or in the barn. I can hear them chirruping.

Maman comes down and starts tidying the kitchen, and shoos us properly outside while she sweeps up our crumbs.

Where shall we . . . Margot begins.

The low meadow, I say. Come on.

As we get to the road we see Josette is standing at the gate, feeding the donkeys bread and carrots and floppy red and green salad leaves. We stop, look and listen, then run over to say hello.

Josette turns to us with a smile, but it quickly dissolves back into her wrinkles. *Mon Dieu!* she says. Then she turns and stares up at our house, as though it has done something very naughty indeed. Come with me! Josette tosses the rest of the vegetables in to the donkeys and then grabs my hand. She crosses us back over, leading us along the road, away from the village, to a small cottage made of *bonbons* and cakes. Well, yes, actually it is just a normal cottage made of stones, with a red roof, like all the houses. But it is very pretty.

We stand at the gate, staring up at her as she walks away. When she notices we are not following she turns around. Come on, she says, what are you waiting for?

Josette's garden is green and full of flowers. From the side of the house, grape vines climb over big dark beams, and underneath is a table and chairs. The grapes, green ones, are hanging down over the table.

I think if we stood on the table we could get those, says Margot.

Now, you wait here, Ragamuffin. And no pinching those grapes, they're not ripe.

It's like she can hear you! I whisper to Margot.

We wait at the table, which smells of honeysuckle and bananas. The honeysuckle smell is not curious because there is a big bush on the corner of the house, all covered in white and yellow flowers. But the banana smell is. I can't see a banana tree anywhere.

Josette comes back. She is carrying a yellow plastic mixing bowl and some scissors. Stay still, she says, sitting next to me. Josette is really old. Her hair is long and the colour of metal. It is pinned up in a bun, held up with a long black needle. I have never touched Josette's hair, but I imagine it would feel scratchy and wiry. Her face is the most wrinkled face I know. It looks like a peach stone sucked clean. Her eyes are a long way inside her head, but they flash like dark wrong-way-round fireworks in a white sky. Josette smells of violets and donkeys.

I look at the scissors and the bowl and I am not happy.

Is she going to make you into a salad? says Margot.

Or a cake made of hair?

Josette puts the bowl on my head. Margot starts to laugh.

Are you a witch? I say. Are you going to make me into cake?

Josette smiles. I'm not a witch, she says. Just an old lady. She takes the scissors and starts cutting at the hair that is sticking out from under the bowl.

Josette's house is not made of biscuits and *bonbons*, and her fingers are not very witchy, but it could all be a big trick and I jump back. The scissors nearly poke my face.

Stay STILL! she says.

I don't want to, I say.

Pivoine, says Josette. Her voice smiles. What happened to your hair?

I am wondering whether or not to tell a lie. Margot is shaking her head but this could mean 'Don't lie' or 'Don't tell the truth'. I shrug.

You cut it, didn't you? As she says this, a very slinky little black cat appears and starts to wind itself around the table legs.

She IS a witch, whispers Margot. I feel my insides go tight. But I decide that in this case it is best not to lie because witches know magic and can probably tell if someone is lying to them.

Yes, I whisper.

It's OK. But let's just make it a bit better, she says.

OK.

Has your maman seen it?

Not yet.

Hmm. Josette snips short snips on my head. I'm trying to make you beautiful again, she says. I look up at her concentrating face and she smiles back down with all of her soft, brown lines. There, she says, done.

I thought it was better when I did it, says Margot.

Josette ignores her, brushing snips and curls off my shoulders and on to the grass. Now, have you had any breakfast? she asks.

I ate the end off the baguette, I tell her. I had to fetch it from down by the road because Maman growled at Sylvie.

Josette nods. Come on, she says, and she takes us to her kitchen, which is yellow and white and smells of cake. On the table is some fresh bread and some sausage. She cuts the sausage into round circles like small pink and white coins. She slices a big slice of white bread. Then she puts them on to a plate and makes a face. The bread is the face, the sausage is the eyes and nose. She cuts me a slice of tomato to make a mouth and pours milk into glasses.

Your house is different to ours, I say, with my mouth full.

How is it different?

You have clean plates, and it smells of flowers and cake, I say.

Josette comes over and kisses the top of my head.

Everything will be all right, Petite, she says. I wonder if she understood what I said.

You're not allowed to kiss me when Maman is not here, I say.

And who told you that?

Claude.

Claude?

Yes, says Margot.

Well now, says Josette, you'd better get back home to your maman. She'll be worried about you.

She won't, says Margot.

And stay out of trouble! says Josette.

Josette's throat is very frisky, says Margot as we walk home. Did you notice?

Frisky? I say.

Yes. When she talks it moves in and out.

It must be because she is old.

When I get old, says Margot, I will have a house that smells of flowers and cake.

When I get old, I say, I will kiss all the people that wanted to kiss me when I was young.

It doesn't matter how quietly we close the front door, because Maman has been watching us come up the path. Her arms are folded, resting on her belly, and in one hand she is holding the chicken scissors, which I had left under my pillow. She looks at my hair, then my eyes. I look anywhere else but at her. It doesn't work; she seems to fill everywhere today. She pushes the scissors towards us.

I don't even know where to begin, she says. What are you going to tell me?

Margot takes my hand. We hang our heads.

Maman, I'm so, so sorry, I say.

It is mumbled to the floor, but Maman is on fire.

Sorry about what? she says. She is already shouting.

About cutting my hair short, I say.

Your hair? I don't care about your hair! You can shave it all off for all I care.

I don't understand, says Margot.

You do not ever take my scissors, says Maman. And what about when the baby is born? Do you think you can just wave a pair of scissors around then?

No, I say.

No, says Margot.

Maman, I'm so sorry. It was supposed to be a good idea, and also to get us some money from a hair fairy, and also I'm sorry.

But Maman has slumped down at the table, her head in her hands.

I can't do it, she says.

We go back outside gloomily. If Papa had been here he would have given me a hug. Papa had a hug for every day, happy or sad. I look at Margot. Margot is good at words but no good at all for hugs and sometimes the words won't do.

We'll go to Windy Hill, says Margot. She always knows what I'm thinking.

We walk without saying anything until we get to Windy Hill where the knots inside me start to unravel. It is late, and the sun is behind me, pushing my shadow out in front of me like another, much taller person. The wing turbines stand like sentinels, but only one is turning. Nothing is going right today. I feel my stomach tighten back up like someone is squeezing me on the inside. I don't know if one is enough. If the wing turbines are not turning, there will be no electricity and tonight I will have to sleep in the darkness. Over the blue-grey *étangs*, the sunlight is making the little seaside houses glitter, their whiteness sparkling like jewels with little red roofs. The moon has come up already, a dappled lemon shape reflecting across the water. If she hurried she could kiss the sun in the sky before he sets, but it is already too late; the sun is disappearing at my back and taking my shadow with him.

# *Chapter 14*

Get out of bed, says Margot.

It's another red-hot day. Already the air in the bedroom is too warm and too sticky. The shutters are open and the light is bright, even with my eyes closed. I press my arm across them and there are red-black sparkles where the world would be.

I'm too tired, I say. I'm going to stay here.

Don't be ridiculous, says Margot, it's too hot. Get up.

Leave me alone, I say. And I roll over so she can't see me.

Margot is being bossy again. The shower's running, she says, listen. Even Maman is getting up today; it's market day.

Hmph, I say, well I haven't slept. I Need My Rest.

It's Market Day, says Margot, and she makes the words in thick crayon lines in the air with her pointing finger.

I don't like market day, I say. It's Boring. And Boring is in thick crayon too and with a line underneath it.

Free food, says Margot.

I roll back again and peer out from over the horizon of my arm. What kind of food? I say.

Olives for definite, sausage if we're lucky, cheese maybe. Let's see if we can get Maman to buy some paella.

She never buys the paella. When we have paella, Maman cooks it herself.

When was the last time she cooked paella?

I can't remember.

Do you like paella? Margot crosses her arms and jigs up both her eyebrows, waiting for me to agree because she knows I do and that I don't like lying. I do like paella, especially the prawns. And the yellow grains of rice, sticky and fishy and many many grains of sticky, fishy, savoury-tasting rice, one at a time, slowly . . . I do like paella.

Yes, I do like paella, I say.

My mouth is watering, here in my bed. I should get up and make breakfast.

The door swooshes open and Maman is right behind it, her hair wet and clipped up, all in white, bare feet, freckles. What are you rambling about? she says. Shake a leg, it's market day.

Margot bounces out of bed and slips past Maman, first to the bathroom as usual.

On the way to the market, we walk slowly. Maman is taking it easy, she says. I am dillying and dallying. As we pass the wall to Claude's garden Margot and I are sly, peering in to see if he is there. It's hard to see anything through the lavender that is overflowing over the wall. Fat moths like humming birds are hovering around it, drinking the nectar with long tongues. The back of my neck is hot, hot, hot. I try to swish my hair over it but the hair is gone and nothing swishes and I feel sorry that I cut my hair at all.

In the market today people are looking at us, more than usual. They stare at Maman's belly as she pushes her way through without a smile. We pass by them, somewhere in the space in between the homey people and the holiday people, until Josette steps into Maman's path by the spice stall. Josette is wearing the floweriest dress I have ever seen and she still smells of violets. There are bees buzzing round her trying her out for nectar. She swishes them away with her brown hand and plants herself properly in our way. She looks up at Maman – Maman is much taller than Josette.

Hello, *Madame*, she says.

Maman takes a step backwards, her hands letting go of ours and flying to her belly. As she steps away from Josette her back bumps into an old lady, who was following us close behind because Maman was walking slowly. Even now, when she doesn't cook so much, she can't walk fast past the spice stall. The smell as you pass by it is like winters in the kitchen, tajines and spice-bread and hot wine. The colours pile up in pyramid heaps out of brown paper bags with rolled-down tops: reds and browns and yellows and oranges but not like crayons, or flowers; like different colours of the earth. The man at the spice stall doesn't shout out like the people with the peaches or the bangles and beads, or the cheese graters. The spices shout out without saying anything and people let themselves be pulled by the smell. Before all the dying, Maman's feet would walk her over to these smells without her promission and she would be stuck there at the stall just like the flowery feathery pictures stuck on our fridge. You'd have to pull really hard to unstick her. After a lot of looking and smelling she would ask for spoons of the magic powders to be scooped into brown paper bags, and they would bring the smell of the stall back to our kitchen. Maman would mix them up, sizzle them in pans, jumping seeds and spitting oil. And later we would sit at the table and taste it together, all our family together.

Now, the old lady who got bumped wobbles a little bit and is caught by someone next to her. They both glare at us and push their way around in the traffic jam of bodies.

Hello, *Madame*, says Maman to Josette.

I live at the bottom of your lane, says Josette. My name is Josette.

I know, says Maman.

Josette looks up at Maman for what seems to be too much time without any words to be polite. Her eyes narrow to small slits in her creased-up face. Then she smiles, pushing back strands of grey that have escaped her hairpins, and showing her brown teeth. She looks down at me. Hello, Ragamuffin, she says.

Hello, Josette, I say.

Maman looks down at me with dark eyes, bad feelings, then back at Josette.

Good day, she says to Josette, in French. And then she says to me in English, Peony, move it. And then back to Josette, Excuse us, please. And I am jostled around Josette and I look at her and hope she can see that I'm sorry.

Josette calls after us, Pay attention. If you're not careful you'll lose everything.

How do you know that lady, Peony? says Maman, still walking.

Careful, hisses Margot, don't tell her about the haircut.

I try and think, but the thoughts are crowding and all I can think of is the haircut, and the breakfast with smiley-face sausage. And also I am trying to look into the basket as we hurry, to make sure that things are not falling out. Everything is safely in the basket. I don't understand what Josette meant.

Donkeys, says Margot.

Peony, says Maman, I asked you a question. Margot shrugs. No one ever listens to her. Except me, of course. It's because you're four, I say.

Pardon?

Donkeys, I say. The donkeys in the low meadow where we play belong to Josette.

Donkeys, says Maman.

Donkeys, I say.

Watch out you don't get kicked.

They don't kick. They just eat grass.

Right.

Ooh look, paella, says Margot, and she is right. In a van across the square, in a flat round pan, a rainbow pile of paella steams smells of the seaside over to our noses. Salty, fishy, yellow smells. My stomach gurgles. Margot laughs.

Go on then, says Margot. I bet you can't get us some.

I wonder what I could possibly say that would make Maman want to buy us some paella. I make lists in my head. It smells good, but we haven't much money. She wouldn't have to cook, but she doesn't eat much these days anyway. She likes yellow. She likes mussels, but not now she's got the baby in her tummy. Papa used to like paella.

That paella smells delicious, I say eventually.

Maman stops and looks over at the big black skillet full of rice and prawns and peppers and shiny black shells. She rests her hands on her belly.

Go on! says Margot.

Papa liked paella, I say.

Maman stares harder at the paella. People are pushing around her all the time. They're cross at her blocking their way through the market until they get around the front of her and see her big baby-belly, with her hard breathing making it go up and down, up and down, and how she is looking at the paella, with the tears coming out of her like rain.

* * *

Pass me the bowl, I say to Margot.

Even the kitchen is hot today. The only parts of me that are cool are the bottom of my feet on the floor tiles. Upstairs Maman and the baby are having a siesta under the fan. Me and Margot have decided to make up for me making Maman cry in the market by getting some lunch ready for when they get up. We have had to use what we found in the fridge and the pantry. This is what we have found:

Cheese, three different sorts. Milk. Cornichons. Jam. Cold chicken. Tapenade. Lettuce. Courgettes. Dried apricots. There are also sausages and pork belly but we can't eat those because they are not cooked.

We also have the bread from the market, and tomatoes.

We need to have goodness and flavour, I say.

And colour and texture, says Margot.

And love, I say. When Maman was still singing she cooked all the time and she taught us the right ingredients for a recipe. You have to have all of those things and also you have to have variety, and you have to smile when you are cooking or else the food tastes bad.

We can make a salad, I say.

You can eat goodness, says Margot, but you can't eat naughtiness.

I think about it, and she's right. You don't get naughty food.

I haven't used the milk because it is too wet, and I haven't used the jam because it doesn't rhyme with any of the other flavours.

I tear up the lettuce and put it in the salad bowl. I can't reach the kitchen sink so I take the bowl outside to the courtyard tap. The water comes out warm, almost hot, and the lettuce shrinks a little bit, but I tip the water away quickly and I think it will be all right.

Margot has already found the grater and put it on the kitchen table with a chopping board.

Thank you, I say.

You're welcome, she says. Today we are being super-polite.

I grate the courgettes into the bowl of lettuce and then we tear up the chicken that is left and put that in too. We find the wishbone and try to pull it, but it is too greasy, so I put it on the side to dry out. I'm not allowed to use the sharp knives so I get a dinner knife out of the drawer for cutting the tomatoes and cheese. The cornichons can go in whole.

The bread won't cut with a normal knife, so I break up one of yesterday's baguettes on a tray and put it out into the sunshine to dry. Papa used to do that. It is midday and the courtyard is hot like an oven, trapping all the heat in the walls of the house and the barn and making us turn pink. I want to take off my clothes but I know that would be worse. My skin is not the right skin for that. I have Maman's skin. But I have Papa's mouth. That is what they told me.

We have to stay out here to keep the swallows and the ants away from the bread while it toasts. Then it will be croûtons. So Margot and I take turns. One of us splashes tap water on our face and throat and hands while the other shoos the swallows away and disturbs the procession of ants. If you put things in their way, like twigs and leaves and crumbs of bread, they get very confused; it's funny to watch. Then we swap. We stay out as long as we can bear, until I think I really am going to toast just like the bread, and then I say, OK, it should be done now. But the tray has got too hot to hold. I run back indoors to get another bowl and pick the pieces off one by one. We spread them with butter and tapenade and toss them in with the rest of the salad. I pour on some olive oil and do the salt and pepper. The salad actually looks very beautiful. I feel quite proud of what we have made. I want to go and wake up Maman to show her, but we decide to wait.

While we wait we sit at the table and play pat-a-cake until we hear the bedroom door open then the taps running in the bathroom.

Quick, says Margot, lay the table.

I set our places and wait for Maman to come down. She is wearing her yellow dress again, floating down the stairs, her cheeks pink, her eyes red.

There is a salad for lunch, I say.

A salad, how lovely, she says, pouring herself a glass of water.

It has goodness and flavour in it, I say.

And colour and texture, says Margot.

And love, I say, although it makes me feel shy.

Maman looks into the bowl. The salad still looks beautiful, although not as beautiful as it did at first because it has been on the table in the hot kitchen for a while and the lettuce leaves look a bit floppy and heavy with oil.

I didn't use the jam, I say. It didn't rhyme.

It looks lovely, she says. I'm not actually very hungry, though. I might just have some fruit.

She takes a peach out of the bowl and rinses it under the tap. The water soaks the skin, making it darker.

Why do peaches have skin that lets the water in? I ask.

Not like apples, says Margot.

Not like us, I say.

I don't know, says Maman. Skin is all different. You have my skin.

I know, I say. And Papa's mouth.

What? Maman's head snaps back to look at me.

Nothing, I say, and watch as she sinks her teeth into the yellow peach.

What are you up to this afternoon? she says.

Just playing in the meadow, I say. Don't worry, I'll watch out for the donkeys.

And wear your hat.

Yes, Maman. Unless you want me to do some cleaning?

Cleaning?

If you wanted?

Cleaning what?

I look at Margot. She mimes mopping.

The floors, maybe?

Peony, you're five years old. Why would I want you to clean the floors?

Sorry, it was just an idea.

Go on, off you go. I've got things to do.

OK.

Margot and I pick the chicken out of the bowl quickly with our fingers and put the rest in the fridge for later.

The cooking didn't work, I say as we walk down through the orchard.

Not salad, anyway.

But she said she didn't want me to clean.

I don't think that's important, says Margot. Sometimes grown-ups don't know what makes them happy either.

Claude is sitting on the grass in the shade of the mulberry tree as usual, smoking a cigarette and listening to the birds. He has one leg stuck out straight and the other bent. Merlin is lying nearby, panting hard. He is wet.

Is Merlin OK? I ask.

He's just old, says Claude. And he's like you; he runs and runs and doesn't slow down much, even in this weather. But it's not very good for him. We'd better be getting home soon.

But we just got here, I say.

I'm sorry, says Claude. Maybe you could play in the girl-nest. Merlin's my friend too and he needs to go home for a rest.

Shall we put on a show for you? asks Margot.

We could do a spectacle, I say. Even better than before.

Maybe tomorrow, says Claude.

I sit down under the shade of the tree, far away from Claude and Merlin. I cross my arms and scowl.

Claude peers at me. I saw you here once last year, he says. You were underneath this tree.

I saw you too, I say.

We weren't scared, says Margot.

We weren't scared at all, I say.

I was, a little bit, says Claude. I thought you were going to pounce on me.

We would have pounced on you if you had come much closer, I say.

I'd better watch out!

Not now!

Why not now?

Because now we know who you are, I laugh.

Claude's eyebrows go up and down, but he doesn't say anything.

Margot makes her eyebrows go up and down too. I laugh some more.

I like it when you laugh, Claude says.

I know some good jokes, says Margot. We can make you laugh too. Knock, knock?

You shouldn't listen to Margot's knock-knock jokes, I say. They're rubbish.

OK, Pea, want to walk with us up to the gate? Claude gets to his feet and Merlin follows with a grumble.

Of course, I say.

As we walk back up the hill I grab on to Claude's finger. I'm tired, you have to pull me up, I say. He doesn't take his finger away. So we go like that all the way up to the road, with Margot holding on to my finger on the other side and Merlin slinking behind us in our shadows.

*Aïe!* says Claude as we pass the brambles on the path. His legs don't fit the path, they are too big and he always wears shorts. The long branches have tangled on to his socks and fresh red scratches criss-cross his legs. He bends over and unpicks the thorns from the sock, threading the long thorny trailer off the path and back into the tangle.

Are you all right? I say.

Every day I get another scratch from these bushes, says Claude. Those blackberries had better be worth it.

I look at the bushes. The blackberries are turning. The red ones now are half black and I think in a few days we will be able to taste them. Green *punaises* are starting to queue up on the leaves. Once the berries are ripe it is going to be a race.

As the path opens out again into grazing, the donkeys pass us at a trot. I look up to see Josette, standing at the gate with a bag of peelings. She sees us coming but does not wave. Claude squirms his finger out of my grip.

I wave at Josette and she lifts one hand off the gate. Still not really a proper wave but I know she has seen me. Then the donkeys have bustled in front of her for their food and she is hidden behind their donkey-bums.

Josette gave me this haircut, I tell Claude.

He looks down at me but he won't stop and squat to listen like he usually does.

Josette cut my hair, I shout. Claude is not listening now, he is walking faster and faster. Merlin is trotting at his side but he is whining.

Never mind, I say, I'll tell you later.

Hello, Josette, says Claude.

Hello, Claude, says Josette, opening the gate for us. What a nice day. She says it is a nice day but she does not smile.

Hello, Josette, I say.

Hello, Ragamuffin, she replies, smoothing the hair back off my forehead.

I have got so many names it is getting very confusing. Most people call me Pea, I tell her.

What are you doing down in the meadow, Pea? Josette asks.

She is standing in front of the sun, so she is mostly just a purple shadow and I have to squint to look at her. We play down here every day, I say. It's more fun than the house. We don't hurt the donkeys and they don't kick us.

I am four years old and Pea is five and a half, says Margot. We are big girls. And we know where all the best shade is, and where the fairies live.

Josette raises her eyebrows. And you, Claude?

I'm walking my dog, since you ask, says Claude. He sounds cross. I've only ever heard Claude sound cross once before, and that was when we were in danger. Unless Josette is a witch, which we decided she wasn't, then we are not in danger. I don't really understand it.

Merlin is magic, I say to Josette, as a sort of test.

A magic dog, incredible, she says. Well, why don't you run off home now? I'm sure your mother is worried about you. I'll see you across the road. This is not a question. So we let her see us across the road and we run up the path. Behind us we hear Josette shout.

Wait!

We turn, but it is not us she is shouting at. Claude and Merlin are heading towards their house and Josette is following them, running, shouting.

Stop right there! she shouts. Claude doesn't turn but she catches him up anyway. For an old lady she can run very fast. Then they start having an argument. Standing there by the fence. The donkeys are watching, we are watching. Merlin is lying down in the grass. It is too hot for him. Claude is waving his arms about. Josette is waving hers too. Their shoulders go up and down.

What's wrong with Josette and Claude? I ask Margot.

Some sort of grownup thing, says Margot. Grownups argue about really stupid things.

Hmph, I say. I'm quite hungry; are you?

Starving, says Margot.

We'd better not eat the peaches, I say. There are hardly any left as it is.

Well there is something delicious in the fridge, at least, says Margot.

Oh yes, I say. I had forgotten about our cooking. I'm tired too. Do you think Maman would notice if we eat it in bed?

I shouldn't think so.

## *Chapter 15*

My room is in the blue half-dark. The frogs are still calling and the crickets too, but there is also the sound of swallows and a cockerel crowing. Papa is melting.

I tighten my eyes as closed as I can make them. Stay, stay! I say out loud as he mushes up into grey, his smile, his smell. It had been perfect. The dream had gone on for so long. I kept waking up then falling back asleep and dreaming the same dream. Papa, smelling of outdoors, of rain and hay and tractor oil. Papa standing in the doorway at the foot of the stairs, his arms open for me, bending as I ran into them. His arms wrapping me tight and lifting me up high for a kiss, to smell his skin, to put my head on his shoulder. I try to stretch my dream, to pull it into the morning, to keep the smells. But trying so hard to keep the dream is making me wake up even more.

Wait, Papa! I haven't told you about the girl-nest and Claude and, Papa, your tractor is all peachy . . .

Where are my tractor boots? Papa's voice is saying. Where are my tractor boots?

Maman had them to kill the scorpion.

Where's Maman?

She's sleeping.

Where is your maman?

I don't know.

I think we've gone and lost her, Pea. Papa's voice dissolves into the colours behind my eyes.

I'm sorry, Papa. I don't know how to find her, I say.

Papa has gone. He didn't even say goodbye. I open my eyes, but there is just the room and I feel ashamed.

I roll back over to face the wall and screw my eyes shut again. I want to go back to sleep but the cockerel is crowing and the swallows are chattering and right now I am angry with them. They are taking away the cool, empty dark with their noise and their hot whiteness. They are taking away my papa and he will not come back.

I feel the darkness inside me, heavy like I swallowed a big cold rock and it scraped my insides on the way down. I start shaking, the sobs come in through my stomach and out through my mouth and I curl tight into a ball and let the sobs shake me wide awake.

After a while, Margot wakes up. Although my back is to the room I can feel when she is awake and I turn over to see. Margot is sitting up with her legs crossed.

Don't worry, my little flea, she says, and I smile. She sounds like Claude and that makes me feel better.

I dreamt about Papa, I say.

Did you? says Margot. What did he say?

I can't remember.

I dreamt about playing tennis at the beach, says Margot. We had orange tennis rackets, but no ball, so it was very funny.

That does sound funny, I say.

Where shall we go today?

Low meadow, I say. Let's go to the girl-nest and see what Claude has left for us.

Just then Maman pokes her head around the door. Her hair is all down over her face and her eyes are still half asleep.

What's all the screaming? she says.

Sorry, I say, it was a nightmare.

Maman sits on the edge of my bed, making it creak. She puts a hand on my leg and looks down at me. What were you dreaming about? she says.

Nothing.

It can't have been nothing.

It was a nice dream, I say. I was scared when it stopped.

Maman's face is waking up. She is looking right at me.

I have those dreams too, she says. Right. The bed creaks as she hoicks herself up again. Her belly is so big now she is definitely going to fall over backwards. If she does I'm not sure what I could do to help, which is worrying.

Get dressed, says Maman. Breakfast.

Be careful, I say.

She smiles with half her mouth and says, OK, Pea, I will. What do you want to wear?

I shrug. I have run out of clean clothes. Maman looks in my wardrobe and pulls out the lilac dress that was my favourite last summer.

This is your favourite, right? You can wear this.

I smile and take the dress. It is a dress for the four-year-old me. When I put it on it is much too tight, but somehow I like how it makes me feel.

While we are having our breakfast, the mouse skitters out from behind the curtain, right behind Maman. I hold my breath.

Margot pouts. We like the mouse. But grownups don't like mice and Maman probably is going to want to kill it.

We're right. Maman sees the mouse out of the corner of her eye and leaves the table to fetch a mousetrap from the pantry. She takes down a sausage from its pointy hook and a sharp knife from the sink. She gives it a wipe. Then she chops off the end of the sausage, leaving on the metal clip and the dangling string, and loads it on to the mousetrap. The mice in our house like sausage.

Maman draws back the curtain so she can put down the trap, but straight away there is a funny smell. It doesn't smell like mice, which actually don't smell much at all. It smells more like our basket of dirty laundry, full of damp towels and dirty clothes still waiting to be washed.

Oh I don't believe it, she says.

What is it, Maman?

A leak, she says. The kitchen sink is leaking.

We are watching her face to see what to do. It hasn't decided yet if it is a fighting face or a face for tears.

Peony, could you bring me a spanner from the barn, please?

OK, I say, hopping down.

Do you know what a spanner looks like?

A big metal dog bone?

More or less.

The barn door is open and we step around the sticky mess, all covered in ants and flies. Inside the barn is shady and cool and in the corner are Papa's tool drawers, where all his tools are put away neat and tidy.

Top, middle or bottom? I say to Margot.

Middle.

I open it and she is right.

Good guess! I say.

I find a spanner quickly. In fact I find three, one small, one medium and one big, but as I am shutting the drawer, the smallest one slips from my fingers and clatters to the floor. When I pick it up I notice something lying nearby in a white crack of light. It looks like a hand.

Agh! I make a little scream and jump back.

That's not a hand, says Margot.

What is it?

That's a glove.

I stare at the fingers and along the back of the hand to where it stops, with the scratchy fastener around the wrist.

A glove. Papa's glove. I pick it up and hold it in my fingers as though I were holding Papa's hand. It is too soft and floppy, but it smells right.

I am going to keep it, I say. I hide the glove under a rock by the barn; it can go and live in the girl-nest later.

When I get back to the kitchen Maman is kneeling on the floor, getting her dress all dirty. But her belly is too big. She cannot get under the sink to fix the leak.

Her face makes up its mind and she starts to cry.

We could phone somebody to come and fix it, I say.

And pay them with what?

I don't know, I say. I'm sorry.

She drops the spanner down by the sink and pulls the curtain back across. She leaves the mousetrap by the side.

Don't touch it, she says, and she goes heavily back upstairs.

We sit at the table for quite a long time, thinking that Maman is going to be back soon. I stare at the mousetrap hoping that the mouse isn't. For a long time, nothing happens. The clock ticks to eight o'clock and goes *ting*.

I've had a very good idea, says Margot. She has something very important to say, you can tell. An announcement. She is waiting until she has got my full attention.

OK, I say, what is your good idea?

I know how to win the challenge, says Margot. What we need is a new papa, and Claude can be it. She smiles proudly. It is a very big announcement.

A new papa? Can you get those?

I think anyone can be a papa. We need someone who can fix things in the house, and who can make Maman smile. If we had a papa she would have to do proper cooking again to make his dinners.

Every day, I say.

Yes, every day.

And you think Claude could be it?

I think he would be perfect.

The birds are very noisy this morning. Some are even in the tree near our heads, chatting and chittering. A woodpecker is drilling holes. It is probably too early for Claude, so while we wait for him we play shops.

I'm the shopkeeper, says Margot, and you are the customer.

OK, I say. Hello, shopkeeper.

Hello. What would you like to buy today?

I would like some cheese please.

Margot shakes her head. I'm afraid we don't have any cheese.

OK, then I would like some coloured pencils.

We don't sell those.

Have you got any eggs? I say.

Eggs? says Margot. What are they? And we both start to laugh.

What do you sell in this shop? I ask.

Lots of things, says Margot. Almost everything you could want.

Have you got carrots?

No carrots. Margot sticks out her tongue and I laugh some more.

What do you have?

We have octopus, clothes pegs, olives and onions, says Margot. She waves her hand across the front of her shop. See, here they are, right here in front of your eyes.

I'll have an octopus and some clothes pegs then please.

Ninety-nine euros, says Margot. She knows big numbers; she is showing off.

We play shop for quite a long time, until the sun is halfway up the sky and even the air in the tree shade is heating up.

Let's go paddling, says Margot. Then she doesn't even wait for me to reply, just slips out of the tree and starts running back through the tall grass towards the stream. By the time I get there, Margot is already on the other side, sitting on a root on the bank.

Slowcoach! she says.

I am not interested in being bossed about today, so I decide to dilly and dally a bit more. I have spotted the evening primroses that I thought had been put there by witches before I knew about Claude. Today I am going to pick them for Maman. Even though the flowers are delicate, the stems are thick and hard to snap. But when I have finished tugging and twisting I have five long stems and there are more than ten flowers and lots of long green leaves.

Beautiful, says Margot. Now come on!

I smile at her and walk straight into the stream in my sandals. It is quite high today and the water sloshes around the bottom of my legs, cold and lovely. For a while I just stand in the same spot, kicking one foot after the other, splashing about. I stare down into the water. I can't see my feet, only my pinky-purple reflection and the yellow reflection of the flowers. I wonder if they will make Maman smile. This makes me think about our leaky sink, and the mousetrap with the sausage, and having no money and needing a papa.

It's getting to be a very big challenge, I say.

Maybe we don't have to fix everything.

But if we don't fix everything, Maman will still be unhappy.

Margot makes her thinking face. If we fix the papa, and maybe the cleaning, she says, I think that will be enough.

OK, I say, then we have to find Claude right now.

Come on, then!

I stop kicking and start to cross the stream. But the floor is slippy and rocky and I nearly fall over.

Oh!

Use the stepping stones, silly!

I put my arms out like an acrobat and take tiny slow steps to get me over to the stepping stones. Yey! I say. I did it! And I am climbing up on to the greeny brown of the first stone and stepping on to the second.

At last, says Margot.

I don't really know what happens next. My feet are slipping off the stones. I am scrambling with both feet and trying to get my balance. And then both of my feet are in the water and so is my bottom and I am wet. That's what's important first, that my four-years-old memory dress and my knickers are wet and cold. But only for a very short time because then I feel the hurt in my foot. Not the scorpion foot, the other one. And when I try to move it to stand up, it hurts more. I feel down in the water. My foot is stuck under a stone. I try to push it, lift it, rock it, but nothing happens.

Margot! I say. But when I look up, she has gone.

The coldness of the water soon starts hurting even more than the rock-squash so I find a way to stand up by twisting my ankle and cricking my knee. The dark purple wetness of my dress is spreading up to my waist, into the lilac parts. I am very alone now. The banks of the stream have shadowy bushes, and I am sure I can see monsters hiding in them. I think about crying, but instead I begin to shout. I shout for Claude and for Merlin and for Josette. I shout as loud as I can and then I stop to listen if anyone is coming. Then I shout again. I am starting to get worried that no one will ever come.

I think I hear a rustling in the grass. When I look up, Margot is back, perched like a frog on the bank.

Don't worry, she says. It will be OK.

Margot, I say, you don't know anything.

It will be OK.

Claude! Merlin! My shouts are becoming quite screamy now. Claude!

Merlin comes first; I hear his bark from far away and then he runs down to the river. He is not galloping as usual, just trotting. He is not in a hurry even though I am stuck. He paddles into the water and I stop screaming so as not to frighten him. Merlin lies down in the water on his belly and looks at me with sad eyes.

Don't be sad, Merlin, I say. I'm not dead, I'm just hurt.

Soon after Merlin comes Claude. His arms and legs are very scratched and bleedy. Even his face has dotted red lines on, welling with blood. He must have hurried fast through the brambles without taking care. He steps straight into the water without saying a word. He leans over and grabs around my waist with one hand, and then his other hand goes down into the water. Suddenly the stone is off my foot and I am being lifted up out of the stream. Claude carries me all the way out and sits me on the bank of the low meadow. I am still holding the flowers. Merlin comes over too and sniffs my face, pressing his head up against my neck. I ruffle his fur. Claude sits down next to me and takes my foot in his hands. He takes off the shoe and presses his hands against the skin. His hands are so hot they feel as though they are burning me.

You're frozen, he says. What happened?

I don't know, I say.

My foot feels like it is being pricked with about a hundred little needles; I don't like it at all.

Claude stands up.

Can you walk? he says.

I don't know about walking. But I am shivering hard. I really want him to hug me. I cling to his legs and wrap my arms tight around them. I look up at him. I wish he would hug me. He tries to unpeel me but I hold on like a monkey.

Claude looks unhappy. Let go, Pea, he says. Claude does not want to hug me even when I am hurt, because he is not my papa. Margot is right.

Claude, I say, I have something important to ask you.

Extremely important, says Margot.

OK, says Claude, sitting down again. Go ahead.

Will you be our new papa?

I'm not your papa, says Claude.

But we NEED a new papa, says Margot.

And you would be the best new papa for us. You don't have to live with us if you want to stay in your house.

How would I be your papa, then?

Well you would have to do the papa things, I say.

Here is our list, says Margot, and she pretends to be unrolling a long piece of paper to read off. There isn't really any paper.

Number One! says Margot.

Papa has to make Maman smile and sing, I say.

Number Two! says Margot.

Papa has to make Maman get out of bed and cook us good food like she used to.

Number Three! says Margot.

Papa has to hug us and read us bedtime stories.

Number Four! says Margot.

Papa has to fix the kitchen sink that is leaking, because otherwise our kitchen will fill up with water and we could possibly drown.

Number Five! says Margot.

Papa has to . . .

Drown in your kitchen? says Claude. How long is this list anyway? He looks impatient, and his face is already saying no.

It's not easy being a papa, says Margot, you have lots of jobs.

The first one is the most important one, I say. I don't want Claude to think that being our papa is too much work.

And the hugs, says Margot.

And the hugs would be nice, I say.

You miss your papa, don't you? says Claude.

I nod.

Claude leans over and gives me a hug, but it is a stiff one, as though he is folded flat like clothes in a drawer.

You're getting too skinny! he says. We'll need to fatten you up.

Like in *Hansel and Gretel*? So you can eat me?

If I ate you, who would I have to chat to down here? says Claude.

No one, so you can never eat me, and that's that, I say.

Claude smiles and gives me another hug. A bit softer but not much.

When you are our papa, I say, you will have to practise hugging. That was quite good for the first time but you can get better.

Merlin is better than I am at all that, says Claude. Hey Merlin, come and give Pea and Margot a cuddle! Merlin gets up and comes over. He flops down beside me with a groan and puts his head in my lap. Margot and I ruffle his tummy and stroke the red fur on his floppy head and ears. His flappy tail whumps softly on the damp grass.

Do you like sausages? says Claude.

We love sausages! says Margot.

We love them! I say.

Well then, it's a deal, says Claude. You come round later and help me eat some sausages, and I promise not to eat you up.

Merlin's tail bangs on the floor.

Yes, OK, says Claude. There'll be one for you too.

When we get home I leave my sandals outside in the sunshine and carry the flowers in for Maman. But the yellow petals are already hanging their heads sadly. I put them flat on the table and try to think how to make them look nice. The phone rings, but I am too tired to answer it. I think I know what Maman means by that now. It's not that my hand is too tired to pick the phone up, it's that my ears are too tired to listen. So the telephone rings and it rings. Eventually there is a bed-creak upstairs, and Maman's door swings open, banging against the wall.

Why don't you answer the telephone, she says, stomping down the stairs, instead of just letting it ring until it wakes me up? Is it because you think I've had enough sleep for today?

No, I say. I'm sorry, I say. I look at Margot, who is kicking her sandals on the kitchen floor, staring at her toes.

I thought it would just be Mami Lafont again, so we should just ignore it.

Maman looks at the unhappy flowers on the table.

Maybe if we put them in some water? I say.

They're dead, she says. Put them in the dustbin.

Maybe I could plant them outside?

Peony, they're dead. Just throw them away.

I grab the flowers from the table and go back outside, letting the door bang hard behind me. Maman does not follow.

Around the back of the barn we sit in the shade with our backs to the cool hard stones. I hold the flowers against my body but the yellow petals are already falling from the heads. I am crying even though there is nobody to see and ask me what is wrong.

What is wrong? asks Margot. She sits next to me, scooching up until our bottoms touch, her hand on my knee.

Maman wants me to throw them away because they're dead.

They're like poppies, says Margot. We shouldn't pick those ones; they just go floppy and die.

I didn't know, I say. I didn't mean to kill them.

Shall we bury them? Margot says.

That is a good idea. Margot is only four but she really has some very good ideas. I nod.

Under the pomegranate tree, we press the flowers down so they fit into the hole that we scraped with our fingers. Then we sprinkle the soil back on top.

Ashes to dust, I say.

It's such a tragedy, says Margot.

I'm sorry, I say. It was my fault. Then I cry some more, until the tears run out. Margot waits.

When I have finished my crying, Margot says, What about the sausages, then?

As we cross the peach orchard I can already taste the barbecue. Smoky wood smells are winding through the trees, pulling us towards Claude's house. My belly bubbles and my mouth begins to water. I'm hungry. Really, really hungry. We start to run. Faster, faster through the trees. When we get to the canal we jump over and through the gap in the hedge. Claude is facing the hole and sees us straight away.

Just in time, he says, pinching the cigarette out from between his lips so that he can smile at us properly.

Claude has laid the table. There are tomatoes cut into slices like wheels, and radishes, and butter and a big loaf of bread. He sees us looking.

Maybe you'd like some bread, he says, just while the sausages cook?

Yes please! we say together, and hold out our hands. Claude breaks off the two crusty ends and passes them over. We sit ourselves down on the grass near the barbecue.

Now don't touch!

I know, it's hot.

Good girl.

The sausages are still cooking a long time later. The more cooked they get the more sausagey smells float to my nose, the smoke stinging my eyes a little bit. Merlin isn't near the sausages.

He's lying under the tree in the shade. Claude has put some water down for him to drink. But Merlin just lies on the grass, dozing and watching us with one eye. His waggy tail isn't wagging today either. He looks so sad that I have to leave the sausage air to go and give him a hug.

OK, says Claude at last. I think they're done. And he brings the first sausage over for Merlin, waving it in the air on a fork and blowing on it to cool it down.

Merlin lifts his head up and looks at the sausage. His tail wags a little happiness, tap, tap, tap, in the dust, but he does not get up and take his lunch.

Claude frowns. He crouches down by Merlin. Here, take it, he says. But Merlin just says, Owwww, and lays his head back down. Claude puts the sausage by his nose and we all stare.

Maybe it's the heat, says Claude quietly.

## *Chapter 16*

I have had enough of these spotty clothes, says Margot.

Me too, I say. Also, I have no clean knickers now and there are some clean ones up there. Well, clean and tomatoey but we can fix that.

Let's clean them, says Margot. We are going to win the challenge today, you will see.

We get on to the wooden table. I have to be the one doing the standing because I am the one with the biggest reach. I still have to do tiptoes, though, which is not easy because of my two bad feet. The one from the scorpion, which is still a bit sore, and the one that got trapped in the stones, which is freshly sore and aches a lot. Also, when I try to reach up to get the laundry I feel dizzy. Margot kneels next to me and holds on tight around my knees, staring up to see what I'm doing.

One by one I unpeg the spotty clothes and let them drop on to the table. It is all going very well until I knock a little pan with my elbow and it falls from the airer with a crash. I try to hurry, so that I can tell Maman I didn't know what the bang was. I pick up the pan and try to hang it back up, but it is very tricky and I keep missing the shiny metal S with the sharp ends. In the end I knock that off too. It bounces off the table, leaving a tiny dint. I don't think Maman will notice it.

Oops, I whisper. Sorry. But it's OK, Margot is not hurt.

I climb down and we fill our arms with laundry and take them to the washing machine in the *buanderie*. I pour in some washing liquid on top of the clothes and shut the lid.

Which button makes it go? I ask Margot.

You could try this one, she says, pointing at one with a picture of some hands dipping in a bowl. That looks like washing.

OK, I say, and I press it. Nothing happens.

Try another one, she says.

I run my fingers along the buttons, pressing them all. When the machine starts up with a grunt it makes me jump even though I should have been expecting it.

Maman will be happy, says Margot.

I hope so, I say.

The washing machine takes a long time, longer than it takes us to give drinks and food to the chickens, and we can't go and play until we have hung the clothes out to dry, so we decide to do dancing. The courtyard paving stones are hot under our feet. I dance slowly and Margot copies me. We are doing the same dance even though the music is in our heads.

Your dance is very beautiful, says Margot.

Thank you, I say, so is yours.

Maybe I'll be a ballerina when I grow up, says Margot.

Not a flamenco dancer?

Probably both, she says. What about you?

I put my arms up above my head and spin. My hat comes off but I keep turning until I feel dizzy and a bit sick. I don't know, I say.

The laundry basket is too big for me to hold and too noisy to drag. Also I cannot reach the washing line, but it doesn't matter.

I have a good idea. I take the wet clothes a few at a time out into the courtyard and hang them over the chairs.

We should go and find Claude now, I say to Margot, and tell him about our successful morning.

Definitely, she says. We are the experts in washing.

And when we get back Maman will have liked it, I add.

She will, says Margot. Today you had good ideas.

Nothing in the low meadow is quite right today. The donkeys are down at the bottom of the field but they don't come over when they see us climbing over the gate. They are more excited by the grass. The apricot spider is not even there and her web is broken. The crickets are still there, pip-popping around my sandal-toes, but only a few and none of them land on my skin.

I don't really want to cross the stream on my own but since we were too busy to have some breakfast I want to go and see what Claude has left us. We hold hands and walk carefully and slowly across together. But the girl-nest is all wrong too. There are no bottles of water by the tree trunk, and up in the nest there are no raisins, no biscuits, nothing. It feels empty and bad and I don't even want to get my tin out to like my treasure. We sit on the ground with our backs against the tree trunk and wait for the grass to move apart to show us Merlin and then Claude.

After a very long time waiting, when I am getting very thirsty and tired, I let the sadness win.

Claude hasn't been yet, I say. And I don't think he's coming.

That is strange, it's nearly lunchtime.

He can't have forgotten. He must be cross with us.

He likes bringing us the treats, says Margot. There must be an explanation.

Maybe he didn't like it that we said he should be our new papa?

He should be pleased, says Margot, then he would be a proper family.

Maybe he didn't like it that I said his hug was rubbish?

It was rubbish, says Margot.

Maybe he didn't like that we said it.

Maybe Claude was invisible today. Maybe he watched us play shops and was laughing at us, we just couldn't see him.

Claude is not very magical but Merlin is, so maybe it is that. I think about it for a while. I look around for clues.

At the bottom of the tree the ground is scuffed up, as though something has been digging.

What made that? I say. That could have been Merlin?

Merlin isn't a very diggy dog.

No. Margot is right. Perhaps it was just rabbits?

It could be rabbits?

Margot makes her eyes wide.

Big rabbits?

Or monsters, trying to climb our tree to get us?

No! I look at the scratching around the tree.

Could be.

The darkness is filling me up. I want to go to Windy Hill now, I say.

The grass is so long here and there are hundreds of flowers – clover and cow parsley and buttercups – pink and yellow and blue. As we walk back to the stream they cheer me up, so even though I am in a hurry because of monsters I pick a posy as I go. I don't pick any of the evening primroses, though.

I have got a nice big bunch and am nearly finished collecting when the grass rustles behind me and I cry out. I spin round to see what it was but my rock-foot doesn't work properly and I fall flat on my back.

Oh!

Sorry, says Margot. I didn't mean to make you jump.

Margot! I say, looking up at her. But I am pleased she isn't a monster. High above us, two buzzards are circling, their fingery wings stretched out, as though they want to hold my hand but can't reach.

When I'm a bird, I will fly like that.

Me too, says Margot. Come on, get up.

Right by the stream, as we are about to cross back to the low meadow, I see a big patch of grey under a tree. I go to have a look and discover more feathers than I have ever seen. They are grey and fluffy, the kind that keep the bird warm, not the kind they fly with. There are one or two flying feathers too, brown ones. I wonder what bird has left these, and so many of them. Then I spot a tiny one in the middle, striped with bright blue. A jay! Then I see another. The blue feathers are scattered like jewels in amongst the grey. I rush to pick them all out, rummaging around to find the treasure hidden underneath.

In amongst the downiness my fingers touch something wet and I pull them out. They are covered in blood. For a while I just look, feeling the darkness again in my stomach, but eventually I use a stick to poke the feathers aside. There is part of a bird's head, with a beak on it, and attached to it is some meat.

That bird's been killed, says Margot.

I start to cry. I am trying to wipe the blood off my fingers and on to my dress. Part of it is coming off, but my hands are still stained red.

Maman!

The word seems to come out of me all on its own. I think it's strange my mouth would do that. The rest of my head knows she's never there.

By the time we got back up to the house and had a drink, the hotness of the day and the badness of the morning were pushing me down flat. The clothes in the courtyard were dry already but I just wanted to go inside for a rest. I decided to put them away after I'd had a lie-down.

It was too hot on my bed, so I slept on the floor with a pillow and woke up feeling woozy and damp. My throat is dry.

Margot is awake too. She is running her finger around the patterns in the floorboards, the circles in the wood. Of course she is counting them.

Do you know how these patterns get into the wood? says Margot.

I don't, I say.

I will explain it to you, she says. When this wood was a tree, someone threw a stone at the tree, and it made these ripples.

But when you throw a stone in the river, the ripples disappear, I say.

That is because the river is made of water, not wood, says Margot. Wood ripples last for ever.

So if we throw stones at the floorboards we can make new ripples? I say.

Don't be silly, says Margot. You can only make the ripples when the tree is alive.

Oh, I say. And I run my finger around the dead-wood ripples as well.

Can you smell the winter? Margot says.

I sniff the air and she's right. Winter smells are coming in the window. I open the shutters wide to see what is causing the muddle, and step back in surprise. There is a smoke monster peeping out from behind the barn, black and billowy. It is bringing a smell so strong that I can taste the burning as though I was drinking it.

Oh no!

I'm going to have a look, says Margot.

You can't, it's too dangerous.

I'll be careful, she says. Maybe I will have to call the firemen.

I'd better come with you then, I say. We do tiptoe-running down the stairs because Maman is still not out of bed, and out of the kitchen door, closing it behind us with a click.

We run around the house and stop at the pomegranate tree. A wolf-wind is blowing, howling through the gaps in the buildings and between the trees. The leaves flap like a rush of birds' wings. Even though the burning smell is close, the smoke is further away than it looked. It is not behind the barn, but there is really a lot of it and it is blowing towards us. The air is crackling.

Windy Hill, I say. Let's go!

A whole hillside is on fire. Not our one but over past the wing turbines. The turbines are turning, their white wings going in and out of the clouds of smoke. At the bottom of the black smoke I can see flickers of orange flame.

Hello, says Margot. But she is not talking to me. She is on the telephone. Yes this is Margot and Pea. We are calling to tell you about a fire. Please can you send somebody to put it out? She looks over at me and sticks her thumb up. Please hurry, she says into the telephone. Then, Thank you.

They are on their way, she tells me.

That's good news, I say.

I told them to come quickly.

I hope they do, I say. I am worried that if they don't hurry the wing turbines will set on fire.

Listen, says Margot, and far away I hear the *pin-pon-pin* noise of fire engines. I am really surprised.

How did you do that? I say.

Margot smiles and wiggles her shoulders. I'm magic, she says.

Just then there is a buzzing in the sky. We look up but the plane is flying past the sun and it is too bright-white to look at even if we squint. Eventually it comes into the blue. It is heading right for the smoke.

I don't think that is very sensible, says Margot.

Nor me, I say, and we stare at the little plane flying right into the fire. It disappears behind a hilltop, but I can still hear the buzzing.

We have to get over there, says Margot, pointing down past some rocks and bushes, so we can see.

The fire doesn't seem to be coming that fast towards us; I think we could run away if we had to, so I agree. There is a sort of a path through the prickly yellow coconut bushes and the lavender, where the ground isn't as rocky, so we follow that. It leads us through big thick bushes covered in flowers like fried eggs. Things skitter away, rustling as we pass.

I wonder where that plane will go when it gets burned up, I say as we walk. Dead oak leaves the colour of bread crusts scrunch under our feet.

It would disappear, says Margot.

But where would the disappeared parts be?

Oh, says Margot. I don't know. I will have a look on the internet.

It can't just be there and then not be.

Why not? says Margot. Lots of things do that.

But it must go somewhere.

No, the internet says they just disappear, says Margot. Think about it. If all the dead and broken things had to be put somewhere then our planet would just be a big pile of dead and broken things and we'd have to be climbing over it all the time.

Well, then what about the dead trees that are our floor?

You ask a lot of questions, says Margot.

The path has taken us up a little hill and in between some pine trees. And here we find a very strange thing indeed. There is a house for a very small person, built out of stones. Not stones like our house, though. This one has only got four stones but they are enormous, like squashed boulders. Bigger than people. They have round edges like pebbles but they are not smooth, they are rough. One of the stones is the back of the house, two are the sides. But the strangest thing is the roof, which is just one very big flat rock, balanced on the not-flat tops of the other three.

This, says Margot, is where people used to hide from tigers in the olden days.

Weren't they worried that the roof might fall off?

They were more frightened of tigers than roofs.

I give the top stone a push. It doesn't budge.

Inside it is shady and cool and feels like a cave. It is just the right height for me to stand up without banging my head. There is a pile of pine cones and pine needles but nothing else.

It is a shame there are no tables and chairs, says Margot.

Maybe no one lives here now, I say. Maybe I could bring the biscuit tin here and then we wouldn't have to cross the stream any more. This could be our girl-cave on Windy Hill and we can come here even when it is hot and shelter from storms and bring Claude and Merlin for picnics. And no one would ever find us. Ooh, look at this!

There is a big red stain on one of the walls. We run our fingers along it to see if it comes off but it doesn't. I wonder what could have made it.

Also we would need to have a proper door, to keep the tigers and the crocodiles out, I say. And a window so that it wasn't too dark with the door shut.

And a casserole, says Margot. And a sink we could reach to wash our hands.

And some electricity for at night. And some books to read.

Yes, Margot agrees.

I sit down at the entrance and look out at the view. You can see everything from here, all of the hills and the wing turbines and right out over the *étangs*. The wing turbines are still turning fast, in and out of the black smoke. The buzzing noise is coming closer. The plane is flying away from the fire and it is not burnt up at all. It is spraying water on to the fire as it goes.

A flying fire engine! I say.

I asked for one of those as well, says Margot, and I laugh.

The plane has flown backwards and forwards to the fire and dropped a lot of water on it but it is still burning. There is a part of the hill that is black and empty, with no fire, but there are still orange flames and black smoke on the hill.

When the plane is here we watch it dropping the water, and when it is gone we look around at our new cave place. There are a lot of interesting things here. For example, in the branches of the nearest pine tree are big balls of cobweb. They look like a place where an enormous spider would live, but they are not. I know what they are, because they are dangerous and Maman has warned me about them a lot. They are where the marching caterpillars live. The caterpillars are fat and hairy. I imagine them all coming out of their cobweb ball and marching in a long snaky line, down the tree trunk and across the floor. They are heading straight for my legs. I wonder what would happen if I did not move. If the hairy caterpillars walked right on to my foot and up my leg. Over my hair and down the other side and off me again, as though I were a bridge. Would I get stung and poisoned and die? Would I disappear for ever, or would I still be here, but dead, so no one would ever be able to make any more ripples on me?

I wonder what it is that's on fire, says Margot.

Everything, I say. We'd better go and check that Maman is OK.

When we get home Maman is in the courtyard with a colander full of chopped-up onions. She is peeling them at the table, sitting under the parasol with her feet in a bucket of water. All around her are the socks and knickers, going very crispy in the sun. She has the kitchen window open, and the radio is playing a song about a blue lady.

Did you have a nice sleep, Maman?

Yes, thank you.

Have you seen the fire?

Yes, she says. And smelled it.

Why are you sitting out here in the smell?

It's worse in the house. Maman rubs the onion tears out of her eyes with the back of her hand.

Shall I fetch you a drink?

Maman looks up at us and smiles. Thank you, she says, that would be lovely.

There is nothing in the fridge to drink, and I don't think the outside tap is a good idea, so I have to find a way to reach the sink. I pull a chair over and climb up to run her a glass of water. Maman spots me through the window and smiles. I smile back. Then, Maman stands up awkwardly, as though she were playing the game where you have to carry a balloon between your knees without dropping it.

What is she doing? asks Margot.

I don't know.

Maman carries the bucket over to the barn, her feet making footprints all the way across the courtyard. By the barn she picks up the yard brush. She dips it in the water and starts trailing it behind her.

Maman's gone potty, says Margot.

Maybe she's cleaning the courtyard, I say.

She would use the hose.

Hmmm, yes.

She's writing letters with the brush.

Letters?

Yes, letters. I . . . L . . .

Maman writes in water on the stones of the courtyard. As she writes, I spell out the words.

I

LOVE

YOU

When she has finished she looks up at me and smiles just like Merlin when he fetches a stick that Claude has thrown far.

Inside I light up like the morning after a storm, and rush back outside to give her a hug. Maman is leaning on the brush looking happy. But as I get closer, her face sours up. She grabs me by the shoulders, staring at my front.

What have you done to your dress? she gasps.

I look down. Oh. It's dead-bird blood, I say. From this morning.

Bird blood? What could you possibly have been doing to get . . . oh never mind, I don't want to know.

The onion from Maman's fingers is prickling my eyes.

Get upstairs, she says. Clean yourself up.

From my bedroom window I sneak a look back down into the courtyard. The sun is already drying up the water. With my finger in the air, I trace over the last dissolving letters of YOU, but then it is as if she had never written it.

At supper time there is a strange feeling in the kitchen. Maman has made ratatouille. She heaps our plates with yellow couscous and spoons the rainbow sauce on top. The food is too colourful for our moods. Maman seems to agree. She doesn't eat hers at all, just sits at the end of the table and fans herself with a table mat. We have glasses of water with ice cubes that crackle and clunk against the glass as they melt.

You're quiet, Maman says.

It wasn't such an interesting afternoon in the meadow, I say. And I'm sorry about my dress.

She nods. Thank you for cleaning the other clothes, she says.

You're welcome, I say.

I wonder how long I have to sit at the table before I can go to bed.

## *Chapter 17*

We have played hide and seek. We have poked around in the fairies' garden. We have picked four-leaved clovers (two) and we have paddled in the stream. We have made guns out of plantain stalks and popped them at each other. It is hot and we are thirsty. We have climbed the trees and eaten some apples, a little bit sour but not too bad. Not enough juice to make the thirst go away, though. We have picked through the blackberries and found some that were ripe at last. We have eaten a handful. Sweet, soft, but still not enough juice. We have eaten handfuls of elderberries, but they taste like lemons and make me even thirstier. There is nothing by the girl-nest again. No water. Nothing. No sign of Merlin and no sign of Claude. It is too early to go home.

What did we do before we had Claude and Merlin to play with? I say to Margot.

It was just you and me, she says.

But what did we do?

This and that, she says. Margot is not so funny today.

The meadow seems empty without Claude. We've been here all day, waiting. I wonder what we did to make him cross, I say.

Perhaps he's sick, says Margot.

He could be, I say, or maybe he died.

Right, says Margot, that's it. We have to say a decision. What if Claude needs help and no one is helping him? Maybe only we know he is in terrible danger.

Yes, I say. We have to investigate.

We cross the road carefully and walk along the edge until we reach his gate. Heat comes up off the road and down from the sky. The tarmac is sticky under my sandals, shining in the sunlight. Claude's gate is open and I click the latch closed behind me. In the driveway is a car. It is the same blue as blue jay feathers; it looks old, but clean. It snaps with Claude. I run my finger along it on the way by.

The car is a clue, says Margot.

By the front door is a spade, a dirty one.

The spade is a clue, says Margot.

I reach up to the metal door knocker and clonk it three times. No one answers.

We are standing outside the door to Claude's house, and I am not sure what to do next. It has been three days now since he came to the low meadow.

What if Claude is dead? I say. There won't be anyone to look after Merlin. If Claude doesn't give Merlin his food and drink, Merlin will die.

Maybe Merlin has a clue, says Margot.

Do you understand his talking? I ask her. I don't.

I can try, she says.

So I call the dog. Merlin!

There is no bark. I shout louder. Merlin! It's me, Pea!

Nothing at all. It is scary-quiet at Claude's house.

This is a big clue, says Margot.

Something is wrong and the darkness is in my stomach.

We have to do something grownup, says Margot. Maybe we should call the police?

How do you call the police? I say.

I don't know, actually, says Margot.

So really there is no deciding to be done. We have to go and see if Claude is dead. I clonk the door knocker again, three times, and then three times harder, and then a lot, very hard indeed. Nobody comes.

I wonder if maybe Claude has been got by the bad men, or maybe he . . . On the wall by the front door a praying mantis lands with a clatter, and then turns his head to look at us. His eyes are like black, unfriendly beads. He lifts a feathery leg and I jump back. I don't like the praying mantis. I don't like the praying mantis so much that I would rather be inside the house with the silence than outside the house with its eyes. The darkness is inside me anyway and I just take it wherever I go. I grab the door handle and the door swings open.

You first, I say to Margot. Even though I am biggest she is the bravest.

Claude's house smells bad. It smells like Maman's room when she doesn't open the windows for days. It smells like cheese left out on the kitchen table to go runny and stinky in the heat. It smells of too-close bodies of people in the market in summer and the hair under their arms. Sour. Cold coffee in a cup. My bone is itching. I scratch, hard, opening some of the old scabs up and making the rest of the skin red and welty. At least the house looks normal. Inside Claude's door is not the kitchen, it is a hallway. The walls have pictures in frames. The floor has four wooden animals' feet on it that belong to a round table, and on the table is a big telephone, mostly hidden under a pile of envelopes. It is like the pile we have in our kitchen, only smaller. Also there are some stairs straight away, going up, up, up with black metal banisters and handrails, twisting up to bedrooms and bathrooms, I suppose. Margot walks ahead down the corridor. She runs her fingers along the walls as she goes.

Any clues? I whisper.

No clues, she shakes her head.

Margot stops at the end of the corridor. There are two closed doors, one by her left side, one on the right.

You pick, she says.

The darkness ties itself in knots. It tightens and it sucks at my insides. The taste of sick comes up into my throat and I swallow it down. It is hot in this house and it smells. The praying mantis is outside. I want to get this over with. I close my eyes. I pick left. I put my fingers on the handle and am about to press it down when the music starts. The music is slow and sad and is behind the other door.

Can you do it with me? I say to Margot. She nods, and together we reach for the other handle.

Margot and I stand side by side in the doorway. It is a living room, it is yellow, and it is dark with the shutters all closed. Claude is sitting on a stool in front of a piano. The stool has gold buttons around the cushion part, and lion's legs. Claude is wearing stripy pyjamas, although it is not morning, or siesta time or even time for bed. His hair is stuck out like a palm tree. His fingers are pressing the piano keys as though they are tired. But they are at least in time with the grandfather clock. It stands by the piano as though it is watching him play and the pendulum is swinging and it makes a real tick-tock. As it does, Claude presses the keys and the sad sounds come. On top of the piano there are photos in frames. There are photos everywhere in this room. On tables and shelves and on the floor and some in frames on the walls. Little girls mostly, and one of a lady. Claude is crying, the piano is getting wet.

Claude!

I say it first, with an exclamation mark (they make the words excited), but he doesn't hear me, so I say it again, a little louder, and then I take a big breath and shout it as hard as I can.

Claude jumps up off the stool and turns around. When he sees us he looks so scared, as though we are big monsters. He looks so scared that I am scared, and I step back a little bit. Margot holds tight to my hand. Claude's mouth is open but no words are coming.

This might not have been a good idea after all, says Margot.

I'm sorry, I say. And then I want to give him a hug to say sorry for scaring him and so that he will be Claude again and not a crying man in pyjamas. I open my arms wide and walk slowly towards him, like you have to do with horses when they're afraid of you.

No! he shouts, and it feels like a thump in my stomach. He looks at the windows, shuttered. He looks at the door behind us, open, empty, then back at the windows again. He starts to shoo us back out of the door and then he gets distracted by his stripy pyjama sleeves flapping at us. He looks down at himself and shudders. He steps back and changes his mind, shooing us into the room. His face is red and teary. He smells awful.

Stay there! Claude says, and goes out of the room, closing the door behind him. We stand there in the dark, bad-smelling room. Claude is not dead, but he has gone strange. He has gone like

Maman, in fact. Crouching here in the dark, smelling bad and crying.

This is no good, I say to Margot. We need Claude. He can't do this.

Maybe his papa died, says Margot, or maybe he is having a baby.

Men don't have babies.

I hear a door slam shut, and feet going upstairs. Two feet, limping feet. One-TWO, one-TWO, one-TWO. Margot suddenly spins around, and again, and again. Where, she says, is Merlin?

I had forgotten about Merlin. Merlin is not here. Two feet, not six feet. One-TWO not one-TWO-patter-clatter. That is not normal. Merlin is always with Claude. He's like a shadow that listens. He is Claude's best friend. The bad feeling comes out of my stomach and crawls over my skin, over my neck and face and right up to where the hairs grow out of my head, making me cold and hot at the same time. I can't say it.

It's Merlin, isn't it? says Margot.

I do a small shrug. But the tears are already starting to prickle. Because I know it is.

I sit down on the tiles, pushing a pile of photos out of my way, and hug my legs to me. It feels a bit better. While I wait for Claude to come back I look at the photos, separating them with my finger. Little girls; lots of photos of little girls. Girls in a garden, Claude's garden. Girls climbing apple trees. Girls on ponies, one white one black, up on Windy Hill, blowing black hair escaping from their riding hats, angel's wings turning behind them. Girls in a tree house; not our tree house. Two girls riding two shiny little red bikes.

Clues, says Margot, lots of clues.

Lots of little girls and none of them are us. I wonder why Claude has not taken a picture of us? Why did those girls get to ride the two little red bikes and we haven't? The girls have dark eyes, like Claude. They are smiling out at us from the photos. Maybe it's their eyes. We are riding the bikes, they are saying. He loves us more. In the smallest picture frame, on the table by the chair, there is a tiny picture of a lady. She is smiling too. I pick up the picture. The lady looks a lot like Maman did when she was still happy, when Papa was alive. The door handle slowly turns. Slowly, slowly. The door opens a crack, a little more, slowly. Claude is here. He is wearing clothes now. Crumpled ones. He has combed his hair. He looks down at me on his floor.

Sorry, Claude, I say.

Claude bends down and starts to pick up the photos. He gently takes one out of my hands. He still smells quite awful. He takes the photo, the one with the bikes. He collects the photos like they are blackberries; press too hard and they fall to pieces in your hands.

Are you OK? I ask. Claude sighs, his shoulders go up and down, his mouth pursed tight. We wait.

It's Merlin, he says at last. He died. So I'm feeling sad.

I know, I say. I feel sad too.

You know?

There were clues, says Margot.

We worked it out, I say.

Oh. You shouldn't have come here, Pivoine.

Another thump in my stomach. Claude doesn't want us here. Maman doesn't want us there. Claude is calling me Pivoine.

Because we weren't invited? I say.

Because it's, it's not . . . Claude loses his place in the sentence and shakes his head.

Claude, I say, I know that you are very sad, but please, can you still play with us. Please don't stay in your bedroom.

Pardon? Claude leans closer.

Like Maman. We like it when you play with us in the meadow.

Yes, he says, I know. I just needed some time. Sometimes people need time to be sad on their own.

Like Maman.

Claude shakes his head. Yes and no, he says.

I have to make Claude feel better. Margot says people die to make way for the other people, I say, so maybe it's the same with dogs. Maybe Merlin is making way for a puppy?

Claude smiles slightly and Margot puts her thumbs up to me. It was a good thing to say.

I'm sure he was, says Claude, but still, he was my friend; I'm going to miss him.

When I am a dog, I won't die, says Margot.

You might.

No. I won't. I will be the kind of dog who lives for ever.

Pardon? says Claude.

Nothing, I say. I point to his hand, the stack of photographs. In the top one the girls are in Claude's garden. They have dark shiny hair and blue dresses.

Who are they? I ask. And how did they get to ride on your bikes?

Claude's face looks just like Maman's when we found out that Papa had died. And when you are that sad it is called having a broken heart.

OK, he says, I'll tell you a story. He is standing in the middle of the room, looking out of the window. We sit on the white tiles at his feet. Those little girls are called Emeline and Sophie, and those two little red bikes? They belonged to those two little girls. Once, he says, there was a farmer's son, quite handsome, who fell in love with a beautiful princess. They got married, and the princess had two children, Emeline and Sophie. They were the most beautiful girls in the whole land and the man and his family were very happy. They lived in a small palace, with a beautiful garden that the princess liked to plant with flowers and vegetables. They had everything they needed.

Claude's voice is very faint. I open my mouth to ask a question but he interrupts me.

One day, he says, in the summer, they decided to take a picnic to the beach. Emeline and Sophie were wearing dark blue dresses with white at the bottom, near their knees. They are wearing the dresses in that photograph there, but you can't see the white at the bottom. It was a beautiful summer, and there were lots of holiday-makers that year. The roads were very busy. Some people were in too much of a hurry. There was a big accident with smashed-up cars, and those two little girls never got to the beach.

Were they hurt?

They died. The lady too. And the man was broken.

Were the little girls very old? I ask. Claude is crying, I have never seen a grownup cry like this before, he is crumpled like paper.

Not very old at all, he says. And I make the joins in my head, because their bikes are not very big either.

I go over to Claude and hug his legs. He crouches down so that I am standing between his knees, and he hugs me back, properly. Quite hard, in fact. I pat his back gently, the way Papa used to do with me. Claude shivers all over, as though he had stepped out into the cold, and lets go of me. He walks over to the window.

It happened a long time ago, he says, before you were born. If they were still alive they would be ladies, not much younger than your maman. They might even have had their own children.

I do not know what to say to this. I know Maman was a little girl once upon a time because there were spiders and bees and wasps but no scorpions and a garden with a swing. She had snick-ets and paddling pools and she ate rocks.

Did they eat rocks? I ask.

Rocks?

Yes, rocks on sticks? Like *bonbons*? Maman did, in the olden days.

Claude's eyebrows do a dance. No, no rocks, he says. In fact Emeline – the little sister – you remind me a lot of her.

So, can we ride their bikes? says Margot.

No one says anything. Claude begins to roll up a cigarette. His grandfather clock tick-tocks, loud in the space between the words. There won't be an answer to the bike question today.

OK then, we shall tell you the news that you have missed, announces Margot, standing up and putting herself in front of the television, which is turned off. First, she says, the evening primroses died and so Maman did not like them.

We threw the dead flowers in the bin, I say. Claude looks up.

Then, we cleaned all the clothes from the kitchen that had the tomato sauce on, says Margot.

She stopped stirring because of the dead fly on her foot, I say.

And Maman loved us, says Margot.

Yes, Maman loved us, I say. Until she saw the bird blood on my dress.

Bird blood?

Oh and there was a big fire and Margot called a flying fire engine.

A fire?

Yes and a flying fire engine.

You don't say things twice on the news, says Margot, that's boring and there is no time for that.

Sorry, I say. And then we wondered where you were and the spider's web has gone and we had nothing to drink when we were in our nest.

Claude looks extra-sad.

But we didn't mind, I add, we weren't really thirsty anyway.

It works; a small smile. A good start.

And yesterday the hills were all set on fire and there were caterpillars in my head. And now for the weather.

But there is no time for the weather report. Three knocks, clonk, clonk clonk. Loud knocks.

Let's not answer it, says Claude.

That's what Maman says, I say. Don't do that. It's not polite.

I think it would be best just this one time, says Claude.

I shake my head. Papa used to say that it is never just this one time. Just this one time is always the first one of lots of times, he said. Let's answer the door.

I know she's in there with you! A shout, a lady's voice. Angry. Outside the house.

Who's that? I say.

I know! I know! says Margot.

Josette, sighs Claude.

Can we say hello? I say.

We have to, says Margot, it's only good manners.

Clonk, clonk clonk. CLONK, CLONK, CLONK! Claude, you open this door right now! Josette sounds furious.

OK! yells Claude. Just stop your yelling. And he stomps to the door and opens it. Josette barges in.

Ha! she says. She is staring at me. She throws her hand out towards me, as though she is a magician and I am the trick she has just done. Ta dah!

Josette, says Claude.

Stop Josetting me, says Josette. And then she looks at Claude's face. What happened?

Merlin is dead, I say. And Claude is sad.

You would have worked it out, Margot says, if you had followed the clues.

Do you really think . . . ? says Claude. Which isn't a proper sentence. And he looks over at us.

Well what was I supposed to think? says Josette.

Excuse me, I say, but what are you talking about? They do not answer. They are nose to nose above us, shouting, angry.

Well I thought you would have known me better than that.

No one knows you any more, Claude. It's as though you died with them.

Well here I am, and I'm not the only lonely person around here. You can take care of yourself, I can take care of myself, who is taking care of her? He points at me.

It's not your job, says Josette.

It's lamentable, says Claude.

Well then someone should do something about it, says Josette.

Right, says Claude. I will.

## *Chapter 18*

The house is asleep and we mustn't wake it. Instead I give it a hug, standing with my skin pressed up against the cool white of my bedroom wall. I am making it grey with sweat. The windows are open but the shutters are closed to keep out the sunbeams. One fat one comes through the crack like an arrow, stabbing at my clothes, which I've left in a pile on the floor. Dust-fairies dance in the light.

Margot is reading books out loud. She can't really read, but she knows the words to most of them in her head, and she turns the pages and tells the story, actually quite well. Her voice makes the silence sing.

Before the doorbell rings I hear the footsteps, a broken heartbeat on the paving stones, and I know that Claude is here.

Listen! I whisper to Margot.

Who could it be? she says.

Well it can't be Sylvie the breadlady, because she's not allowed at our house any more, I laugh.

And it can't be the peachman because this isn't the day he comes! says Margot.

And it can't be Papa, because . . . I have had enough of that game. I stand up and go to the window to be sure it is Claude.

Because he's got his key, says Margot, firmly.

Claude is standing a few steps back from the door. He looks strange at our house. A bit wrong, like strawberries on toast. He is holding a big basket, with newspaper stuffed down the sides, all around a big pile of fat pumpkin-tomatoes.

I pull open the shutters and lean out. The stones are warm against my skin.

Boo! I whisper.

Hello, little flea, says Claude. I have come to visit your maman. Is she there?

Hang on, I say, we're coming. I don't want to shout in case I wake her up.

I put on my dress from yesterday and tiptoe down. When I open the door I see Claude's eyes are still red and he looks worried.

Come in, I say.

I'll wait until your maman invites me in, if you don't mind, says Claude.

She's in bed, I say.

Hmm, what time does she usually wake up, do you know?

You can never tell, I say. Maybe when it's supper time; it depends if the baby has been doing a lot of exercises.

Would you check if she's asleep? he asks.

I feel a bit sick. I don't want to disturb Maman, but she does like tomatoes.

Are you here because you want to be our new papa? yells Margot.

Are you going to make Maman happy? I say.

Well, I brought some tomatoes; does she like tomatoes?

She does.

Well then maybe I will make her a little bit happier.

OK, I say, I'll go and check. Margot, I announce, you can stay here and entertain our guest.

Certainly, says Margot, and she grabs Claude's hand.

I am pleased that Claude is here, especially if he is going to be our papa, but I am not pleased about having to wake Maman up. Her room is dark, the ceiling fan whirrs and buzzes. Maman is lying on her side, pressed up against a stack of pillows. Her eyes are closed, her head is covered in tiny drops of sweat, like dew on the grass. She is panting like Merlin. My heart thumps. She will be furious if I wake her, but then if I don't Claude might be cross and Claude is already sad. That is too much darkness all at once. Also, if Maman won't meet him then there is no chance he will be our new papa and make her happy. It is cool under the fan. I could lie down on the floor by her bedside and sleep here too. Instead I kneel.

Maman? I say under my breath. She opens her eyes, she is not asleep. Good. Maman, I say, we have a visitor. They need to see you, it's extremely important.

A visitor? Is it your grandmother?

No.

Is it about the peaches?

No.

Well then who is it?

It's our neighbour from across the peach orchard. Claude.

Claude? Pea, I'm trying to rest. Did you tell him I'm trying to rest? Does he know I'm pregnant? What does he want?

The questions pour out from her scowling face. She is not looking at me, she is looking at her belly, which is rising and falling like waves on the ocean and with each wave she pauses to groan.

He has brought you something. To make you happy.

What is it?

Can you please come? I say.

Dammit, says Maman, and starts to heave herself out of bed. She sits on the side for a while. She is just wearing knickers. She lifts her face up to the fan and takes deep breaths. Her belly is lopsided and shiny, her doorknob sticking out where her belly button used to be. Her breasts are big, with blue veins all over them and big dark nipples about a hundred times as big as my nipples. Her legs are puffed out, big and shiny too, and so are her feet. She looks like she has been blown up all over like a balloon. I hadn't noticed all this before. Just her big baby-belly.

Are you all right? I say.

I'll be better when this baby decides to be born, she says. Can you pass me my dress, please?

I pass her the crumpled-up white dress off the floor and she pulls it on. Come on then, she says, clipping up her hair. Let's go and see what this neighbour – what does he call himself?

Claude.

Claude. Let's see what Claude has brought to make me happy.

Maman goes ahead of me downstairs to the kitchen, where Claude is standing in the open doorway, leaning on the doorjamb, his basket on the tiles at his feet.

Maman stares. She looks at his face and the bit of his head with no hair. She looks at his legs, the scratches and the scabs where the thorns have gone in and made him bleed. She looks at his shoes that are like Wellington boots except not boots. And she looks at the kitchen floor, with dust and the onion skins, the crumbs and the outside dirt. It must make her feel the crumbs and the dirt on her feet because she rubs each foot on top of the other, one at a time. Maybe this makes the bottom of her feet feel better but now the tops of her feet are dirty too.

Hello, *Madame*, says Claude. I'm sorry to disturb you. I'm your neighbour.

Have you just moved here?

No, *Madame*, I've lived here all my life.

Oh.

Maman rocks from side to side, one foot then another. She doesn't like standing up if she doesn't have to.

Why don't you sit down, Maman? I say.

Not now, Pea.

Margot slinks around from Claude's side to come and stand next to me.

My name is Claude. Claude frowns. I think he can't think of anything important to say. I scratch my arm.

I'm Joanna, says Maman. So what did you want? Peony says it's important.

Beh . . . I brought you some tomatoes, says Claude. I mean, I have too many. My garden is big. I thought . . . would you like some tomatoes?

Maman is staring at him again.

Five years, she says.

I beg your pardon?

Five years I have lived here. And you have lived here all your life. And now you have chosen today, when I was sleeping, with Amaury dead, to come and bring me tomatoes? Her voice is getting louder, her hands are on her belly, the air in the kitchen is being sucked down into her so that she can shout out whatever is coming next. I can't breathe. Claude can feel it coming too. He opens his mouth to say something but it is too late.

Tomatoes! she yells. Who sent you? Was it his mother again? Why can't you all just leave me alone?

Claude is shaking his head. Really, he says, it's not like that at all. I met Pea, I mean Pivoine . . .

What? Maman is still shouting.

Maman, I say, it's just . . .

Not NOW, Peony, she yells, and then she bends over again, over her belly, over the baby.

Get out, she says quietly.

I'm truly sorry, says Claude, and he turns, limping away across the courtyard. We slide past Maman and try to follow him, but he looks back over his shoulder and holds up a finger.

Not today, he says.

We watch him leave. Behind us the door slams shut.

Papa used to tell me when you get angry you should count to ten before saying anything. So I stand in the sun, my eyes screwed up against the brightness of it and stinging with the sweat that is already running into them from my head. One, I say out loud, two, three.

You should maybe say hippopotamus, says Margot.

It's not a game, I snap back. I'm angry.

I know, says Margot.

I finish counting to ten and turn back to the kitchen.

Shall we just do up to twenty? says Margot.

No, I say. Papa said ten and I did ten and I am still angry and now I am going to tell her.

Are you sure? says Margot.

She isn't being very useful. I am sure and I am angry and I don't care what she thinks any more because she is . . .

The door opens and Maman is standing there. Get in the house, she says. What are you doing standing out there shouting? Get in here.

But I am boiling and I run at her. You're NOT a very good mother! I shout at her. You don't look after me, you don't say please and thank you. You're ALWAYS grumpy. You're a BAD mother and I'm not your friend.

Her hand slaps me so hard that I am knocked sideways into the chair. The chair moves and I land on the floor on my bottom. My bottom hurts from the floor. My shoulder hurts from the chair, and my arm stings from the slap. She was trying to smack my bottom but my arm was in the way and now a cherry-stain handprint is stuck there, as though Maman had just been playing with paints.

I start to scream, not because it hurts as bad as all that but because I am really, really cross. As I scream she backs away from me. I get up off the floor and I scream some more and right at her face.

You DON'T do that! I shout. And then I scream some more until my throat hurts and my screaming turns into crying. Proper crying, that I can't stop, that shakes me like the wind, with tears.

Let's go to the girl-nest, Pea, says Margot.

I don't want to go to the stupid girl-nest! I shout.

OK, let's climb the apple trees, then, she says.

I don't want to climb the stupid trees.

We'll go to Windy Hill, says Margot. Come on.

I'm tired of stupid Windy Hill. I don't want to go to the stupid meadow! I'm FED UP!

Margot looks at me. Maman looks at me.

As I take breaths between sobs, the clock ticks loudly. The handprint on my arm burns, and I hold it against my mouth. Her hand is there, and hot.

Then, as though I were throwing a stick over the rainbow, I bring my arm back and slap her back, hard. I am still not very good at aiming. I was trying to hit her leg but instead I hit her in the belly. I know straight away, before she can say anything, that I haven't hit Maman. I have hit the baby inside. In the space where the sorry should be, I wait to see if the baby starts to cry, to see if I have hurt it.

Maman grabs me by the arm, her fingernails digging into the red slap, and scowls down into my face.

You're just like your father! she screams at me.

Her face is fire and thunder, but my voice comes out loud too. Papa was . . .

Not Papa, your REAL father!

Maman clutches the belly. The belly with the baby in it that she made with Papa, and then I realise that it is me that is not good enough. The baby in her belly is coming to take my place.

Am I going to die? I ask.

Get out of my sight, says Maman.

So I go. I feel like I am turning inside out.

Running down the stony path away from Maman and away from the house, I am a small dark cloud in the blue sky and Margot is the wind that blows me along.

## *Chapter 19*

I didn't mean to hit the baby, I say to Margot.

I know, says Margot. Anyway, I'm sure you won't have killed it.

No, I say. I run my finger over my arm where it hurts, feeling the crescent-moon dents where the fingernails stuck into my skin. Maman hit me, I say.

Margot nods. Yes. She didn't mean that either.

Yes she did, I say. She meant to hit me. I meant to hit her. I just didn't mean to hit the baby.

We are sitting at the bottom of the path, by the pavement. I am sulking. My arm has the big pink slap on it. I want the cars to come by and the people to look out of the windows and ask why I have a big pink slap on my arm. I want Josette and Claude to come and ask why I have a big pink slap on my arm. Then I will tell them all. Because Maman is a bad mother. Because she doesn't look after me and she is rude to my friends and because she is making up lies about my papa.

What did she mean about Papa? I ask Margot.

Margot stretches her arms up above her head. I think, she says, that you must be a princess.

A princess? I say.

Yes, says Margot. It all makes sense now. You are an English princess, and Maman stole you when you were a baby and ran away with you to France. Maybe the King and Queen tried to stop her and that's when your itchy bone got broken, because she had to TUG you away from them.

And Papa?

I don't think Papa knew. Maman probably pretended you belonged to Papa.

So in the photo, that is Maman stealing me, when I was a baby.

Yes, it must be.

Why would she steal me and not just have her own baby?

Margot shrugs. Maybe all Maman's babies die, she says.

It is getting too hot and there is no shade here. I am starting to feel thirsty and also a bit dizzy. No one is coming to look at my arm, and the handprint is starting to disappear as the rest of my skin gets pink in the sun.

Let's go and get a drink, I say.

Even before our feet have landed in the grass on the other side of the gate, the donkeys have come over to say hello. It's like someone called them to say that we were coming and that we were not in a good mood. They push up close, nudging at my hands with velvety muzzles and fluttering their long donkey eyelashes. The donkeys smell kind.

Thank you, I say. And I stand next to the grey one for a long time, stroking the dark line down his back and his shoulders, smelling his grassy donkey smell.

That donkey likes you best, says Margot, and the brown one likes me best.

Yes, I say. And I stand some more.

The donkeys follow us down to the stream and stare over to the other side. Someone has been here and given the low pasture a haircut. It is lying flat, turning yellow in the sun, and it smells like you could eat it. I'm sure I can hear the donkeys' tummies rumbling. We wave goodbye to them and go very carefully over the stepping stones. The field looks different now, bigger and cleaner, like it wants us to run in it, so we do. Right along the long rows of cut-down grass. It feels funny running on the stubbly leftovers, no flowers, all empty. The grass spikes scrunch under my sandals.

Claude has been to the girl-nest. There are bottles of water and a packet of biscuits waiting for us. But Claude is not there. I drink some water and start on the biscuits. They are soft and sticky and full of figs. I wonder if I should save some, because I haven't decided if I am going to go home yet. I am tired and need to think about it. The nest is shady and soft. Margot and I curl up together and try to make nice dreams come.

When I wake up my dream is still behind my eyes. I was dreaming of a jar of beads, red at the bottom and then orange and yellow and blue all the way up to the top, with all the colours, even the boys' colours. The beads were spilling out one by one. I knew when the last red bead was gone and the jar was empty something very bad would happen, but I couldn't scoop them up as fast as they were tipping out. It wasn't a nice dream and I am very hungry. I shake my head to make the dream be gone.

Pass the biscuits, I say to Margot.

Pass the water, PLEASE, Margot says back.

I pass her the water and when I take the biscuits from her I say a very big and polite THANK YOU. I have nearly finished the whole packet before I remember to offer her one.

I'm terribly sorry, I say, how rude of me. Would you care for a figgy biscuit?

Margot smiles. How kind, she says, but no, really I'm not very hungry. Would you like some water?

Oh yes, I would LOVE some water. THANK YOU, I say.

After all this I feel better – not dizzy any more and less cross. But I don't think I want to go home.

Shall we go to Claude's house? I suggest.

We can't, says Margot. He put up his finger and said not today.

Hmm, I say. Well what about Josette then?

Why should we say we have come?

To say hello?

She might be disturbed.

I don't want to go home! I say. I can shout at Margot, it doesn't matter. She isn't allowed to get cross with me.

Right then, says Margot. Off we go to Josette's house. Shall we take her some flowers?

That's a good idea, I say. Yellow ones.

Josette is pegging out the laundry in her garden. She has a pink basket sitting on the grass full of unusual clothes. We are sitting on the grass and watching her. We arrived quietly and she doesn't know we are here yet. She takes a pair of trousers and floofs them so that they uncrumple. A pair of frilly knickers fly out from the leg and I laugh.

Pivoine! says Josette. Good heavens, you gave me a fright! What are you doing here? Is everything OK?

I hold out the flowers. Hello, I say.

We hope we are not disturbing you, says Margot.

Are you hungry? she says.

No, I say. Claude left us some biscuits and water.

Did he now? Josette folds her arms.

In the girl-nest, Margot says.

In the low pasture, I say.

I hope it wasn't meant to be a secret, says Margot.

Maman yelled at Claude, I say. So we have no one to play with.

Who? says Josette.

Me and Margot, I say.

Suddenly I hear music, and we look up to see a band walking up the path to Josette's house. There is a man with long hair and a trumpet. A man wearing a hat with a green ribbon around it and holding an accordion. There is a lady with long dark hair and rings all over her fingers and a shiny brown guitar. There is a big boy, with thimbles on his fingers, who is carrying a big tray and scratching the thimbles on it.

Are you having a party? I ask. Josette laughs.

It's the *llevant de taula*, she says.

The what? I don't know those words at all. But Josette doesn't speak English.

That's Catalan, she says. In French it's the *lever de table*: it means dessert.

These people are a dessert?

Josette laughs again. They have come to play us a song, and to invite us to the village fête tonight.

I remember now, how last year they came to our house. It was the day I saw Papa smoke a cigarette. Papa followed the band up the path on his tractor. They all arrived in the courtyard and Maman was hanging out clothes, just like Josette today. Papa asked them to play a song, and the words kept saying *Je t'aimais, je t'aime and je t'aimerai*. That is in French and it is telling about how the singer used to love someone and still does and always will. It sounds like it should be a happy song, but when they played it, it came out all sad. I thought maybe they had played the wrong song. But Maman and Papa danced to it in the courtyard, so close they looked stuck together, and Papa sang and Maman cried. Afterwards, Maman went back into the house, and Papa and the musicians drank some pastis and smoked some cigarettes and they made their glasses chink.

Everybody kisses Josette, and the man holding the accordion gives her a big hug.

So, what song would make you happy today? asks the man with the trumpet.

'La vie en rose', says Josette.

That is a song about life being pink, says Margot.

That's silly, I say. You have to have all the colours.

Everybody laughs as though I have made a joke.

But I'm serious! I say. They laugh some more, and then they begin to play. It's quite a happy song and Josette sings the words while we listen.

Sit down, says Josette when it is finished. So the musicians sit around the table and Margot and I sit on the grass and look at them. The man with the hat has taken it off and put it on the table. Underneath he has no hair! He takes out a red handkerchief and wipes drops of sweat off his shiny bald head.

Josette comes back with a bottle of wine and puts some coins into the hat with the green ribbon. Then she whispers in the ear of the man with the accordion. He smiles with his yellow teeth, then squats down next to me.

What's your name? he says.

Pea, I say.

Pi? Like the number? he says.

Or *Pie* like the bird? says one of the ladies. Everybody laughs and I feel shy.

Pea just like pea, says Margot.

My name is Pea, I say. P, E, A. And this is Margot. I am five and a half years old, I say, and Margot is four.

The musicians all have their eyebrows up.

She is tall for her age, I say. They laugh.

Well then, he says. Your house is next, so come on, we'll walk back with you.

The band has a white truck, like the peachman's only bigger. It is open at the back and they all climb in and pull me up. Come on P, E, A, Pea, they say, come on Margot-Tall-For-Your-Age. And we get into the truck with the drum and the accordion and the trumpet and all of the people and we drive along the road. And they are playing happy music. A car passes us going in the other direction and the people wave at us. I wave back and do my best smile. I feel like a princess at last.

The musicians follow us around the house into the courtyard. They are still teasing me.

Shall we get your maman? says the man with the long hair and the trumpet. His hair is shiny and I would like to touch it to see what it feels like.

Better not, I say. She prefers it inside and she's probably asleep.

Maybe we shouldn't play, then, he says. We shouldn't wake her up.

I think about it. I am still extremely cross with Maman. That's OK, I say. She's deaf.

Oh, says the man. OK then P, E, A, Pea, what song would you like me to play?

I try hard to think, but I can't think of anything.

I don't know, I say.

Well, says the guitar lady, bending down and taking one of my hands. She has a soft, kind face. She is very pretty. Well, she says, when is your birthday?

My birthday is on the seventeenth of September, I say. I will be six years old.

Well then you are more than five and a half years old, says the lady. You are nearly six.

I suppose that is true. Papa told me I was five and a half but that was a long time ago.

How many days is it to my birthday? I ask the lady.

More than you can count on your fingers and toes, she says. But less than if we used my fingers and toes too.

But how many? I say. The fingers-and-toes thing is very complicated. Why do grownups complicate things all the time?

Pea can count to a hundred, you know, says Margot.

Thirty-five, says the lady, smiling.

Three and five, I say. And I draw it in the air with my finger.

Very clever, says the lady.

That's not such a long way off, is it?

No, not so far at all.

If you took a car you could get there faster, says Margot.

I could get there really fast on an aeroplane, I say.

The lady laughs. Come on, let's celebrate a little bit early. She strums the guitar once and then the band starts to play. They play 'Happy Birthday' and the lady sings. I have never had a band play

'Happy Birthday' to me before. It makes me feel a little bit shy. But Margot is not feeling shy.

Come on! she says, and she grabs my fingers and starts to twirl me around, so I twirl her back. We dance to 'Happy Birthday'. Not like Papa and Maman danced, but more like ballet dancing or flamenco dancing, or both. Our special colourful, sparkly dresses spin up around our legs so we look like the ballet-dancer on Maman's musical box.

When the song is finished, everyone smiles at me. I know we are supposed to give them some money now to say thank you, or a drink. I suppose they won't want to drink from the outside tap.

The peachman has not left us any money, I say.

That's OK, says the man with the hat. It was nice to meet you. The long-haired lady comes and holds his hand and he puts his arm around her.

Bye, Pea, she says.

Don't forget Margot, says the man.

Bye, Margot, she says with a smile, and then they all start going away.

We'll see you next year, they shout, and they wave at us. Margot and I stand and watch until the truck has gone down the path out of sight and the dust has fallen back out of its cloudiness on to the ground. I look around us.

We'd better water the plants, I say. They are looking sad and thirsty.

Yes, we should, says Margot. But I don't know what we can do about the hanging baskets.

The hanging baskets are by the door. The leaves are yellow and crispy and there are dead flowers on the ends of dried-up stalks. But I can't reach them to give them a drink.

If we had Claude he could bring a ladder, I say.

Maybe we could get the ladder from the barn, says Margot.

Do you think we could carry it? I say.

Well, it is a silly idea putting flowers up so high anyway, says Margot, if you want the children to water them.

Yes, I agree, let's just leave them.

I look up at Maman's bedroom window. The shutters are closed, which means supper is whatever we want, and bedtime is whenever we say. To start with I thought those things were good but now it is quite boring. It is quite late and I don't want to go out again, but it is too early to go to bed. It has been a long and complicated day today.

What did you like best about today? says Margot.

Best about today, I say, was it being my birthday. What did you like best?

I liked best about today, says Margot, the man's hat with the green ribbon around it.

That was my next favourite thing, I say.

And what didn't you like about today? says Margot.

Nothing, I say.

Nothing? says Margot.

I don't want to talk about it, I say.

Margot waits for a while, and when she sees that I am not going to ask her, she says, Well, what I didn't like about today was the . . .

Shush, I say. And she does.

After a while, though, I feel sorry for being rude. I hope Claude is OK, I say to Margot.

I hope he left the tomatoes, she replies. And then she winks at me.

We go back around to the front door and the tomatoes are still there in the basket on the doorstep. They are hot from the sun, almost cooked, and their skins are tight. When I bite into one the sweet warm juice squirts out straight away on to my chin. For a while we just sit there and eat the tomatoes, staring up at the pink-blue sky, and the swallows diving past the window every now and then, catching insects as they go. A lizard scurries down the wall and around the corner to where we found our specimens.

Shall we go and look for more specimens before bed? I say. I would like to find another butterfly wing to match the one in my tin.

That's a very good idea, says Margot, and I say, I know.

The problem with following insects is that they are flying, so you are looking up into the air instead of where you are going. This is why we chase the blue-green damselfly right into the nettles. First I notice the jaggedy leaves brush my legs with a kind of tickle. I stop looking at the damselfly, and look down instead, wondering why I didn't feel any sting. But then it comes, the hot stinging right by my knee. I open my mouth because I am going to cry hard and loud, but then I see Margot in front of me. She has been stung much worse. My leg has a small pink patch, with white dots bubbling up. But Margot is smaller and she has the nettle stings all over her arms as well.

Oh, help me! she says.

OK, I say. Don't worry. We will find you a dock leaf. My arm is stinging, but I am being brave, and when I find the dock leaves I make sure Margot is all rubbed better before I have one for myself.

By the time I am in bed the nettle bumps have gone, but I still cannot get to sleep. I can hear the thumping of faraway music in the village. People there will be dancing and being happy. I have never been to the fête in the night-time but I have seen the posters that are put up on the road to the village. There are men standing on stage wearing white trousers with gold on. They have microphones and trumpets and there are ladies in sparkling swimming costumes doing dancing behind them. There are people listening to the music, waving their arms and smiling. The faraway music doesn't sound like I imagined it to sound. Still, I can imagine all of our neighbours, the people from the village, Tante Brigitte and Sylvie, the priest who buried Papa and the man from the post office, holding up their arms and dancing. I wonder if Claude is there, because Claude probably is rubbish at dancing and also he doesn't have many friends. Maybe he went with Josette and they will do the slow dancing. There is also food. Party food, I think. I am hungry now, but I don't want to get out of bed.

Instead, I plan what I would have for my midnight feast if I could make it appear magically in front of me. I would have ham and butter sandwiches. I would have the leg parts of roasted chickens that you can pick up with your fingers. You can always find a bit more chicken on them even after a long time. I would have pain au chocolat and lemonade, pizza and peaches and avocados and chips. Imagining my midnight feast makes me feel better. I am pretending to taste the butter and the fizziness. I am starting to half-dream things. People are coming to my picnic. Claude is there with Merlin. Some rabbits. Margot. We are on Windy Hill and all the wing turbines are turning but it is not windy. I watch my turbine number five and start to breathe with the turns. My breaths turn to yawns.

Outside my room the floor creaks, jumping me awake. I can feel my heart thumping inside. I wait to hear a flush from the bathroom but nothing comes. I listen carefully, but everything is quiet. Then the floor creaks again.

Margot! I whisper.

What's up? she replies, straight away.

There's someone out there.

Another creak. There is some shuffling of my bed sheet and Margot climbs into bed with me. Margot has never been in my bed. Normally I like to have my bed all to myself like a big girl. I can turn my pillow over when it gets too hot so that I can feel the cool side against my cheek. I like to have the cow that Papa gave me on the side nearest the wall, and on the other side I have the blue bear that I have always had. I would share my bed with Maman or Papa if they asked, although their bed is bigger, but otherwise it is my bed and on the wall above it there is a little plaque that says Pivoine and tells what my name means in French, just to prove it. But now I don't mind Margot sharing because it is late and someone is standing on the other side of the wall. It is nice to have somebody close. Margot is clever and she is not afraid of anything. It's just her personality.

OK, says Margot, don't panic. Let's think about this sensibly. Has there been a flush?

No! I say.

Hmmm, she says. Were they big creaks like a monster would do, or small ones like a very heavy cat?

Now I am not sure.

I hear something soft bump up against the wall. I sit up in bed and I try to scream, Maman! But my voice comes out a whispery nothing.

There is another creak. Margot wraps her arms tight around me. There must be a perfectly reasonable explanation for this, she says. She talks like a grownup.

Then the door swings open, letting light slip in on to the floor. I hold my breath in the dark, staring at the slice of light and hurting to know whose face is going to appear in it.

It is Maman who creeps in.

I remember a surprising thing. How, when I was four years old, the door would open every night. The creak would wake me up but I used to keep my eyes closed because I always knew it would be Papa and Maman. I had forgotten that. They came every night, together, bringing their smells of tractors and cooking and shaving cream and face cream. They would whisper to each other and pull up the covers. I would stick my leg out again, the way I like it. Sometimes this would happen twice and Maman would make a soft tiny laugh. Then there would be two kisses, one on my forehead (Papa) and one on my cheek (Maman). And I love you, and *Je t'aime*. The door would click closed and the creak would creak and I would stop being awake again. I have remembered this and it makes me feel sad for everything.

Now, though, I am not pretending to be asleep, I am sitting up by the end of my bed with my eyes open. Maman jumps when she sees me, as though I were the monster.

Oh! she says.

Sorry, I say.

She comes over and sits down on the bed, lowering herself backwards with one hand on the bed and the other on her back.

I'm sorry, Pea, she says. She tries to pull me to her to cuddle her but the baby is in the way. I move around the side and do it like that.

Maman, I say, because the question is too big for me to keep in my mouth, is Papa not my papa?

Maman is crying, her tears on my cheeks, bothering me, so I uncuddle from her. She shakes her head. Peony, she says, Papa will always be your papa.

So who is my Real Father that you said . . .?

You know, Pea, it's a long story. Once, before I came here and met your papa, I lived a long way away in England, and people were not always very nice. I mean, not that people in England are not nice, but where I lived there were a lot of not nice ones . . .

Maman's nose is running. She wipes it on her sleeve.

Am I a princess? I say. Did you steal me?

Did I steal you? She laughs a little. No, Pea, you grew in my tummy, just like this. She smooths her hand over her big round belly.

So you are my real maman?

I'm afraid so, she says. Warts and all.

Witches have warts, I say.

Yes, says Maman. Big ones on their noses. Have I got one, could you have a look please?

I look closely at her face. Margot too. Her face is normal. Her nose is normal.

You don't have a wart, I say.

So it's decided. I'm not a witch, just your maman.

And Papa?

Pea, I will tell you all about it one day, she says, but for now all you need to know is that Papa loved you. I love you.

Even though I get in your way?

You don't get in my way, she says. Her belly goes up and down when she sighs. She tries to tuck my short hair behind my ears, but it won't stay. The tears start to come, and she gives up and wipes them off her own face instead.

I'm sorry I'm always so tired, she says. It won't be long now. When the baby is out it will be better.

It's OK, I say. Even though it isn't really OK, because Maman is crying. I don't know what else to say.

Ask about the photo, whispers Margot.

No! I whisper back.

What is it? says Maman.

I'm so sorry I hit the baby, I say. I didn't mean to.

I know, she says. But, Pea?

Yes?

Don't ever, ever, do that again. Your baby brother is so tiny and so fragile and . . .

It's a baby brother? I say.

Yes, says Maman. It's a baby brother.

Oh, I say. Maman is looking hard at my face now, waiting for me to be happy.

What is his name? I ask.

His name is going to be Pablo, and Amaury like your papa. We are going to take care of him, you and me.

Now I start to cry a little bit too. I wanted a sister.

Get some sleep now, Maman says, and she kisses my forehead. It is the wrong place, but still it feels nice. I lie back down and she stands up and pulls the sheet over me. I stick my leg out, the way I like it, and behind her tear waterfall is half a smile like a slice of rainbow.

## *Chapter 20*

Our band marches from tree to tree, cheering everybody up and having drinks and collecting money. We cheer up the ants and the fairies and the apricot spider who has made a new web. We cheer up the apple trees and the cherry trees and the mulberry tree. I have two sticks. When I clock them together they make good marching music. Margot has a guitar, a pretend one. Also, she has a tuba. The cuckoos join in too, and the doves. Our music is really clever and we are trying to get everyone to come to our fête that we are having later.

At our fête, I say, everyone will dance and so will we.

When we are not being the band, of course, says Margot.

We make up some songs to sing to go with the music. I have made up one about Maman. It is not especially cheerful.

That's enough of that, says Margot. Your song is extremely boring and not the right song to make people happy and come to our fête.

What shall we sing instead then? I ask.

I have made up a better song, says Margot. It is about a dragon called Grimpy and a wizard called Merlin.

Merlin is a dog, now, I say.

Yes, says Margot, I know. Merlin is a dog-wizard.

So we sing her song. We make it up together. In the end the dragon gets killed with a killing-spell for being grumpy and Merlin stays alive.

The best thing about making up your own songs, says Margot, is that you can decide how you want things to happen.

In the low pasture the hay has been bundled up into parcels. Margot and I run around the field, making sure that we sit on every one of them. They are spiky and make my legs itch a bit but they smell sweet and warm. When we have sat on every bundle of hay we run instead over to the girl-nest. I am happy to be home at last. I take out my things and look at them and like them – the lonely photo, the feathers, the smooth round stone, the seashells, Papa's glove. I can't see the fairy but I say hello to her and I think maybe I can hear her singing. The feathers are beautiful and feel nice. Papa's glove feels nice and smells nice. The shells are beautiful and smell like the seaside. The lonely photo doesn't smell nice at all. It doesn't feel nice, either. Even so it is the one I look at the most.

Why do I keep playing with something that doesn't look or smell or feel nice?

Like Claude? Margot pretends to be smoking a stinky cigarette.

Not Claude, the photo. I don't even like the photo.

But we like Claude.

Yes, but Claude feels nice on the inside.

Yes. Margot scratches her head. It's a puzzle, she says.

I don't think I am an English princess, I say.

You could be, though, says Margot.

I could be. But maybe I am just a normal girl. Maman isn't a queen and she said that she is my real mother.

Unless she isn't telling the truth, says Margot.

Why would Maman lie about it? I say. But as soon as I say it I can think of lots of reasons, like her not wanting me to call the police.

We will have to think about it like scientists, says Margot. What is the first thing you remember about Maman?

I try to remember being a baby, but I don't remember it at all. Maman says we came from England, so I try to remember another house, another orchard, a different bedroom. I can only remember our own house that we live in now. My bone is itching and I rub it hard against my knee to make it stop.

I can't remember, I say.

You are remembering all wrong, says Margot. You have to think backwards.

So I try. Margot is right, it is easier to think backwards.

I close my eyes and I think about last night. I think about the argument. I think about the trip to the seaside when I asked for the watermelon and the day she threw the peaches at the tractor. I think about the day she broke the glass with her belly, when she chose my jam instead of Margot's and, before that, the day when all our clothes got spotty, when she had the fly stuck to her foot. I think fast over the bits that are dark and I think slow over the bits that are nice. I think about her at the church when Papa had died, and before that, when Papa still lived with us, and the food she would cook for us all to eat. I think about the day she came home from the hospital without the baby, and before that, when she was happy. She really did used to be happy. I think about all the kisses goodnight, when I was four years old and three years old. I remember birthday parties and picnic days at the beach, and walks in the low meadow. I remember one day in the low meadow, we were just walking. We had eaten peaches so it must have been summer. We were holding hands and all the sticky peachiness was gluing our hands together. We washed our hands in the stream and we practised naming all the trees and flowers and birds. Maman knew them all, so she would let me guess first. And that day I remember I found a ladybird and I wanted to show her. She got down on the ground beside me. It didn't matter to her then that she was dirtying her dress, pressing her face close to all the different flower smells in the middle of the dewy meadow, where donkeys have weed and spiders spun webs. I remember that on the way home I was tired and she carried me on her shoulders up the hill. She didn't mind. She was singing.

Well? says Margot.

Leave me alone, I say. I'm busy remembering. Margot taps her fingers and I open my eyes crossly.

I'm not a princess, I say. And I tidy everything away into the box. I wrap up all my rememberings with a yellow ribbon and I put that in there too. I can look at them again later.

Margot's hair is getting longer again. Mine is not. It's not fair, really. She is twizzling it round her fingers, trying to make it reach her mouth so that she can do thinking.

I have been reading a book, she says, about a girl who was not a princess. It is a good story. If you sit down nicely I will read it to you.

I am sitting down, I say. Margot rolls her eyes.

Once upon a time, she says, there was a girl who was not a princess. But she lived in a castle anyway, up on a hillside, far far away from here.

I close my eyes and listen to Margot's story.

The castle was also far far away from all of the normal people in the kingdom. The girl, who was not a princess, was lonely, because her maman, who was not a queen, was very busy looking after the baby in her tummy. So the girl had no one to play with.

What happened? I say.

The baby was born and then the little girl had someone to play with and then she found her maman a new papa and they all lived happily ever after. The end.

And now, Margot says, it is time for the baby to be born.

I have taken the rug from the bottom of the girl-nest and pushed it inside my green dress with the daisies on, so it looks as though I have a baby in my belly.

I am the doctor, says Margot. Welcome to the hospital.

Thank you, I say.

You're welcome, says Margot.

I want this baby out of me please, I say.

Ah, yes, says Margot, I see. OK, well come with me and we will get the baby born. Lie down!

I lie down. The floor of the girl-nest is cool and rough.

OK, says Margot, let's see your door. She lifts up my dress.

Aha, aha, right, here it is! she says. Then she takes out the rug and cuddles it up like a baby. I sit up to see.

Oh dear, I'm very sorry, *Madame*, says Margot. I'm afraid it's a boy.

But I wanted a girl, I say.

Well, let's see, Margot says. I'll go and fetch my stethoscope and my needle for sting-y injections.

Pea would like a sister, I say, so please can you sort it out?

Hmmm, says Margot, and she stethoscopes the baby and gives it sting-y injections. And then she says, There! She passes me the baby.

Oh! I say. It's a beautiful baby girl! Thank you, Doctor.
You're welcome, Margot says.

Hello, says a voice.

Claude! It's you!

He is standing under the tree. Without Merlin next to him he looks like a picture that hasn't been finished. I want to draw Merlin in, in red pencil, hairy and clever.

Hello, Pea, says Claude. How are you today?

I am fine, I say.

Pardon? Claude cups his hands to his ears and stares up at me. I lean over so he can see my mouth.

I am FINE! I say.

And how is Margot?

Margot is a very good doctor, I say loudly. She can make baby brothers into baby sisters, which is very clever and useful.

Yes it is, isn't it? says Margot.

I can imagine, says Claude, with his eyebrows up.

How are you? I ask.

Well, says Claude, I'm OK. It's very nice to see you.

I like it best when you are here, I say, and not when you are not.

I miss you too, says Claude. He looks around the low pasture. Maybe he is checking that Merlin hasn't come back after all.

I don't think he will, I say.

Pardon? says Claude. He doesn't hear me.

Can I come up? he says suddenly.

Into the girl-nest?

Yes.

With us?

Yes. If it's OK?

Yes of course, I say.

Claude climbs the ladder slowly and gets into the girl-nest. He sits next to me. There is not a lot of room and we have to squeeze up. The squeezing-up feels nice, and I squeeze even closer than I have to. Claude smells of smoke, which is not a nice smell, but he is very comfortable.

This is what swallows do, I say.

Claude looks at my mouth. Swallows? he says.

Yes, I say, because they don't have fingers or arms for hugging and holding hands. Would you like a biscuit?

That would be nice, says Claude.

I pass him the tin and he opens it.

Oh! he says. And I laugh, because in the tin there aren't any biscuits any more, just my treasure.

Fooled you! I say.

What have you got here? says Claude.

It's a specimen, I say.

He picks up the crispy yellow thing in his big fingertips and looks at it. Aha, he says, an egg-case.

That's what I said it was, says Margot.

Do you know what made this? Claude asks.

Was it very small wasps?

Claude laughs. Not very small wasps. A praying mantis. It's where she laid her eggs.

But praying mantises are bigger than wasps, I say.

Yes, says Claude.

So why do they make smaller nests?

Well, it's not a nest, but an egg-case.

But the wasps make bigger holes. Those holes are tiny.

Yes, says Claude. Sometimes you think a rule would make sense and it doesn't. He puts the praying mantis egg-case specimen back in the tin but leaves the lid open. His eyes look around the tin. In the places where biscuits should be there are feathers and the sad photo, Papa's glove and a butterfly wing. Claude nods as he looks, as though he is agreeing with the things in the tin. He is not cross that we ate all the biscuits in the tin and there are none left for him. He likes my treasure.

For a minute we just sit and listen to the birds and the crickets. We forget to talk. Even Margot doesn't have anything to say. Then, Oh, my arm is trapped, says Claude.

Oh, I say, leaning forward a bit, and Claude moves his arm so it is around my shoulders. It feels nice. After a little while longer he starts to squeeze gently. It is like a one-armed hug. I put my head on his chest and think about being hugged. I can hear my breath. I can hear Claude's breath. And I can hear the bumping of his heart. I am remembering Papa now. Papa's hugs, the way he made breakfast in the morning, the way his kisses were too scratchy in the afternoon.

Can you feel sad and happy at the same time? I say.

Yes, says Claude. I feel just like that now.

Me too, I say.

We cross the stepping stones and walk together back up through the low meadow.

When the baby is born, says Claude, I'll come back and see your maman. It will be all right.

It's a boy baby, I say.

That's great! says Claude.

No it's not, I say. I wanted a sister.

Oh yes, says Claude. Of course.

We stop by the apricot spider, because Margot wants to count how many crickets she has caught for her supper. The spider is sitting in the middle of her web. Margot leans down to do her inspection. She has caught three.

Yes, says Margot, that is enough.

Well, says Claude, who is still thinking about Pablo, wait and see. Brothers can be good too.

Have you got one? I say.

No.

On the path, the brambles are everywhere now, making big loopy knots in the spaces where we want to walk. In some places they come so far over that we can't really get around them any more without falling off the edge on the other side. We have to pick our way through them, or go underneath. I can do that easily but Claude is too big. He tries to hook them up out of the way as he goes so I can pass through, but they keep falling back down.

Halfway up the path I bend down to look at a bright green *punaise* that is sitting on a blackberry, and the thorny part tangles in my hair. It scratches my face and I try to wriggle out of it but it just gets more scratchy.

Ow! I shout.

Claude looks back. Stop! he says. Don't move!

I stand very still, and just move my eyes from side to side. What? I say.

Don't move, says Claude. You don't want those thorns to get in your eye.

His rough fingers go into my hair, untangling the brambles. You have to be careful, he says. It's just like the jungle here!

Except not so many elephants, says Margot.

Not so many elephants, I agree. Still, you could bring your elephant knife, I tell Claude.

You know what, says Claude, that's a very good idea. He ruffles my untangled hair, and opens his other hand, which is getting purple skin because he has filled it with surprising blackberries. I reach out and pop one into my mouth. Claude tips the rest into my hands. There are so many I have to use both.

Really, says Claude. Why didn't I think of that?

## *Chapter 21*

Maman is cleaning everything.

The laundry basket from the bathroom is empty. All the clothes are clean and wet and hanging out on the spinning dryer in the courtyard, turning white in the sun. In the house, the floor is swept and still shiny-wet from the mop. The mop and bucket stand drying by the door. The windows are all open, letting the house breathe all the warm afternoon smells of sage and jasmine, and pushing out the old smells of suppers and sadness.

Maman is in the baby's room. There is a big heap of clothes and she is sitting there, taking up all the space on the floor, making piles.

Can I help? I ask.

She looks up at me, her eyes doing most of the lifting. Her cheeks are pink.

No thanks, she says. Why don't you go and play?

Maman has earrings in that look just like pomegranate seeds.

Maybe I could just sit with you, I say, or do folding?

Maman shakes her head. I won't be long, she says. I just want to get this over with. Off you go.

We wander into Maman's room. There on the bed is a suitcase, half full on one side and half empty on the other. I peer in. Slippers, pyjamas, a book, shampoo, a toothbrush and toothpaste, dresses, knickers, a hairbrush . . .

She's leaving us, I say to Margot. The darkness fills me up and I climb on to the bed with the suitcase and curl around it. The bed sheets are soft and pressed into a shape of Maman and my tears fall into her smell. I close my eyes.

She can't be, says Margot quietly. There must be an explanation.

She's packed all her knickers, I say. And she is busy getting all the baby clothes ready too. She's going to leave us and live with the new baby.

Don't be silly, says Margot. She takes me by the hand. Come on, we'll go and ask her.

No! I yell. We can't do that, she'll get furious.

Well what does it matter if she's leaving anyway?

What would we do? Claude could come and look after us?

He could but not if he kept smoking; it stinks.

I want Maman, that's all, I say.

Come on, says Margot, and drags me off the bed.

Maman is still sitting in the big pile of clothes. Her face has been crying.

Please don't leave us, I blurt out.

Peony, I to – What? she says.

Please don't leave us. Please can you stay?

Pea, sweetheart, Maman says, I would never leave you. Never, ever. Why do you think I would leave you?

Because you've made a suitcase, I say. It's going to be for you and Pablo. But I want you to stay here, I could look after you better. I can teach the baby to climb trees.

Maman smiles a sad smile. A breeze blows in through the half-open shutters, fluffing up her hair.

We need to pack you a suitcase too, Pea, she says.

Where are we going?

Nowhere yet, but one day soon we will have to go to town, to the hospital.

For the baby?

For the baby.

Maman, I say.

Don't say it! whispers Margot, poking me.

How do you know . . .?

Don't say anything about the dead one!

Why?

What? says Maman.

Nothing, I say, and I bend over and wrap my arms around her shoulders.

When we go to the hospital we will have beds. One for me and one for Maman. Margot will be there too. It is going to be soon, but we don't know when. We will go in an ambulance because Maman says you can't drive a car when the baby is trying to get out.

I have a suitcase now. Well, it is a plastic bag because we didn't have another suitcase. It is packed with clean knickers and my cow. My blue bear has to stay in my bed because if I pack him then who would I sleep with?

I am thinking about this and working out the answers. It is nearly supper time but I am too busy thinking and looking to go home yet. I am lying on the bruisy ground on Windy Hill. I am watching the small white clouds, the ones you draw in pictures, get pushed along by the wind, and the angel arms turning fast, white against the blue, upside down over my head, looking big.

I am feeling better and dizzy at the same time.

Yuck! says Margot.

What?

This.

Margot holds out her arm. She has got a tick on her. I know what ticks look like because the cats that visit our house sometimes get them, and once Maman got one on her too. This tick is near Margot's shoulder and it is like an old yellow pea. It has got eight wiggly red legs near her skin. We do like insects normally, but I think it is rude that ticks want to drink your blood and I don't like the way their bodies look when they are stuck on.

Maman doesn't either. When she got the tick on her she screamed. I found her in the bathroom, looking back at herself over her shoulder. She was holding up her hair with one hand. The tick was on the back of her shoulder.

What is it? I asked her.

Don't worry, Sweet Pea, she said. It's just a tick.

It looks like a fat insect, I said. But it has eight legs, I've counted them. Does it hurt?

No, it doesn't hurt. I didn't mean to scream, sorry. I was just surprised.

Do you want me to brush it off? I said.

It won't come off, she said, we have to do it carefully. We have to get Papa.

But Papa was out at work, so we had to go and fetch him. She couldn't wait until he got home. We went together, quite slowly. She wasn't as fat as she is now, but she still had a round belly. It was the other baby was in there. The girl baby. The not-good-enough one that we didn't get to keep. As we went, Maman was shouting. Amaury? Amaury! It didn't take us long to find him.

He was only in the peaches and he hurried over when he saw us. Maman went soft against him and he kissed her forehead. Papa wanted to pinch the tick off with his fingernails, but Maman had brought tweezers with her.

When the tick was off, Papa put it on the floor and trod on it. That killed it, and then Papa showed us what was left. There was hardly any tick at all, just a splat of Maman's blood on the ground. I crouched down to look at it and Papa came down next to me.

Make sure Maman puts some antiseptic on when you get her home, he said.

I promise, I said. Then I got a head-kiss too.

OK, I say to Margot, I will be Papa and I will get it off you.

Margot holds her arm out. Use the tweezers, she says, not just your fingers.

Of course, I say, I have the tweezers. There is nothing to worry about.

And there isn't. I get it off first time and drop it on the floor. It is too fat with Margot to run away, so together we stomp on the tick. Like a stompy dance.

Ooh, says Margot, look at the blood!

Yes, lots of blood. That tick must have drunk nearly all of you up. It's a good job I got it off.

Thank you for looking after me, Pea, she says.

You're welcome, I say.

## *Chapter 22*

We have fed the chickens and brought the bread up to the house. We have had our breakfast and waited for Maman for a long time, but it got very boring and I want to go and see Claude, so I have tidied away our breakfast things and left the table set for Maman.

We are trotting down through the peach trees on our horses, jumping over logs and winding through the trees. The edges of the teardrop leaves are already turning orange. Margot looks back at me over her shoulder.

My horse is dappled grey and it is called Bolter. What's yours called?

Saskia, I say. And she is black like Black Beauty.

As we get down towards the road I hear a strange noise. It sounds like someone calling my name and I stop to listen.

Come on, says Margot, giddy up!

Don't you hear that? I say. Isn't that Maman shouting?

I doubt it, says Margot. We did all the jobs. What else would she want you for?

Maybe she got another tick?

Could be. Margot gets off her horse and pats his neck. I do the same. Let's leave our horses here, she says, so they don't fight with the donkeys. We can go and see Claude and not take long. Then we will go back up and check if Maman has a tick.

Yes, I say, that's a good idea, because I really want to see Claude and check again about him being our papa.

We cross the road and climb the gate into the low meadow. I can see Claude, right down at the bottom of the path.

Look! says Margot. He brought his elephant-tracking knife!

Claude is slicing at the brambles, cutting away the loops and trailing parts. As he swishes them, the bushes are getting flat edges, and thorny bits, blackberries and little brown *punaises* patter on to the path. Even the ripe blackberries are getting chopped.

Oh no! I say.

Let's go and save the blackberries! says Margot.

Definitely! I say, and we run down the hill. Claude hasn't heard us yet.

Peony!

I stop running and turn. It really is Maman. She is by the gate and she is waving her arms over her head.

Peony!

I must be in big trouble for something, although I can't think what it is. Unless Maman really has got a tick too. But even if she has I don't know how to help her. My tweezers are only pretend ones and I'm still only five years old.

Maman walks slowly down the path. I stand still and watch her coming.

Peony, come here! she shouts. But I'm scared. After only a few steps she stops and leans against an oak tree. She presses her head against the trunk and her shoulders go up and down.

Is she cross or sad? I ask Margot.

She looks sad, maybe, says Margot. Or else sick.

We'd better go and see.

Yes, Margot agrees.

We turn around and start back up the path towards her. We don't run.

As we get closer I can see there really is something wrong with Maman; she has walked a few more steps but has stopped again. Tears are running down her face and she is roaring like a lion. It is worse than the day she attacked the tractor with the peaches.

Margot grabs at my arm. Don't, she says.

Margot, is Maman after us?

I don't know, says Margot. We should ask Claude; he will know what to do.

Margot takes my hand and we pelt back down the path to get Claude. He is still cutting the brambles.

Claude! I shout.

Swish, chop.

He seems cross with the brambles.

Claude! Margot shouts.

Chop, swish.

They scratched him a lot, it's true.

Claude!

If Merlin had been here he would have been barking by now.

Swish, chop.

We are really close now, my breath is puffing. I reach out my arms so I can stop myself against his legs.

Chop, swish.

Claude! I shout.

At the same time, behind us, Maman shouts, Peony! Peony!

We are so loud that even Claude can hear us now, and he looks up from the brambles, turning to see where the noise is coming from. But his knife is still swinging.

Swish.

And we are still running.

And it is too late to stop.

I see the knife coming straight towards my face.

## *Chapter 23*

Blood is pouring from my forehead like rain. It falls into my mouth, sticky and surprising. Maman is running towards me. Her face has opened so wide it looks as though the sunlight is coming right out of her. Her eyes are saying, Sorry, sorry, sorry, and she is still screaming my name. Beside me, Claude is shouting Oh! Oh! Oh! The noises swirl together and behind my eyes it bangs.

Maman's arms are stretched forward as though she is trying to catch me. I open my mouth to say something, but my breath is sucked out of me like a slamming door. Margot lets go of my hand and I feel myself fall away from her, backwards on to the path.

I am caught by gentle hands. There is a lot of quiet. I am in a beautiful white place, it is smiling at me. The air is happy and cool. I'm so comfy, maybe I am on a cloud, or tucked in under a cloud. It's hard to say. It doesn't really matter. I feel dozy and light and that is good enough.

Wake up! Wake up! Wake up!

I don't want to wake up.

Peony, you have to wake up. Peony, open your eyes. Come back to me, Pea.

Maman is walking in the whiteness; she is calling for me.

It would be nice to walk with Maman. Or not.

Peony, look at me. Peony, don't leave me!

The whiteness is colouring in, I can feel my body wrapped in body. Am I somehow back in Maman's belly? I reach out but there is no baby here, just softness. My head is aching, my mouth tastes sour. I pull back, I want the happy place again.

Peony! Peony! Peony!

It is Maman. I am laid against her by the gate to the meadow. She is curled around me, her hand pressed against my forehead. She is holding a rag against me that smells like Claude. It is hot and wet. I feel dizzy.

Stay here, stay here, Pea, she whispers. They're coming to get us, it won't be long.

Witches? I say. Do we have to run?

Not witches, Pea. Help. Help is coming. Hold on, baby.

We are in the sun on the road. Sitting like we are having a picnic. Maman has her arms around me. I still feel like I am being sucked back inside her. I'm thirsty. A car stops by my feet. The wheels are silver stars.

We are in a car with the windows open. I am leaning against Maman. Her dress is red with my blood. She will be cross. Everything smudges together, washing in and out like the sea. I close my eyes to make it stop.

We are away from the village, passing big buildings all blurry through the windows. Claude is driving. He has no shirt on. His face is a grey mountain and his tears are the streams.

* * *

Papa is carrying me against his hairy chest. He smells salty like Windy Hill. His big arms are around my back and under my legs and his big rough hand is holding my head. Hold on, Pea, he whispers and his breath is a warm breeze. There are voices all around, and far away. Shouting.

I love you, Papa, I say, but he does not reply.

## *Chapter 24*

The hospital is white and smells of mops. I am lying on a bed staring up at a square light on the ceiling, and at the hairs in the doctor's nose. He wiggles his fingers at me and peers into my eyes, which are blurry with tears but I don't remember crying.

Maman is by the bed, singing. She does not know the words and is making up the song as she goes along. One song spills into another and she does not stop. She grips my hand tight, leant over the bed, whispering. I'm sorry, Pea. I'm sorry, Pea. I'm sorry. Her own tears fall on to my belly.

When we got here there were lots of injections. The first one went right into the cut that Claude made with the elephant knife. It hurt much more than the knife did. After that I was sewn up like torn trousers. The nurse gave me a syringe to play with and I injected everybody, but the game wasn't so much fun because being sewn up was tuggy and scary and made me feel sick.

I still feel quite sick.

The doctor sits me up slowly.

OK, Little Fighter, he says, you're all set. And he turns to Maman.

It's a lot of blood, he says. They're like that, heads, but your daughter only has a scratch. He looks at me.

You're lucky it was only the flat part that hit you, he says. You'll not go running up behind people again, now will you?

No, I whisper.

The doctor looks back at Maman. She is going to have a big bruise, he says. Keep an eye on her, if she is sick or . . .

He stops because the nurse is jiggling his elbow and nodding at the floor. We all look down. Maman is standing in a sudden puddle.

## *Chapter 25*

Pablo is here. After Maman wet her knickers in the doctor's room, they took her away for him to be born. I got taken to a room with a bed and a television and a lady brought my dinner on a tray. There was bread, a yoghurt, a peach, and some meat with vegetables. Claude stayed with me while I sat up in my bed and ate my dinner and watched television, and sometimes looked out of the window into the car park where people in cars came and went.

I'm sorry, Pea, he kept saying, which was quite boring really.

Does my bandage look good or stupid? I asked him. And then, Is that knife really for hunting elephants? Because I have been wondering if that was a made-up story. Claude didn't want to talk about his knife.

After dinner, a lady in pink clothes came to fetch me and take me to Maman and Claude went home to fetch us our suitcases.

Maman is sitting up in bed. Pablo is asleep next to her in a plastic cot called a *bassinette*. He is orangy-coloured and his hair is black. He doesn't really look like a proper baby.

I sit on the bottom of the bed and Maman holds my hand. Can I see your tummy? I ask her.

My tummy? Yes, OK, but why?

I was just wondering if the door is still there now that Pablo has come out.

The door? But Maman lifts her nightshirt and I lay my hand on her belly. Maman jumps a little as though I have tickled her. There is no door, not even any sign of one having been there. Her belly is much smaller now, and squashy. How did Pablo get out? I ask.

Pablo was in a hurry to come out, she says. He wanted to meet his sister. The doctor helped.

She pauses a while and reaches out for me, one hand around my middle and the other raking back my hair gently so she can see the bandage on my forehead.

I'm so sorry, Pea, she says again.

It wasn't your fault, I say. It wasn't Claude's either really; he's deaf you know?

Maman shakes her head sadly.

I mean I'm sorry I left you all alone.

I wasn't on my own, Maman. I had Margot.

What did you say? Maman asks, and then Claude walks in through the open door.

Hello, Pea, he says, and hands me a baby doll, pink and round-headed and still in its box. It looks like a proper baby, and it is a girl. I get down from the bed and hug Claude around his legs. He doesn't hug me back. Still.

She was with me, too, he says to Maman.

Well that's quite far from a consolation, says Maman, her voice staying quiet but at the same time getting shouty.

I tried, says Claude. I knew how it might appear. I did try to speak to you. I thought maybe my keeping an eye on Peony would be the next best thing.

She's a little girl, says Maman. It's not normal!

Claude's face is getting angry but his voice stays quiet too. Pablo is sleeping.

Your daughter has been running around in the meadow all summer, he says. She plays hide and seek with herself. I found her alone under a tree in the middle of a hailstorm. For God's sake she even has to make up imaginary friends so she doesn't get too lonely. I know that it's not easy for you but Pivoine needs her mother.

What did you call her? Maman says, with glassy eyes.

I called her Pivoine.

Her name is Peony.

Actually, my name is Pea, I say.

I'm sorry, Pea, says Claude. Is Margot here?

No, I say. Margot is gone.

Maman has a white face and her kaleidoscope eyes are looking at me through tears.

I know I have done something very bad this time.

Claude looks at Maman, and looks at me. I hang my head and look at my shoes.

The baby that . . . you lost, he says finally.

I don't think she was lost, I say, she was . . . but Claude is shaking his head at me. Maman is crying a flood of tears, her shoulders shaking, her face red and her nose running. Pablo is still fast asleep.

I go back over to the bed, slowly.

I'm sorry, Maman, I whisper.

Maman opens her arms. I charge at her, knocking her back against her pillows. She hugs me tight against her whole soft-bellied self.

No, she says, I'm sorry.

I climb back up and curl up on Maman's lap as though I am a cat. Maman strokes my hair and my eyes fall closed. A cool breeze from the open window blows across my face. While I doze I can hear their whispered voices above me.

I'm a father.

I'm her mother.

I didn't want to see you lose her.

Will you stop staring at me?

I'm reading your lips.

Oh.

I lost my hearing in the car crash.

Oh.

No one should lose a child. I should know.

You lost a child?

My whole family.

Oh. I'm sorry. Maman is quiet.

I know I'm no picture, but I mean well.

OK.

Look, we all know that Amaury's mother wants the farm back. Even if many people think you're a bit stuck-up, no one wants to see you kicked out. Amaury loved you. But you have to make some friends if you're going to stay here.

Maman is quiet again. So quiet I can hear Claude breathing.

Maybe you could start with me? he says.

Maman has to stay in the hospital for a week. I am allowed to stay with her, in her room, because there is no one to look after me at home, although I think I would be OK. I have a bed in the corner and Pablo has his *bassinette* right next to me. Pablo sleeps quite a lot and when he does Maman sleeps quite a lot too and I watch her. She lies on her belly and she sighs small sighs. Her eyelids flicker.

Every day the doctors and nurses come in to look after Maman. They take her temperature with thermometers and her blood presser with a pumpy sleeve and stethoscopes and they give her medicine because she has some aches and pains. And they do other things too. Because of this I don't have as many questions as I used to and I can tell you now that actually ladies do NOT have a door where the people go in and out. The truth is stranger than that.

Pablo was a success. He is all finished, except for his belly button and we are finishing that off together. Every day Maman cleans the place where his belly button is going to be and I pass her gauze to wrap around it. And we bathe Pablo in the big sink. We scoop water up on to his head, which is fuzzy like the skin on a peach. Maman says he looks like Papa, which is the silliest thing that she has ever said. Papa was tall and had a bristly chin and rode on tractors. Pablo is so tiny he has baths in the sink, he is a funny orange colour and his skin doesn't fit yet. He really looks nothing like Papa at all.

People come and visit us. Mostly it is Claude, but today Mami Lafont is here. Claude has brought her. When she comes into the room her face is grumpy and her lips are tight. Her witchy hands are holding some blue flowers, which she puts down on the bed.

Hello, she says, without looking at me or Maman. Then she rushes straight over to Pablo's *bassinette.*

Let's have a look at this baby, then, she says.

He's sleeping, says Maman.

Mami Lafont peers in. Pablo is lying on his back; he has his arms up by his head with his hands in fists, as though he is cheering, as though he has won a race.

Oh! says Mami Lafont. And her face cracks open like the shell peeling off a boiled egg. Hard on the top, soft underneath. Tears start to come down. She pulls a tissue out of her handbag and mops herself up.

What's wrong, Mami Lafont, I say, don't you like him?

But Mami Lafont cannot stop staring at Pablo.

My Amaury, she says, he looks so much like my Amaury.

Yes, says Maman softly, he does look like his papa.

Why does everyone keep saying that? I will have to ask Claude later. He is the only one who has not said it.

Then Mami Lafont looks at Maman and Maman looks back. Their faces are twitching, eyebrows, mouths, wide eyes narrow eyes, but they are saying nothing. They look like two dogs who have just met each other. Next they are either going to do the sniffing part, or else one of them is going to get bitten.

We're staying, says Maman eventually.

I know, says Mami Lafont. Thank you. He's beautiful. You look after that baby.

Maybe you could help, says Claude, who has been standing in the corner, watching them like TV.

If you would like? says Mami Lafont.

You're his grandmother, says Maman.

Are you my grandmother too? I ask. Everybody turns to look at me, as though they had forgotten I was there. My mother looks fiercely at Mami Lafont, who nods slightly. She comes over and gives me a hug that starts off thin but gets warmer and tighter.

Of course I'm your grandmother, she says.

Mami Lafont turns as she is walking out of the door. Can I come back tomorrow? she says.

Of course, says Maman.

## *Chapter 26*

Today is the last day of summer. Tomorrow I am going to my new school. I have a new backpack with wheels, to put all my books in, and new clothes and even a new haircut, which is much prettier than the one that Josette gave me. My scar peeps out from under the fringe, bright pink and shiny as my two little red bikes. Claude has brought them to our house. One is for me to ride and one is for my schoolfriends when they come to play. Everyone says I will make lots of friends at school.

There are four beds in the courtyard with no mattresses on. Claude has painted them yellow and is sitting next to them, watching them dry. He has Pablo asleep in his arms. Pablo sleeps all the time now, except at night. But then he only wakes up for milk. He isn't as much fun as I thought he might be. He hasn't done one somersault since he was born. Maman says he has forgotten, and when he gets a little older I can teach him.

What Pablo likes best is to be taken for walks. If you do not take him for walks then he cries and cries and cries. This is excellent. Because of this we go for walks, Maman, Pablo and me. We bump the pram down the track and on to the village road. Maman walks with her chin held up and pointed down the road and we walk past people and I say hello and Maman says hello too and she smiles a big smile because she is proud of Pablo. And everybody stops us to say hello, and isn't he beautiful, and doesn't he look like Amaury. Why do people keep saying that? Are they all crazy-mad? He really doesn't look at all like Papa.

While they stop and congratulate Maman and say their silly things and ruffle my hair, my job is to rock Pablo's pram – jiggle, jiggle – so that he doesn't get cross that we are not moving. Then we set off again, parading through the village as if we were kings and queens.

People come to our door now too, visitors, and we welcome them. Claude comes every day. He brings food and flowers from his garden and he has been doing some mending. Every day Maman says things like, Really, that's enough now, I'll never be able to pay you back for this, you've done enough. And Claude just ignores her. It's not that he can't hear her, but that he is ignoring her. Sometimes he will say things back like, That's enough, you just worry about yourself and that baby.

Mami Lafont has also visited a lot, and Tante Brigitte. They come and they pass Pablo around and jiggle him and talk nonsense to him. They bring jam and cakes and olives and sausages. Every day. Mami has done washing and pegged it out. She has cleaned the windows. She has even sneaked into the barn and cleaned the peachy mess off Papa's tractor.

Josette has been here twice. The first time she brought a quiche and some beer. She said Maman should drink the beer. It would be good for her and good for her milk. Maman has not drunk the beer, but after Josette left she cried a little bit and said how nice people were being. That was the sadness you feel when you're happy, I think. When Josette came the second time she brought me a bunch of her grapes, which were only just ripe and they tasted sweet and sour and burst in my mouth. She also brought a cardigan for Pablo. It is yellow and red; she made it herself. It is a funny cardigan because it is very tiny, but at the same time it is much too big for Pablo. Josette says he will grow into it in time for autumn. Like his skin maybe.

Autumn is not far away. The holiday people in the market are not so many and the days are not so hot, hot, hot. But they are still sunny. The yellow beds are going to be for the holiday people. Claude has already organised it and we have two people coming next week. They are going to pay Maman some money to sleep in the summer rooms and to have their suppers with us. Maman has been stewing the last of the tomatoes to make sauces.

Tonight we are having our supper outside. On the green plastic table is the yellow oilcloth, covered with black olives and blue gentians. Bread and tomatoes and olives are all laid out in bowls, and on a big white plate is the fruit that Maman has already cut up for our dessert. Each fruit has its own curving stripe on the plate – strawberries, cantaloupe, yellow peaches, grapes, blueberries, plums and figs.

The smell of sausages and honey-covered pork ribs sizzles up from the barbecue and paints smoky patterns in the air. Maman is standing by the barbecue. She has a fork in her hand but she is not turning the sausages. She is singing. So softly that you can only just hear the tune, and the words are lost, all tangled up in the rising smoke. She is swaying like a flower in the breeze.

Acknowledgements

Writing a novel is very much a solitary business, but bringing it to life has been the work of many and I am filled with gratitude.

My heartfelt thanks to Antony [illegible], my agent, and Helen Garnons-Williams, my editor at Bloomsbury, who have been enthusiastic champions of this novel and this author.

A huge thank you to the whole team at Bloomsbury and to the copyeditor Sarah-Jane Forder, for their meticulous and patient suggestions [illegible] so delicately [illegible] pencilled [illegible]. Thank you all.

Many thanks to the friends who read early drafts of this novel – Janet, Tracey, Alison and Mary – for their encouragement and enthusiasm; and to all the other friends who didn't even read it (yes, that means you!) for encouragement in various ways. The greatest of these has been Charlie, my best friend and confidante, who understands it all. Thank you.

Finally, many people have asked me if *[illegible]* is pure fiction or if there is some truth hidden in there. Did any of this really happen? As Pea would say, the truth is stranger than that. A word of thanks, then, to my mum, Jenny, who taught me through example that even when you don't think you can go on, you can, and you will.